CLOAKED

CLOAKED

THE ASCENSION MYTH BOOK 7

ELL LEIGH CLARKE
MICHAEL ANDERLE

DISRUPTIVE IMAGINATION

LMBPN Publishing
PMB 196, 2540 South Maryland Pkwy
Las Vegas, NV 89109

First US edition, September 2017
Version 2.03 October 2018

CLOAKED TEAM

JIT Beta Readers

Kelly O'Donnell
John Findlay
John Raisor
Jed Moulton
Paul Westman
James Caplan
Keith Verret
Erika Daly
Alex Wilson
Joshua Ahles
Micky Cocker

If we missed anyone, please let us know!

Editor
Joe Brewer

To everyone who ever dreamed of making a dent in the universe.

— Ellie

To Family, Friends and
Those Who Love
To Read.
May We All Enjoy Grace
To Live The Life We Are
Called.

— Michael

ZHYN POLITICIAN

THE KURTHERIAN (tm) GAMBIT

ZHYN SOLDIER

THE KURTHERIAN (TM) GAMBIT

CHAPTER ONE

Aboard the *ArchAngel*, Commons Lounge

Giles ambled up to the young man sitting with his back to the bar in a booth. The lounge was mostly quiet and empty, on account of the early morning hour.

"Uncle Lance?" Giles approached him, looking a little worse for wear.

Lance looked up from his coffee as if awoken from a day dream. "Giles. Morning. Er... do sit down," he said, gesturing to the seat across from him.

Giles shuffled in, and nodded to the server at the bar offering him coffee. He turned his attention immediately back to Lance. "You okay?" he asked, noticing the chewed cigar abandoned on the table.

"I'm fine," Lance answered. "I've just been up a while."

Giles paused, waiting for more information.

Lance pushed his coffee mug forward a little, and wiped his hand over his face. "It's the Federation stuff. It's all getting a little... silly... if you ask me."

Giles tilted his head, questioningly. The server had come over with a fresh cup and the coffee. He poured one for Giles and then

1

topped up the General's before quietly disappearing out of earshot.

Giles grabbed for some whitener at the end of the table and started stirring it into the tar-black nectar. "What's going on?" he asked, concerned.

Lance shrugged. "Oh, the usual. The Leath for one. Pressures for us to disarm generally. Meanwhile, others are assembling their forces month by month, like they think we don't know what they're doing."

He shook his head in disbelief. "Anyway," Lance continued, "nothing for you to worry about. I just wanted to speak with you before you disappeared off on one of your goose chases."

Giles eyes brightened in interest. He took a slurp of his coffee and then set the mug down. "Oh?"

Lance had a little twinkle in his eye. "Yes. And don't pretend. I know you're heading off to Orn with or without my blessing."

Giles started to protest, but Lance held his hand up. "Ah, now, now. Come on. I've known you since you were in diapers. I've witnessed or had reports on every stunt you've ever pulled, remember."

Giles settled his indignation and resigned himself to hearing the General out.

Lance smiled gently. "So, I was going to give you my blessing for Orn. But," he continued quickly before Giles could get too excited. "I need weekly reports from you on this."

The General paused, and Giles took the opportunity to clarify. "Meaning, it's an official trip?"

Lance nodded. "It is. And if you're right about this talisman stuff, it affects the Federation directly. But it's a complex situation. The Zhyn are friends now, but they still haven't joined the Federation, proper. Bottom line, you need to tread *very* carefully out there - which means no inciting hostility."

Giles nodded obediently.

"Plus," Lance continued, "after what you put us all through

with getting yourself taken hostage, I'd be more comfortable being kept up-to-date with your whereabouts. Remember, the whole Federation may report to me, but when you're on one of these hair-brained missions, I end up reporting to your mother."

Giles sniggered, carefully placing his coffee mug down again, for fear of spilling or snorting it. He took a moment to compose himself. "Okay, Uncle Lance. I hear you. Loud and clear."

Lance smiled. "Good. Coz heaven forbid, anything happens to you, we'd all have our heads on the chopping block."

Giles bobbed his head and took another sip of coffee. "So... Moons of Orn, and then Estaria?"

The General suddenly looked a little confused. He frowned. "Estaria?"

Giles nodded. "Yeah. I mean, the parent talisman I had there and then took to Estaria was one I found on Earth. It's a long story. That means we haven't found any more pieces that originated in the Estarian culture proper. And with what I showed you and Molly about the similarities in the genetic make-up of the Zhyn and Estarians, it seems only logical that there will be one in Estarian culture."

Lance grunted and Giles continued. "Well, Arlene and I both believe that there are cultural similarities too. Like similarities in their ascension myths..."

Lance frowned. "You mean, you think they're both talking about the same phenomenon?"

Giles's face lit up. "Exactly!"

Reynolds rubbed his chin, his elbows resting on the table. "Hmm. Yes, Molly had mentioned as much."

"Molly?" Giles asked, curious.

Lance nodded. "Yeah, she was also interested in getting answers about this."

Giles thought for a moment. "You mean, because of her realm jumping thing?"

Lance took a slurp of coffee, and then pushed the mug away,

3

deciding he'd had enough. "Yes, I believe so." He paused, watching Giles's reactions carefully. "Do you think it's related?"

Giles nodded. "Almost certainly. There's a bigger picture we're not seeing yet. I think gathering these two fragments, the oracle from Orn, and whatever the Estarian equivalent is, will give us some definitives to work with."

Lance took a deep breath. "Well, you have my blessing." He paused, settling back in the seat. "You'll be taking Arlene with you, of course?"

Giles looked resistant for a moment before quickly realizing that the suggestion Lance had made wasn't quite a suggestion. He gathered his thoughts. "Yes, Uncle Lance. I'll be taking Arlene to babysit me," he teased.

Lance's face relaxed a little. "Very good," he acknowledged. "So tell me, this 'do' your mother is organizing tomorrow. What time does it start?"

Aboard the *ArchAngel*, Comms Room AA19

Arlene sat immersed in her holo screens, her audio implants tuning out the sounds around her, and playing a brain synch track to help her focus. She scrolled through one of the holo documents, trying to figure out if there was a connection between that and the other account she had been reading.

She felt a nudge on her shoulder.

She turned, half expecting it to have been a random muscle spasm. Or even a sensation from the realm jumping she had been doing earlier. When she concentrated hard, she could sometimes lose her grounding.

But then she saw that there was someone standing there just behind her.

She flicked her audio to ambient and looked up. "Oh, Giles... you scared me!" she said, a hint of annoyance in her voice.

Giles pulled up a console chair next to her. "No, I didn't," he told her. "You could have an armed warrior sneak up next to you and you'd be ready to poke his eyes out with your elbow.

Arlene turned back to her document, her face perfectly straight. "That is true."

Giles chuckled. "So, I have news," he offered.

Arlene continued studying her screens, flicking between one and another as if she were on the brink of a meaningful break-through. "Uh huh," she muttered.

Giles leaned back in his chair. "Yeah. You want the good news, or the bad?"

Arlene leaned up a little, and turned her head towards him. She narrowed her eyes. "Gimme the bad first. Always."

Giles grinned. "The bad news is, I need to take you with me."

Arlene tried her best to look annoyed. "And the good news?"

Giles's grin spread a little wider. "The good news is the General has put us onto the Orn thing. We can leave whenever we want." He rocked a little in the console chair, waiting for the praise to follow.

Arlene didn't answer and went back to her screens.

Giles sat up suddenly. "What? What's the problem?" he pressed.

Arlene put her holo screens down and turned to him. "What's the problem?" she repeated his question, a hint of frustration in her voice now.

Giles eyes opened in bewilderment. "Yeah."

Arlene clasped her hands together on her lap. "I'll tell you what the problem is! Apart from the fact that not a matter of weeks ago you went and surrendered your sorry ass to a known terrorist organization. Apart from that, and the hell you put us all through... you left me."

Giles's eyes wrinkled up in confusion. "What? When?" he asked, searching his memory.

Arlene frowned at him. "Seventy years ago. We had a row, and

I thought we were going to figure it out. And then I came home one evening and you were just... gone."

Giles's mouth dropped open. "I left because you told me to!"

Arlene scowled at him. "I did no such thing!"

Giles was caught completely off guard. There was a second's silence while his brain scrambled to recall the events of that night.

"You did!" he protested. "You said that if I wasn't ready to settle down, and stop the juvenile adventure trips where I'd disappear for weeks on end, you thought that it would be better that I didn't come back. So, I took you at your word."

Arlene shook her head. "Those things... we say things like that in arguments. That's just what people say in the heat of the moment."

Giles shook his head, taking his glasses from his face. "Well, I didn't know that. I thought you wanted me to go ..."

Arlene shook her head, her anger lifting to reveal the old pain. "No. It was... silly. And, in the Estarian way of doing discussions, it's just a point of negotiation."

Giles suddenly seemed to disappear from behind his eyes.

Arlene tapped him on the leg. "Hey. Where did you go?"

Giles's mouth hung open for a moment before he returned to his senses. "I've just realized... a whole bunch of interactions have just made sense. Although ..." he added, cleaning his glasses and putting them back on his face, "The common denominator wasn't the Estarian thing. It was more the female thing."

Arlene didn't hesitate. She slapped the side of his leg. This time quite hard.

"Owwww!" He protested, rubbing the point of impact hard. "That's-"

"No less than you deserve!" she said, finishing his sentence for him.

He looked down at his leg where he was rubbing. "That's going to give me a painful lump," he told her.

"Humpft," she scoffed, turning back to her work. "Don't forget, alien-boy, I know about the nanocytes. Your exaggerations and fibs aren't going to work on me, like it works on your floozies."

"Floozies?" Giles repeated, looking shocked, and yet vaguely amused at this revelation.

Suddenly his mood changed, and he scooted his antigrav console chair a little closer to Arlene. "So, er... do I assume from all of this that you still have..."

Arlene scooted her chair back from him. "No. No, it does not. Not even a little bit. That ship has well and truly sailed."

Giles backed his chair up a little too. "Well, erm... okay then." He removed his glasses again, and started cleaning them, a little embarrassed this time.

Arlene smiled. "No," she concluded. "Too much water under the bridge," she explained more gently now. "And though you're easy on the eye, your boyish charm just doesn't do anything for me anymore."

Giles sighed and slumped back in his chair. His eyes looked a little dull, as if he'd suffered an actual disappointment.

Arlene turned back to her holoscreens. "Anyway, no need to look so glum," she told him. "From the sound of it we have another mission."

Giles eyed her carefully. "So, you're okay with working with me again?"

Arlene nodded, still not looking at him. "Oh yes," she answered simply. "I just needed to clear the air."

"The air I didn't know was smoggy," he mumbled.

Arlene half turned her face as if responding to his comment, but didn't manage to peel her eyes from her holos. "In fact," she told him, "I've been doing a little cross checking with your nursery rhyme."

Giles sat up and pulled himself closer again, peering over at her holos. "Oh yeah?"

Arlene picked up one screen. "Yep. I think I've narrowed it down to three possible moons. We'll know more when we get close and we can see the exact arrangement of the moons now. I think this data we're using is pretty old, and then we need to wait for the alignment... or calculate it... but in any case, I think we have a way forward."

Giles looked at her, half smiling. "You mean, you've been working on this without telling me? All this time?"

Arlene nodded. "Not just a pretty face, you know."

Giles got up. "Right then," he announced.

Arlene spun around, her clever discovery forgotten. "Where are you going?" she demanded.

Giles grinned. "We're going to need some wheels. With gate capabilities."

And with that, he strode out of the dimly lit comms room, and disappeared into the bright corridor beyond.

Arlene shook her head, sighed, and returned her attention to her screens to set up her calculations.

Gaitune-67, Base Gym

Thump.

Thwack. Thwack. Thwack. Thwack. THWACK.

Sean hit the deck for the third time that session.

Joel padded over to him. "You okay?" he asked, offering him a hand up. "Want a break?"

Sean, panting, lifted his head up, and then pulled his arms underneath him. A second later he sprang to his feet from a laying down position, ignoring Joel's outstretched hand. "No. I'm good," he said, looking fatigued, and more than a little irritated. "Let's go again," he affirmed.

Joel nodded, and stepped back a little, waiting for the agreed signal to attack. Or rather, in this instance, waiting for Sean to lunge forward and try to blitz him.

This time Sean hung back and switched stances a few times. Joel edged in a little further, looking loose and relaxed in his movement. Sean tried to copy his relaxed air, but he was just too tired. And invested.

A second later, he was on his back - again - realizing that Joel had just moved in and swept him as he bounced, contemplating his next move.

Crash had appeared in the doorway. "Ouch. That's got to hurt!" he muttered under his breath. Neither Joel nor Sean realized he was there.

"Okay. What have you done?" Sean asked, gazing up at the ceiling from his lying down position.

Joel looked innocent. "How do you mean?" he said, ambling over again.

Sean was sweating. He put his hand out for Joel to help him up this time. Joel took his hand, heaving him up to standing.

"You've done something," Sean insisted. "Like upgraded. There is no way you can just suddenly start moving that fast."

Sean thought about it a moment more. "In fact, this extra speed only happened since we got back from the *ArchAngel*. You've had another implant!"

Joel pretended to look offended. "*Another* implant?"

Sean narrowed his eyes. "Oh yeah. I know about your original upgrade. Fuck knows how you managed it because it was before you knew anyone on the *ArchAngel*. But those sudden increases in your performance... no way that's natural, mate."

Joel smiled knowingly, but didn't respond.

Just then Brock arrived at the door next to Crash, and the two warriors became aware that they were being watched.

Joel looked sheepish, but clammed up. Sean realized there was no way he was going to admit anything in front of the others. He changed the subject, wandering over to the edge of the mat to grab his towel. "You guys want in?" he called over to Crash and Brock.

"Helllz no!" Brock called back to him. "I'm working my sweet ass to get fighting fit, for sure. But no way am I gonna risk messing this pretty face up with some macho bravado."

Crash was quiet, still hanging on to the door frame. His muscles bulged a little more than Joel remembered.

"Hey," Joel called over to him. "You been working out more since we got back?" he asked Crash. "Or are you just pumped?"

Crash bobbed his head and glanced at Brock. "We've been hitting the weight room most days since we got back."

Brock did a little swing of his hips. "Yeah. I'm gonna be ready next time we get sent over to that APA again!"

Joel raised his chin. "Ahhhh. I see. It's the Were Cat thing, eh?"

Brock nodded vigorously. "Yeah. I dunno what hope we're supposed to have against one of those cats even if we train, but I figured our odds are better if we're in condition. Plus, the better the skills we have, the more chance we have of surviving."

Sean was taking a long drink from his water bottle. He finished and put the lid back on. "Yeah, that's always my philosophy. So how's the six-pack coming, Brock?"

Brock laughed. "Ha! More like a jelly pack right now. But I'm working on it!"

Crash chuckled and patted his friend on the back. "He's doing great," he told them.

Brock slapped him playfully on the arm. "You're teasing me."

Crash opened his mouth to protest, but Brock had already changed the subject. "Hey, anyone seen Molly this afternoon?" he asked.

Crash stuck out his lower lip and shook his head. Sean and Joel shrugged. Then Joel remembered something. "Ah, yes. I think she's out auditing a lecture or something on Estaria."

Brock frowned. "Auditing a lecture. What for?"

Joel shrugged again. "No idea. Have to ask her when she gets back. Later tonight, probably. Think she put a food order in with Paige, so she should be around later."

Brock nodded his understanding. "Alrighty then! Thanks Joel." He turned to Crash. "I'm gonna hit the shower."

Crash slapped him on the back. "All right, bud. I'm going to do a round with these guys. Time to start pushing myself," he said, stepping into the room.

Sean was drinking water again. He took the bottle from his lips and pointed at Joel. "Go against him first," he said. "I'm having a time out."

CHAPTER TWO

Aboard the *Scamp Princess*

Giles arrived on the *Scamp Princess* through the cargo hold. "It's okay! I'm here!" he called through to Arlene. "Scamp, you can close up the doors now," he added.

The computer-generated voice spoke to him over the in-ship communication system. "Okay, Giles. Closing doors. Did you get your message sent okay?"

"Yes, thank you," Giles frowned, fixing his single pack of luggage to a rack. "How did you know?"

Scamp responded matter-of-factly. "Arlene wanted to know where you were. ADAM would only tell me you were in the comms department, and that you were on your way over. I assumed you were sending someone a long-distance message before we left on our adventure. I mean, mission."

Giles smiled at the EI's dig at him and his attitude towards missions. "Ah ha. Arlene wanted to know where I was?" he repeated, like a grownup talking to a child.

Arlene turned her head as he wandered into the cockpit. "Arlene did," she confirmed.

Scamp clicked on again. "She also wanted to know what you

were communicating to whom, but ADAM wouldn't give us clearance for that."

Arlene looked suddenly guilty. Giles looked vindicated. "Well, it's good that at least ADAM has some integrity around here," he jested with them. "So, are we all set?"

Arlene spun back around in her console chair. "Yes. We were about to miss our window, but I think we'll be okay if we leave now."

She flicked a switch, starting the engines.

Giles could see she had the pilot's console up. Normally, with anyone else, except maybe Sean Royale, he might argue. But today, with Arlene... he was quite happy to be a passenger. He made himself comfortable in the next console over and strapped himself in. "Okay. Well, what are we waiting for?"

Arlene rolled her eyes, and gave the command. "Okay, Scamp. Let's get going, now that his royal *tardie-ass* has arrived!"

The *Scamp Princess* lifted up off the hangar deck of the *Arch-Angel* and made its way out into the blackness of space.

"The Giles Kurns Adventures continue," Giles muttered to himself as he relaxed back in the chair, interlocking his fingers behind his head.

Staðall University, Spire, Lecture Theater 21

The lights along the walls of the lecture theater flashed, signaling to both the students and teacher that the allocated time had come to a close.

Professor Abigail Von paused mid-sentence, before finishing her point.

"And for those who have volunteered for the next Think Tank session, make sure you review chapters twenty through to twenty-two. It will make the decision-making and discussion much easier on your counterparts when you plug in if you've done the reading!"

The theater erupted in activity as students scrambled to their feet. Molly was sitting quietly, dressed all in black. She was in the back row and out of the way, watching, expecting a mass exodus.

But that didn't happen. At least a quarter of the two hundred and something students raced towards the front and seemed to gather around Von, hanging on her every word.

Molly frowned, watching carefully, waiting for the activity to clear. When it didn't, confused, she allowed herself to also be drawn down to the front of the room.

"...Yes, and if they had considered that in the first place, you could say it would have been another variable. But as it was, it was indeed forgotten. Well spotted though, Johnny."

Abigail Von seemed to be having a discussion with one of the students as the others listened in rapt attention. As soon as she finished responding there was a respectful clamor for her to choose them as the next question.

Von glanced up at Molly as she made her way down the steps, obviously a little old to be in the class she had been teaching. Von was distracted for a second, but then turned her attention back to the immediate consideration. "I'm afraid we're out of time, folks. You need to get to your next lecture, and I need to eat something before supervising a discussion. If you don't have a class next, you're welcome to attend."

The remaining students started to disband and make their way up and out of the doors at the back of the theater.

Von packed up her things and started to head out herself, too. Molly battled against the current and managed to catch Von as she headed towards the doors on the lower level, presumably reserved for the faculty, Molly guessed.

"Professor Von?" Molly called over the hub of activity as she landed on the ground level.

Abigail turned around and looked at her.

Molly quick stepped over. "I was wondering if we might speak. I have a proposition for you."

Von was already biting into an apple. She kept walking towards the door, now with Molly in tow. Clearing her palate, she leaned against the door and nudged it open. "Are you okay to walk and talk? I need to be across campus in twenty minutes, and I'd like to eat as well."

Molly smiled, helping her through the door as she shuffled without a free hand between her bag, water flask and half-eaten apple. "Sure. Let me help you," she offered as she pushed the door.

Von led her through what seemed to be a dumping ground for old equipment and abandoned experiments. Then, through another two sets of doors, they seemed to arrive in a corridor that was beyond the lecture theater and back in the main building, only another level down from where the students had spilled out.

Von glanced over at Molly since more of her attention was available now that they were en route. "So, how can I help?" she asked.

Molly had considered her pitch and began speaking immediately. "You're the foremost authority in interplanetary negotiations. I need someone like that for a special project. Someone like you," she clarified.

Von frowned. "You're not planning on starting a war, are you?"

Molly chuckled, having never considered that that might have been why she was asking. "No. Not in the slightest. I'm looking for someone who can help avoid future wars."

Von glanced over at her as the two women strode purposefully down the stark white corridor. "Oh, I'm not taking on any consulting gigs right now," she said dismissively.

Molly shook her head, looking straight ahead of where they were going. "Not consulting. Teaching."

Von's pace slowed a little. Molly could feel through the space, using her new abilities. She could tell the academic was curious.

ELL LEIGH CLARKE & MICHAEL ANDERLE

"I have a job teaching," she told her, gesticulating with the remains of her apple at the surroundings as way of evidence.

Molly smiled. "I know," she responded simply. "A different teaching job. But still here."

Von's pace slowed again as her mind worked to put the pieces of information together. Her slim brown eyebrows furrowed together.

"Here, at this university?" she asked, looking confused.

Molly nodded. "The long-term goal is to start a university for the next generation of leaders."

Von started walking again, this time a little more slowly than her initial, harassed pace. "We already have places that do that. Like the military. And the elite universities that educate the best and the brightest in law, history and politics."

Molly bowed her head respectfully as they journeyed down another corridor. "Yes, I'm aware of that. And what they're taught doesn't coincide with what they *could* be taught. Things that will ultimately lead to making better decisions - decisions that aren't based on greed, or fear, or commerce. But on methods to resolve conflicts and create stability for the whole population, not just the few who can afford to buy influence in politics."

The corridor opened out into a stone building, and the two headed through the foyer of what looked like an original piece of architecture from when the university had been founded.

The foyer then gave way to a hall, which in turn turfed them out into a quadrangle. "So what are you suggesting they be taught instead?" Von pressed, tossing her apple core into a refuse disposal chute as they passed by.

Molly clasped her hands behind her back now as she spoke. "The practical strategies that actually mean a better life for all involved. The policies that mean a sustainable system which don't rely on versions of financial enslavement. How to build economies so they are healthy rather than corrupt. How to ensure justice for all, no matter what their background, gender or skin color."

Von almost smirked. "That's sounding a little... ambitious. Which organization did you say you were from?" she asked a little suspiciously now.

Molly stopped walking, forcing Von to turn and look at her. "I'm not from an organization. But I do have the means to fund this venture. And in the first instance, all I want to do is prove a concept. Prove that this is something that can work, even just with one course."

A gaggle of students walked by, laughing and joking loudly. Von shot them a look, and they quietened down a little.

She turned her attention back to Molly. "So why me?"

Molly shrugged, watching the students head across the rest of the quadrangle in the direction they had been walking. "You're the capital city's leading authority on Estarian-Ogg trade relations. I checked you out. It's because of you that there is an ensuing peace between these two inner system planets, which could otherwise have been disastrous without your mediation a couple of decades ago."

A frown appeared across Von's perfectly manicured human eyebrows. "So you want me to teach trade relations?" she deduced.

Molly nodded. "Yes. But as a container for this bigger vision. Making it clear that this is why the method of negotiation is important. Why co-operation is always the most beneficial to all sides."

Von looked thoughtful for a moment. "Well it is true. I can think of several instances during my career that would support that conjecture..."

Molly's face was serious. "I've read a number of your papers. I believe your work is instrumental in not just the fate of our inner system, and Sark, but beyond, too. But it needs a platform. We

ELL LEIGH CLARKE & MICHAEL ANDERLE

need more people who understand it, and can operate from this place effectively."

Von started walking again, and Molly quickened to keep up with her.

Molly continued talking. "I'm advocating we start a course. Right here, within your department, to test the concept. If it gathers traction, and we think it's worth continuing, then we'll expand. If it doesn't, we'll never need run it again."

Von glanced over as they headed up the steps into another building. "Sounds reasonable," she said, non-committally.

Molly followed her through the door. "Have a think about it, and then reach out and let's talk. Here are my holo details," she said, pulling up a screen on her holo so she could bump the information over.

Von hit a screen, and then held her wrist out. Molly bumped her holo against Von's. The professor looked down, checking it had registered. "Okay. Got it," she confirmed.

Molly noticed another horde of students heading in through another door. Probably a classroom. "What's up next?" she asked, curious as to what all the excitement was about.

Von lifted her eyes to the ceiling as she shifted her bag on her shoulder. "Think Tank time," she explained.

Molly looked puzzled.

Von explained quickly. "The folks involved in the discussion plug into a hive mind of their colleagues and discuss the solution to various historical problems."

Molly turned her ear as if straining to hear.

Von grinned. "It's group-think at its most advanced." She hesitated. "Trouble is, it needs to be limited and supervised. The effects produce quite a high, and then there is a come down when it's time to unplug."

Her eyes dropped to the floor for a moment. "We had a problem a couple of years ago where students were plugging in

18

for days at a time. Missing classes. Missing meals. And then of course when they had to deal with the disconnection."

Her face turned grim, and she lowered her eyes. "Well, you can imagine..."

Molly nodded her understanding, amazed that such technology was now being used in education.

Von made her way through the door behind the students who were gathering to be a part of the session. She called back to Molly. "You're welcome to join us. To observe... if you like," she offered.

Molly beamed. "I'd love to!" she exclaimed, following her new contact into the fray.

Erm. I hope you're not considering hooking us up to this... thing. Whatever it is.

It had crossed my mind.

That was what I was afraid of.

Come on, Oz. What's the worst that could happen?

Er... you allow all these students to access your thoughts. And me? You overload the system with the data we manage? You fry their brains. Need I go on?

Molly went quiet.

Okay.

...

...

We'll just observe.

...

...

For now.

Molly disappeared into the room, and the doors closed behind her.

Gaitune-67, Base conference room

"Why don't you just take them out? You have the resources. The firepower."

Molly was nearly an hour into a briefing with the General, and only just starting to understand the deeper problems the Federation was facing.

Lance sighed as he leaned in closer to the holo. "We do. Except we don't know what else is on there. We don't know what they're planning, or who truly is behind it. We have a hint that the Leath are involved, but we haven't got enough physical proof to go to war."

Molly's brow furrowed as she grappled with the problem. "And blowing up the ship would be an act of war?"

Reynolds nodded. "Plus, it gives them the scope to say that there was nothing untoward going on there. We know there tends to be paperwork to support these missions. Papers that say that it was straightforward commercial goods, like farming equipment, or whatever."

Molly thought for a moment. She cocked her head. "But your sources say it's equipment for fracking?"

"Yes," Lance confirmed. "But of course, ADAM can't be physically on the ship to verify that, which is why we need people with bodies to go and check it out."

Molly narrowed one eye, still thinking. "But fracking isn't illegal on an uninhabited planet you have the rights to."

Lance chewed on his cigar. "This is true. But the shipments have been ending up on Teshov."

Molly nodded her head slowly in realization, mulling what that meant.

After a moment she had another thought. "I take it you don't want us to stop them and board them, in an official capacity? You'd have people to do that, if that were the case."

Reynolds smiled. "You catch on fast. I am suggesting you do this... under cover."

Molly eyes lit up in secret excitement.

Lance seemed to read her thoughts. "You'd need to stay out of it, of course. Just in case they need your leadership from outside the ship. Or in case they were discovered. You'd need to have a way of getting them out, without bringing the federation into it."

Molly's eye crinkled up in concern. "You wouldn't back us up?"

Lance sat back. "I can't be seen to. It would drag us into a war. And that's exactly what we're trying to avoid. That is why the Sanguine Squadron exists, remember."

Molly sat back in her seat, subconsciously mirroring his movements, and taking a deep breath.

After a moment she spoke again. "Okay, boss. Let me talk to the team, and see what kind of plan we can come up with. The exit strategy seems like it might be the sticking point here."

The General nodded. "Okay. Let me know how you get on. The ship leaves in two weeks, and you'll need time to infiltrate the crew before it leaves from Estaria."

Molly stood up. "Yes sir," she confirmed, giving him a salute.

The General returned the salute and ended the call.

"Close holo," Molly said, giving the instruction to fold the holoscreen away into the table. She rearranged the chair she'd been sitting in, tucking it away under the table, and then wandered out of the open door.

Neechie was standing there, watching her leave.

"Come on Neech," she chirped, wiggling her fingers to encourage him to follow. The pair wandered down the corridor, Molly deep in thought, and Neechie looking like he was considering his next realm jump with his apprentice.

CHAPTER THREE

Gaitune-67, Molly's conference room

Sean and Oz had been verbally jousting. Sean's face firmed in tension as he shifted in his chair. "That's not what I'm saying, Oz. All I said was that you have an ability to change how you 'feel' about things, and so it's not that important to worry about your feelings being hurt."

Oz spoke over the room's comm system. "I don't see how that follows. If I were an organic entity, would you be saying that?"

Sean's brow wrinkled in frustration. "Yeah but you're not, so it's pointless considering it."

Jack raised her eyebrows. "Actually..." she started.

Joel was observing from the other end of the room. He folded his arms and leaned against the wall watching with interest.

Jack continued. "I think the point that Oz is trying to make is valid. If you had a human who was adaptable, or just thick skinned, would you be more considerate of their feelings?"

Sean dropped his head into his hands, defeated. Joel continued to watch. He knew Sean was old, but surely not old enough to have been around before EIs were designated Entities with rights and personhood.

Just then, Molly breezed in. "Greetings folks," she said brightly.

Sean looked up an expression of relief on his face.

Molly plonked herself down in the chair nearest Sean. "Looks like we've got a new puzzle to crack," she told them. "One that includes some undercover work." She grinned like the cat who had got the cream.

Sean's eye brightened too. "Do tell, our esteemed leader!" he said, turning to look at her, and then shuffling his chair round.

Joel pushed off the wall and came to sit at the table with the others. Jack swiveled her chair to face Molly, her conflict of opinions with Sean relegated to off-duty kitchen talk for later.

Molly called out to Oz. "Oz, could you bring up the shipping route the General just shared with us please?" She tilted her chin up so that she could hear him through the room's intercom. She found that she was talking to Oz out loud more and more so she didn't have to explain herself for the purpose of those who didn't inhabit her synapses.

"Of course," Oz responded, activating the holoscreen against the safe house conference room wall.

Molly glanced at each of her team members as she spoke. "This is a shipping route between Estaria and Teshov. It's mostly used by heavy industry carriers. Equipment, technology and the like. This one here," she indicated by highlighting a route and a profile picture of a cargo ship, "is a ship that does a run every four months or so. We have no idea what is truly being transported. The ship's manifest says it's farming equipment."

Joel leaned his arms on the table. "And is there a reason we suspect this *isn't* the case?" he asked, looking for the reason that this was an assignment.

Molly lowered her head. "A number of reasons. Lemme run you through them."

She pulled up a screen on her holo. It had a lot of graphs and numbers on it. Sean scratched his head as he studied the hologram.

Molly began her explanation. "This is seismic activity that has been occurring on Teshov. What we're looking at is the base line activity that has been happening naturally for the last few hundred years."

She opened another screen, pushing it over to sit next to the current one. "This is recent activity, in the last six months. As you can see, it is much more regular, and more destructive. In fact, when ADAM noticed this, he cross-referenced it with known profiles for this kind of planet and found that the activity is consistent with core mining."

Joel frowned, pulling his eyes from the screen to Molly. "Core mining? But there are people living on Teshov. Surely that's—"

Jack finished his sentence. "Illegal? Reckless? Immoral?"

Molly nodded. "All of the above," she agreed, her face looking more serious now. "Which is why we need to find out what's going on. The Federation suspects this shipment may have something to do with it."

She flicked some more data up on another screen. Then another two screens, each with profile pictures of people on them. "This is Lana Rey. She's been support personnel on legal core mining expeditions on various rocks in the asteroid belt."

She nodded in the direction of the second image. "This is Dr. Ainstel Brahms. He is one of Estaria's foremost seismologists. He specializes in energy from geological events — earthquakes, glacial movement, magnetic pole drift. The works."

Jack sat back. "So what? They're involved?"

Molly shook her head. "They've gone missing. Brahms hasn't shown up for work at his government research project in over eight days now. Rey is also missing from her job in Uptarlung."

Joel leaned forward, looking concerned. "And how have we linked them to the shipment?"

Molly flicked back to the original screen with the shipping

data on it. "ADAM has done some analysis of transportation paths, and looked at what has coincided with the seismic activity. Allowing for two to 21 days to set up equipment and start drilling to place the charges, he's filtered through the ships arriving at Teshov, and taken into account only those that were large enough to be transporting equipment. He noticed a pattern. And their point of origin was always Estaria. And actually — always one ship — the one we looked at several screens back."

Sean watched the details on the screen with intense concentration.

Molly waved her arm over at the hologram. "We think that the personnel have been kidnapped to help on this project. ADAM estimates that if they make even the slightest error in their drilling works, the outer core could create enough environmental disturbance that life on the planet could be wiped out in a matter of days after the event."

Jack's mouth dropped open, her eyes fixed on the screen trying to make sense of what they were hearing. Joel leaned forward, as if trying to hear better.

Molly continued her discourse. "ADAM has also advised us that the most likely ship for this next trip with the scientists, and probably more equipment for boring deeper, is this one."

The screen changed, displaying an image of a cargo ship. Molly shifted slightly in her chair, looking over at Jack and Joel. "It's the only one that is leaving this month. It's unlikely they would want to hold the hostages for longer than this. Personally, I'm surprised they're possibly holding them this long. If I were in their shoes, I'd be wanting to do the snatch just ahead of the ship leaving."

She shrugged, thinking for a moment before continuing. "Unless they've already sent them on in a people carrier. ADAM suspects not, simply because of the large distances involved, and these guys don't have access to our travel tech."

Joel had put his hand over his mouth as he listened. He removed it to speak. "You mean, our pods?"

Molly closed her eyes and nodded once. "Pods, or whatever. Meaning we have an advantage." She took a deep breath and leaned back in her seat, dimming the holograms, and raising the lights from her holo. "The thing is if we just blow the ship up, we kill the hostages. If we board, we lose the opportunity to find out what is really going on and who is behind this operation."

Jack raised her hand at shoulder height, as she leaned on the desk. "But isn't that preferable to letting them continue on?"

Molly bobbed her head. "Yes, and ADAM is concerned that whoever is behind this might be doing it in other systems too. It's not just the Teshov population that is at risk. And if one shipment goes missing, the operation will still survive. This makes it more of a weeding exercise." She looked off to one side, pulling her mouth onto one side of her face, considering her own words.

She didn't correct herself.

Sean turned to her. "So what you're suggesting is that we go undercover on this ship, as... crew?"

Molly nodded. "Yes. Oz will create personas for you. He'll make sure you have proper cover stories and reasons for being there, and then once on board you can dig around and see what's what."

It was Joel's turn to chip in. "You're using the second person a lot here. Does this mean you're not coming with us?"

Molly nodded, unaware she was sticking out her bottom lip. "The General has recommended that I stay in a position off the ship, in case you need an extraction."

She paused and looked at Joel. "In fact, he's recommended that at least some of the team stay back."

Sean started to speak, an air of agitation taking over his demeanor. Molly's look of sadness lifted and was replaced with humor in her eyes. She quickly held her hand up to him. "It's okay Sean. We'll make sure you're in the undercover crew," she said shaking her head. "But we need a plan, and then we'll select who else is best placed to follow that plan."

She looked to Joel. "This is your op, chap. I'll take your recommendations once you and Oz have had a chance to review the intel from ADAM. It's unlikely that the crew are going to need military skills, though. Generally. From what Oz has already looked at, the more 'normal' these folks are, the more chance they have of going undetected in this cargo shipping scenario."

Joel nodded, snatching a glance at Sean, before looking back at Molly. "Understood," he said, quietly pleased he might be able to stay and protect Molly from the outside should she need to get into the fray at some point.

"Great!" Molly said, brighter now that the information dump had been complete. "Let's meet back here tomorrow with a game plan, and then we can bring the others in on our next move."

The warriors nodded their agreements and started getting up to leave.

Molly was the first one up and out of the door.

Why are you in such a hurry?

Conference call with Von.

Of course. I'd not put that on your official schedule, since it's technically an off-book hobby.

Good thing you're not my PA, eh?

Hmmm. I'm sure your holo has a function for that.

It does. That's why I remembered! Unbelievable. I have an AI in my head and I'm having to separate which things are projects and which are work.

She tutted to herself as she strode out to the kitchen to grab a protein drink, and then headed back down to the ops room.

Gaitune-67, Ops Room

Molly sat in the ops room on her usual console.

"So what did they say?" she asked, sitting back in the invisible, movement-responsive sofa, her cup of lemon water in hand.

Von responded over the enhanced holo connection. "The board is agreeable. Well, they *became* agreeable, after they were reminded how it would make the institution look like a trailblazer." Abigail chuckled to herself, in a way that reminded Molly that beneath her academic seriousness was once a young person like herself.

Molly grinned. "And they agreed to fully acknowledge the course?"

Von nodded. "Yep. Full credits for the discussion work and the examination."

Molly sat up a little. "This is great news!" she said, her face lighting up even more.

Von nodded, her smile showing she was rather pleased with her powers of persuasion. "The only thing that remains," she added, changing her tone a little, "is how to recruit the students."

Molly uncrossed her legs and poked at the holo in front of her, sharing her screen. "We almost have that covered as well. My team has worked up a campaign to use through the university Ethertrak. It's designed to have maximum resonance with our key demographic."

Von's eyes scanned the material on the screen.

Molly continued. "What we need to do next is recruit ourselves a spokesperson. Someone who knows the material and understands the power that this insight has in negotiating peace. Someone who is also articulate and can relate to the students who will be taking the course."

Von stopped reading, and looked off into the distance. "I can probably reach out to a number of people who would be keen to represent this program. Counselors, board members …"

Her voice disappeared into her throat as she realized that Molly was shaking her head. "No, no," Molly chuckled lightly. "You misunderstand me. We've got a short list already."

Von's eyes widened, and she began to apologize.

Molly beamed at her again. "A very *short* shortlist," she added.

Von looked intrigued.

Molly continued. "Professor Von, I was hoping that you might be agreeable to being our spokesperson."

Abigail suddenly looked a little taken aback and flustered. "You mean... you want me to talk on recordings and... for the campaign?" she tried to clarify, a little flustered.

Molly nodded. "Yes. Exactly. You're the person who is the most qualified."

Von took a deep breath, collecting her thoughts. "I... I don't know what to say," she said, her face flushing beet red.

Molly sat back on the couch again. "Well," she said, her voice giving the sense of being more serious now, "I was hoping you'd say 'yes.'"

Von's eyes were alive as she stared into the camera. "Yes! Yes, I would love to. Yes!" she exclaimed, her serious professor-like demeanor abandoned.

Molly smiled, feeling the older woman warm to her the more interaction they shared. "Well, good then," she said, satisfied. "It's just as well. My team has already started pulling together some scripts that might work. I'd hate to have to make them rewrite them for some stuffy board member."

The two women chuckled as co-conspirators.

As their humor subsided, Von brought them back on point. "So how do we go about doing this then?"

Molly tilted her head, contemplating their next move. "I think what we need to do is start filming. What say you if I bring my team over to capture the footage? I'm sure they can get the scripts over to you in the next few days. And then perhaps we film after that?"

Von nodded enthusiastically. "Of course. That sounds wonderful. We have a semester break coming up next week so the campus will be quiet."

Molly bobbed her head, considering whether they actually might want students in the reel at all, but then figured it was a detail they could resolve later if they decided that they did. "Great. That'll work," she agreed.

Von's face changed suddenly, as she seemed to look around her university office before bringing her eyes back to her holo. "Tell me. I know you said you were well funded, but I'm curious where the funding is coming from to do all this?"

Molly took a deep breath. "Well, we have some private funds from parties interested in educating our leaders to make more informed decisions. And a number of industry leaders who have been adapting their working practices in line with some of the principles you've been advocating. They want to make sure that they can select their workforce from these informed leaders, too."

She realized she was being vague. "You know, as we work together, I'll be able to show you more and more. For now, just know that this is all above board, and being done for the right reasons. After all, there is no way this kind of strategy can benefit those who would have motive to exploit the population. And you know what a positive effect your strategies have on civilizations as a whole."

Von seemed to take comfort in the reassurance. This Molly Bates was right. There is no way that anyone could be using these strategies for bad intent. It just wouldn't be of any benefit to them. Von smiled. "Okay. I'm happy to proceed."

Neechie had managed to find his way into the ops room as Molly had sat talking with Abigail, and just then jumped up on the invisible sofa.

"My ancestors!" exclaimed Abigail. "Is that …?"

Molly nodded, stroking his head as he nuzzled up to her thigh and then jumped into her lap. "A sphinx. Yeah. He's our mascot around here."

Von leaned forward, trying to see him better. "He's a little cutie!" she remarked.

Neechie looked up at Molly as if to say, *See, told you so. I am, aren't I?*

"Yes you are, Neech," Molly agreed, pulling her hot mug out of the way so as not to burn him. "You are ..." she repeated, stroking him with her free hand. Suddenly she felt a little light headed.

"Okay," she said, looking back up at the screen. "I need to head out and get back to my people. We'll get some scripts over to you in the next day or so, and if you're happy to continue working on the syllabus, feel free to send it over when you're ready for me to take a look."

Von snapped back into business-mode. "No problem. I'll do that." She grinned and waved at the Sphinx. "Bye Neech!" she said. "Bye Molly," she said, looking a little more grounded and waving to Molly.

The call disconnected, and Molly put her mug down immediately.

"What is it Neechie? Are you trying to show me something?" she asked, looking down at the Sphinx in her lap.

He meowed, and then Molly felt herself start to drift through realms. She saw images of places she had never seen before. An image of a series of planets in a weird array, balanced in a cluttered orbit.

She saw an entrance to a tomb, and some old markings that reminded her of the Zhyn characters, but ones that she didn't recognize.

She felt like she was losing consciousness, and she put her feet on the floor, causing Neechie to jump off her lap and onto the console floor. She focused on her breathing, allowing the images to come and go, but putting her attention on the present, on the sensations in her body, keeping herself grounded in this reality.

She saw space. But a space cluttered with stars. She looked around trying to recognize a constellation. A feature. Something that would tell her where she was.

She recognized nothing.

ELL LEIGH CLARKE & MICHAEL ANDERLE

Breathe, she told herself.

She was aware of Oz, and words coming from Oz. But she was too far into the realm visions to really understand.

Then she felt like she turned back over her shoulder, and looked behind her, and she was no longer in space, but in a bedroom, looking down into a drawer, near a bed.

Breathe. You're safe, she told herself.

Then everything grayed out a little, and she became aware of the lights in the ops room through her eye lids. She felt herself hyperventilating as her awareness in the present world came back, and she kept breathing, feeling a little nauseous and out of sorts.

Molly? What's happening?

Molly heard Oz's words this time.

It's okay, Oz. I'm back. I'm right here.

'Nother realm jump?

Yep.

I'm blaming the Sphinx.

Molly breathed heavily through her nose in a half snort. The Sphinx sat looking at her, unimpressed, as if trying to assess her condition.

Me too. I think we should rename him Mercury - the messenger.

Gaitune-67, Safe house, Kitchen

Joel looked over at her, his eyes full of concern. "So, you really think it was a message?" he asked.

Molly shrugged, leaning back against the counter top. "I don't know what else it could have been. I mean, unless I'm just seeing random scenes that are neither past, present, nor future."

She moved over to one of the chairs and sat down at the kitchen table. "I just don't know what to think anymore. I just know what I feel. And it felt like a message."

Joel folded his arms, and shifted his weight to his other foot.

32

"Shame there's no way to get in touch with Arlene. This was precisely what she was meant to be helping you with."

Molly cocked her head. "Hmm... but *is* there no way to get in touch with her? I mean, they headed off to ancestors know where... but we can call anywhere from that ops room. Distance is irrelevant. So, assuming they're on a Federation ship they must be reachable.

At that moment Molly heard someone sitting down in the common area, and then the noise of a game playing on the holo. She looked towards the door.

Joel frowned as he watched her get pulled out to the common area by the noise.

He followed her, standing in the doorway.

Molly had stepped through to look at who was sitting on the sofa. "Sean?"

Sean looked up, surprised that anyone was around. "I was... I was just chilling out for ten minutes. I needed a break from cataloging the—"

Molly shook her head, dismissing his excuses for slacking on the job. "It's okay. We were just talking about something, and I thought you might know about this. Giles and Arlene went off on some mission. Giles didn't tell me where exactly, but I can take a guess. If he's in a Federation ship, how would I get hold of him?"

Sean shrugged. "Ops room. Ask ADAM which ship, and then connect a call with that ship's EI."

Molly looked confused. "Okay. And do you know how it is these EIs can be in touch over such ridiculous distances?"

Sean nodded nonchalantly. "Sure."

Molly waited, dropping her head, and raising her eyebrows pushing him to explain.

Sean sighed. "Tech-no-lo-gyyyyy, of course," he said, patronizingly.

Molly rolled her eyes into the top of her head as she turned and headed back into the kitchen.

Joel's smirk turned to full on laughter as he headed back in ahead of her. "That goon," he chuckled.

Molly laughed away to herself, her chest bouncing as she tried to keep it inaudible. "I never know if he's being earnest, or if he's just fucking with us!" she admitted.

Joel shook his head and retrieved his mocha from the counter where he had left it a moment before. "Yeah, me neither. The guy is a mystery," he added, still laughing quietly to himself.

Molly leaned against the fridge. "Okay. So I'll give them a call and see if Arlene has any suggestions. And beyond that I think I should probably spend some more time with the little guy. See if I can get some practice."

Joel's face crumpled in confusion. "Little guy?" he asked, crossing his legs, and folding his hands in front of his crotch.

Molly had opened the fridge and was taking out the remains of one of her shakes. "Yeah. Neechie," she responded, without looking up.

"Oh. Right. Of course," Joel agreed quickly, relaxing instantly.

Molly closed the fridge door and turned to leave. She spun back to look at him. "What did you think I meant?" she asked.

Joel blushed and shook his head. "I... had no idea," he lied, picking up his mocha and hiding behind a slurp. A slurp that was way too much, and way too hot.

He swallowed, ignoring the pain, as Molly bobbed her head once, and drifted out of the kitchen, oblivious.

CHAPTER FOUR

Administration House, Staðall University, Spire
Dean Alfred Radcliff sat comfortably in his chair reading on his holo. There was a timid knock on the door.

"Enter," he said brusquely, swiping away the screen and sitting up a little.

His assistant poked her head into the office. "Dean Radcliff, there is a gentleman here to see you. He says you have an appointment, but I don't see anything on your schedule."

Radcliff sat up properly and flicked through to his schedule. He was blocked out until his meeting with the heads of the Science Department at four. He looked up, frowning. "Nothing on my schedule. Who is he?"

His assistant looked awkward, stepping gently into the room, intending to close the door so she couldn't be heard. Before the door was closed it was pushed open again, and there stood a rather tall Ogg, in a smart-looking atmosuit, not altogether unlike one that Radcliff owned for meeting and greeting visits he often needed to do.

"Greetings of the day to you, Dean Radcliff. Allow me to introduce myself." The Ogg spoke with a refined accent. A lilt of his native Ogg-tongue but with the precision of excellent schooling in Estarian ways.

The Dean, too curious to insist he schedule an appointment, beckoned him into the room, and indicated at the chair in front of his desk. "That will be all, Amy," he told his assistant.

The Dean sat down again as the Ogg made his way into his office and sat down.

The Ogg continued his introduction. "My name is Raj Ghettie, of the Northern Clan of Cambodrian. My family has extensive ties and business here on Estaria, as well as an interest in supporting the education system."

The Dean had worked with many enterprises and representatives with big trust funds and contributions that needed to be allocated for philanthropic causes. His face brightened at the thought of where this might be heading.

The Ogg continued. "We have a heavy interest in maintaining what we call 'vallitseva tila.' The balance in all things." He paused, studying the Dean's reaction carefully, as if his next word were dependent on how he responded.

The Dean leaned his arms on his desk, nodding with interest.

Raj Ghettie took it as a cue to continue. "We feel that the education sector is a huge part of this process. So much so, we would like to pledge some financial aid in exchange for lending some direction to some of the material taught."

The Dean smiled, satisfied that his first reaction had been entirely accurate. "Of course. This is something I'm sure the board would be open to. However, I must ask — what kind of influence are you expecting?"

"Oh, nothing too drastic," Raj explained with a dismissive wave of his hand. "We're mostly impressed with the breadth of study available. But we'd be keen to ensure that the university remains... traditional. None of these newfangled courses like Media Studies, or Reinterpretive History, or Journalistic Methodologies." He chuckled at the thought of the subjects.

Radcliff nodded sympathetically, his fake smile playing across his face. "Yes, I concur with that sentiment entirely. These people will argue anything to give a degree away these days."

"Quite," Ghettie agreed. He paused for a moment before continuing. "I assume you'll want to do your due diligence before you accept our contribution. But I think in essence we can work to move this forward fairly quickly."

Ghettie stood up to leave. Radcliff stood too, and walked around his desk to see him out politely. He stopped, thinking of something new. "Mr. Ghettie. I'm grateful for your interest, and I look forward to accepting your generosity. But I wonder …?"

Ghettie finished his sentence with a knowing look in his eye. "Why now?"

Radcliff bowed his head a little. "Indeed."

Ghettie's confidence suggested he'd anticipated the question. "We live in uncertain times. Times where we all have a responsibility to ensure our crafting of the future. I myself have suffered a health challenge, and swore that when I was able enough again I would do everything in my power to make that change in the world that I would like to see before I die."

He placed his hand on Radcliff's shoulder as if he were a longtime friend. "I know that for those of us in the game of educating young minds we are very in touch with this concept. And our own impending mortality.

Radcliff nodded, sympathetic to the gentleman's health problems. "Yes. Yes, of course," he muttered. "One has to ask, though."

Ghettie removed his hand from Radcliff's shoulder and turned to leave. "Yes. One must," he agreed. "I'll have my people send you over some material to consider. We should talk again in the next week or so."

And then he strode out of the office, leaving the door open.

Radcliff could see Amy sitting in her desk, watching a little awe-struck by the stranger who was able to walk into the university and speak with her boss without an appointment or a good reason.

Her eyes remained on the door out of her office.

"Amy," Radcliff called through from his office.

Amy's attention snapped back to him. "Yes sir?"

Radcliff's voice was enthusiastic and motivated. "Have the board meeting scheduled for the end of the month brought forward to next week. There are some pressing matters for us to consider."

Amy had already started pulling up the details to alert the board members and their assistants.

He ambled over and closed his door, and her attention was pulled from her screens as she heard it clunk shut.

Curiouser and curiouser, she thought to herself, returning her eyes to her task.

Gaitune-67, Base conference room

"Okay, how did we get on?" Molly asked looking over at Joel.

Joel straightened up and then stood up, regarding the assembled team in the base conference room. "Looks like we have a plan," he reported, pulling up a screen on his holo.

Each team member looked a little more on edge than usual. No one had been told who would be going undercover, and apart from Pieter, everyone else was at least part excited by the possibility. Pieter sat looking morose, like a kid who didn't want to play this game.

Brock noticed. "Hey, cheer up buddy. May never happen!" he said, slapping Pieter's arm, and only then realizing how what he had just said was totally not true.

Pieter glared up at him. "Fifty-fifty chance I have to do the whole undercover thing. I tried to tell Joel it just wasn't my bag."

Brock lowered his voice and leaned in. "And what happened?" he asked, concerned.

Pieter shrugged anxiously. "I never got past rehearsing what I would say in front of the bathroom mirror."

Brock giggled. "You loon. You should know you can just talk to Joel. I did, back when there was ops stuff I didn't want to do."

Pieter turned his head so they wouldn't be overheard. "And what happened?" he asked softly.

Brock shrugged with his easy relaxed way. "He took me out of it until I got enough training to feel good about it."

Pieter considered it for a moment. "I also didn't want to let the team down. I mean, surely no one else wants to do it either."

Brock pointed around the table, sweeping his finger, and encouraging Pieter to look. "See all these folks here?" he asked.

Pieter mumbled to the affirmative.

Brock posed his follow up question. "Notice the air of excitement in the room?"

Pieter nodded.

Brock grinned down at him. "Every single one of them is excited by the prospect. There's no shortage of people who want to volunteer. If you're not ready, you're not ready. You shouldn't feel like it is any reflection on you, or on your commitment to the team."

Pieter nodded again, his shoulders relaxing a little. "Thanks, man," he said quietly, nudging Brock on the arm.

The two sat up straighter and started paying attention to the meeting that was getting going.

Joel pulled up a screen with a bunch of names.

"Okay," he told them. "Oz has gone in and created back stories for each of the folks who have been selected for this mission."

He glanced at the screen and then his notes. "What you see on screen is the ship's manifest. This is the crew that is down to take the ship from Estaria to Teshov. Those who have been selected for the undercover part of the mission are: Sean..."

Sean fist pumped the air near his body, in silent jubilation.

Joel continued to read off his list. "Brock, Maya and Jack."

ELL LEIGH CLARKE & MICHAEL ANDERLE

Maya grinned.

Jack nodded politely, only her eyes betraying her secret lust for a good undercover mission.

Brock's eyes widened as he wobbled his head from side to side in a silly gesture of excitement. At the same time his mouth was chewed up in pretend anxiety — probably covering his actual mixture of anxiety and excitement.

Pieter's relief was palpable. He slumped in his chair as if he'd just escaped being abducted by little gray aliens.

Joel allowed a second or two for the muttering and excitement to subside, and then continued. "Learn your back story and make sure you collect your ID cards and make them look like they've been used. Carry them around with you. Get used to answering to your cover ID name. I and others will be testing you."

Maya was still grinning, her fists clenched in thrill under the table so that she didn't undo the somewhat professional air she had been cultivating of late. Paige noticed though, but said nothing. Her expression was a little more serious.

Joel was still talking. "If one of you gets caught, the strategy is to remain undiscovered for as long as possible, unless you need to prevent real harm from coming to your team mate. Once the ship docks, we will be there to meet you, and as long as we have the intel we need, we will have Federation arrests made."

He scanned around the room. "This means we need to keep the ruse going for the duration of the journey. Which is *several* weeks." His face was deadly serious. "This could be the most difficult task you've ever undertaken."

"For those not undercover, your role is support any which way you can. Paige and Pieter, you will be responsible for monitoring all communications and feeding them intel or back story prompts as they need. You'll also be looking at any clues they gather and running checks to build up our picture of this organization, to make sure we get what we need. Once we have it, you need to alert me so that we can make necessary arrangements with the Federation to come and step in when we dock."

Paige nodded, and Pieter even sat up a little to acknowledge his role.

Joel glanced around the room, engaging with each team member. "Molly and I will be reviewing everything as it comes through, making necessary adjustments."

"Crash," he said, turning to their pilot, "we need you to work on any contingency plans in case one or all of the operatives are discovered. We need a way of pulling them out, without endangering the rest of the team, or the kidnapped scientists."

Crash lowered his head for a moment, and then raised his hand to get Joel's attention.

"Yes, Crash," Joel acknowledged, lifting his eyes from his holo and his next item.

Crash shuffled his butt cheeks forward in the chair. "Joel, if one or more of our team is discovered, is it under our remit to extract the hostages too?"

Joel glanced at Molly before answering. "We should run through a list of the scenarios. It depends on how much they know about us. Innocent life is, as always, at the top of our priority list to preserve."

Molly nodded her head silently, her eyes on the desk in front of her. Crash sat back, satisfied he was going to receive more input before he needed to hatch his hair-brained master plans of transportation badassery.

Joel began to wrap the meeting up. "We have twelve days before the ship leaves. Those undercover need to arrive there a day before departure for vaccinations and medical evals. There's also a bunch of admin that needs to be done before a trip like this, so read the packs the company sent to your server addresses that Oz has marked. Any questions, let me know."

He glanced around. "All good?"

Everyone nodded.

"Okay folks. Let's move out," he announced, dismissing the team in his usual manner.

Gaitune-67, Common area

"Who did *you* get?" Brock asked Maya.

Maya was studying the back story to her new identity on her holo. "I'm called Marissa d'Senigle," she announced proudly. "How about you?"

Brock tilted his head, trying to read the name on the ID card. "I'm Mr. Tallus Copernican," he said slowly, mouthing out the sounds.

Maya smiled congenially. "Well, I'm very pleased to meet you, Tallus," she said, bowing with a flourish of her hand.

Paige watched from the sofa. "Honestly. You make it sound like it's just a game!" she snapped.

Maya spun round. "No, we're not. We're just having some fun," she explained.

Paige huffed, and went back to her holo. "It says here that you studied economics before dropping out. I mean, what if someone asks you about the economic situation in the inner system?"

Maya sat down next to her friend and linked her arm, resting her hand on the top of Paige's forearm. "Well then, I'll tell them there was a reason *I dropped out*," she said gently, but smartly. She paused, then spoke with a little more gratitude. "I understand you're worried. But it's all going to be okay. I promise."

Paige looked up at Maya, the anger melting from her eyes. "I hope so," she agreed, not entirely convinced.

"Besides," Maya continued, "this is not much different from what I would do nearly every day when I was working on a case. And then I didn't have any back up. Just an editor who would come and bail me out if I got arrested or something."

Paige looked horrified. "You know, I never know when you're joking or serious when you say shit like that."

Maya grinned, and winked, moving the conversation back to Brock. "So... *Tallus*," she said emphasizing the use of his new name. "Where you from?"

Sean wandered into the common area, looking perplexed. Brock turned as he approached, his city of origin as Tallus forgotten. "You okay?" he asked the uncharacteristically emotional Sean.

Sean scratched his head. "Yeah. Looks like I've been placed on the highest risk role."

Brock frowned. "Thought you'd be pleased about that?"

Sean nodded slightly, flipping his ID over. "Yeah. I would normally. But this looks like ..." His voice cracked a little. "It looks like it's a desk job."

He practically gulped as soon as the words left his throat. He looked up bewildered, only half seeing Paige and Maya in front of him.

Maya giggled. "Dude, it looks like you've just been handed a pile of turds. What's the problem?" She watched him, unable to contain her mirth at his expression.

Sean looked tired and stressed. "A *desk* job," he repeated, this time more emphatically.

Paige started chuckling. And then Brock joined in. Sean glanced over at him, horrified.

Brock patted him on the back. "Welcome to the world of 9-to-5!" he chuckled. "It's okay. We're here for you. You *will* get through this," he said in his best therapist's voice, pretending to counsel him through the traumatic realization of what was to come.

Sean shuffled over to the arm chair and allowed his knees to collapse him onto it. His eyes scanned and rescanned the ID card. "How could they do this to me?" he muttered in disbelief under his breath.

He became vaguely aware that Maya had leaned forward and

was doubled over laughing her head off. Paige put her hand on her back, as if trying to soothe her bouts of hysteria.

Brock sat on the mocha table in front of Sean. "Bump me your back story," he suggested, holding out his holo. Sean pulled up the document, and then bumped holos with Brock.

Brock got up and ambled over to the arm chair on the other side of the holoviewing area, reading as he went.

He sat down. "Says here your name is Rex. Sounds kinda badass to me," he said encouragingly. "In fact, Rex sounds kinda tough. You might get a chance to show this posse who da boss is... desk jockeys or no."

Paige rolled her eyes. "You make him sound like such a meat-head!" she exclaimed.

Sean looked up, his eyes still half glazed and wider than they normally would be. "But I AM a meathead. If I'd wanted a desk job, I'd be somewhere like the *Meredith Reynolds*, or the *ArchAngel*, organizing battles and maintaining the Empress's forces." His eyes lost focus again and his attention dropped back to his holoscreen.

Brock cocked his head empathetically. "Well, it sounds like you're the best person to do this. If they said this was high risk, it's likely you're the only one who has enough operational experience to deal with whatever is going down in that area of the ship. Plus, if any of us get found out, we need you in a position to come rescue our asses!"

Sean bobbed his head, warming to the idea.

Maya pulled herself together after her fit of laughter and managed to feign some sympathy. "Yeah. And I suspect that there will still be an opportunity for you to do meathead stuff. The ship must have a gym. And other meathead operatives for the heavy lifting and stuff. I'm sure you'll find your groove."

Sean glanced over and nodded appreciatively. "Maybe I'll tell them my nick name is 'Meathead'... just so they don't get the wrong idea."

Paige shook her head, sniggering to herself. "I think we might be missing the point of going under cover!" she said gently.

Sean didn't hear her, his spirits lifting a little. "Yeah. I'm going to call myself Meathead for this one," he declared a little more decisively. He stood up, pulling himself to his full height. "I think I'm gonna enjoy this gig," he said. Then he turned and walked out, with his usual Sean-cyborg-Royale swagger.

Maya started giggling again. "Meathead!" she said, shaking her head.

Brock started vibrating with silent laughter too. "Wait till he realizes that his role is the Head of Administrative Services, as a representative for an external auditing company!"

"Oh shit," Paige snickered. "Let's not break that to him just yet. Let him get used to the desk job thing for a day or two."

Brock put on his I'm-not-taking-the-blame-for-anything-that-happens look. "Well, it's right here in black and white on his briefing doc."

"I wonder how long it's going to take *Meathead* to read it," Paige chuckled.

CHAPTER FIVE

Gaitune-67, Base Ops Room

The call connected on the console holo and two smiling faces came into view.

Molly sat up a little on her invisible chair, shifting enough to encourage Neechie to jump down from her lap. "Greetings, gentlefolk," she called out, as if her voice needed to travel further because she knew they were connecting from a long way away.

"Greetings, Molly," Arlene called back, warmly. Giles made some greeting like "Hi, how are you," but his voice was a little fainter on account of him being a little further from the holo.

Molly felt happiness lift inside of her as she looked on the two old friends over the connection. "I'm good. How are you both?"

Arlene responded for the two of them. "We're doing okay," she told her. "Giles obviously is grumpy about the tedious workload, but we're doing well. Making progress," she summarized.

Giles protested. "We're working through the moons one at a time. And there are eleven of them! Arlene's calculations sucked ass."

Arlene grinned and tilted her head at him. "See?"

Molly smiled. "So you're in the Orn system?" she asked.

Arlene pulled her console chair a little closer, pushing Giles out a little. "Yes. I must say, the moons are rocky and deserted for the most part. But when you look out at the system, in almost any direction, it isn't half beautiful."

Giles interjected. "It is, but what is more fascinating is how eleven of these moons ended up in such an intricate orbit so close together. And so similar in size. There's no physical way it could have occurred naturally. It just doesn't make sense. Unless …"

Arlene frowned. "Unless you buy into the conspiracy theory!"

Giles huffed. "It's not a conspiracy theory. It's just physics. Occam's razor, etc., etc."

Arlene shook her head at him and smiled back at Molly. "See what I have to put up with?" she joked playfully.

Giles pretended to be offended and folded his arms. "Well, I shall just be quiet then, shall I?"

Oh my ancestors, they're like an old married couple.

You noticed that?

It's hard not to!

It's humorous.

It's sweet. As long as they don't end up killing each other.

That is a consideration.

"So," Arlene said, changing the subject. "You had information for us?"

Molly shifted in her seat a little. "Well. Kinda. It's like …" she took a deep breath before continuing again. "I had a realm shift, and I saw some things. I had no one else who might know what it meant, so I thought I'd reach out to you. In case you can help."

Arlene was listening intently. Giles had sat back a little but was still paying close attention, too.

Arlene leaned on the console in front of her, and had her hand by her chin. She waved it a little. "Go on," she said, encouraging Molly to share.

Molly took another deep breath. "Well. I'd just finished a call and Neechie was hanging around, which is why I knew at first that it was a realm jump. So the usual started happening. Feeling ungrounded and so on. And then I saw an image, as clearly as I see you in the hologram before me. It was a series of planets in a weird array, all in this cluttered orbit."

Arlene started poking at her console, her attention no longer on Molly. Then a second holoscreen appeared, with the exact same image Molly had been describing.

"Something like this?" she asked.

Molly's mouth dropped open. "How did you do that? Was Oz able to pull an image?"

Arlene chuckled lightly. "No, no, no. This is where we are. This is the Orn system we were just telling you about."

Molly's mouth dropped open. "But that's *exactly* what it looked like."

Arlene bobbed her head. "Well, good," she confirmed, matter-of-factly, unmoved by the fact that Molly's visions actually meant something.

"So what does this mean?" Molly asked.

Arlene looked back at the camera. "Well, for one, it suggests that your realm jumping is getting more precise and useful. I wouldn't be surprised if Neechie was helping you access aspects of your higher self that knows everything from past, present and future."

Molly allowed the new paradigms to float into her consciousness, cognizant that Oz could always give her a replay later.

Arlene continued. "As for what the scene means specifically, what else can you tell us?"

Molly closed her eyes, trying to recall the incident again. There was a pause on the line while she summoned the sequence in her mind's eye.

"I saw some kind of doorway. In stone. Like an entrance to a tomb. Or a temple."

She imagined herself there, recalling the details. "There was a smell of how the air goes when it's hot outside, but cold inside the stone walls. And there were markings. Like the Zhyn characters. But not. Maybe a different language. Or older. And they were worn away a bit, making it hard to make them out for sure."

She moved her head as if looking up and around, her eyes still closed, her mind lost in her memory. "The constellations were strange, but that would make sense if it were in the Orn system, an area of space I'm not familiar with."

Arlene whispered to Giles. "So it's a tomb, above the ground."

Giles nodded, his eyes not leaving the holo of Molly.

Molly could hear Arlene's voice again. "Anything else in the sky?" Arlene asked.

Molly shook her head again. "No, just a beam of light falling on it. Lighting up the glyphs."

Arlene's voice seemed a little more excited. "Can you see where the light is coming from?"

Molly shook her head. "No. But then I was somewhere else." She paused a moment, as if reliving the experience. "I turned, and looked down, and I was in a bedroom… looking at a drawer next to a bed. A bedside cabinet."

"Whose bedroom is it?" Arlene coaxed her into revealing more information.

Molly shook her head, a strand of her blonde hair dropping in front of her face. "I'm not sure. I feel like it's a girl. But a little girl who is quite… precocious. She feels as if she's beyond her years, or something. She's… strange."

Arlene's voice reached out to her. "What else can you see in the bedroom?"

Molly's brow creased up, as if she were trying to see closer. "There were red curtains over by the window. And outside… a building like the Capital Building in Spire. The room was sparse. Like a religious dorm or something. There were some Estarian beads on the wall."

She paused, her head looking downwards now. "But on the bedside table, there are tablets. That aren't being taken."

Arlene's voice penetrated her consciousness. "How do you know they're not being taken?" she asked.

Molly answered simply. "I just know."

Molly was silent. Giles and Arlene waited, watching. Wondering if there was any more information to come.

Molly suddenly opened her eyes. "That's it," she told them. "That's all I saw."

Arlene had been taking notes on her holo. She flicked up and down the screen, making sure she had everything she needed.

Molly watched the holo screen waiting for Arlene's opinion. "So, what do you think?" Molly pressed, a twinge of anxiety in the corners of her eyes.

Arlene pursed her lips, and then closed her holo. "I think," she told her, "that you've been seeing things that may help us narrow our search down."

Molly's face brightened. "Well, that's great then!" she said. Her face dropped a moment later. "But why?" she asked.

Arlene took a deep breath, and then glanced over at Giles, who was cleaning his fake glasses.

Realizing he was now being invited into the conversation, he sat up a little and pulled the chair forward. "I believe that as you're becoming more proficient in your realm jumping, you're able to access more and more intelligence out of time."

Molly frowned. "Out of time?" she asked.

Giles nodded, placing his glasses back on his face. "Yeah. So as humans... or any organics I know of... we experience time in sequence. Like frames of a movie."

Molly nodded her understanding and Giles continued. "Thing is, all these frames exist at once. Plus, there's an infinite number of possibilities, which all have their own track of frames."

"Okay ..." Molly agreed, slowly. She'd read her fair share of theoretical physics. The only problem she'd had with it was that it was purely theoretical.

Giles continued his point. "So imagine all of these frames, and then not necessarily being tied to them. So you're able to look at all of them out on a table in front of you."

Molly bobbed her head. "Yeah, okay. I get that."

Giles decided not to belabor the point. "Right. So. When you're realm jumping, you're basically accessing these other frames, from that altered perspective. What I've been calling 'out of time', or more precisely, 'outside of time.'"

"Hmmm," Molly mulled the idea for a moment. "That sounds... plausible. And it certainly explains all the different things I've been experiencing with the jumping and drifting."

Giles smiled, and then leaned over to speak quietly to Arlene, well aware that Molly could still hear him. "It's unnerving how quickly she accepts these things."

Arlene nodded with a detached smile on her face. "I know. It freaked me out a little when I first met her. I still haven't figured out if it's personality or just rapid processing of new paradigms."

Molly eyed them playfully. "Erm, hello? Still here," she called waving. "Even *I* know it's rude to talk about someone in the third person as if they're not there."

Arlene smirked a little. "My dear, we thought you were beyond such social conventions."

Molly relaxed in her seat. "Well. Yeah. That's true. I only mentioned it coz I thought it would be funny," she confessed blankly.

Arlene and Giles burst out laughing.

Molly looked at them, completely puzzled and missing the unintentional joke. "I don't understand," she said, as their laughter subsided.

Giles wiped an eye from behind his glasses. "It's funny because you tried to make fun of yourself and we didn't get it, and then you explained it , which was hilarious. And then it was a

ELL LEIGH CLARKE & MICHAEL ANDERLE

double whammy when you didn't understand why we found it funny in the end."

Molly's expression was still deadpan. "I think my head is about to explode."

Well, you wanted to try your hand at organic-peoples' humor!

True. I wish I hadn't now.

"Okay," Molly said brightly, "this has been useful and enlightening. What's next?"

The conversation continued for a few minutes longer, and eventually they said their farewells.

Giles clicked off the call, and sat back thinking.

Arlene glanced over at him. "You didn't want to talk to her privately then?"

Giles frowned. "Whatever for?"

Arlene rolled her eyes and moved her console chair back across the cockpit to her usual spot. "No reason," she said, a hint of humor in her voice.

Giles couldn't tell if Arlene was having a dig, or genuinely encouraging his interests in Molly. Plus, she had her back to him as she made the comment, making reading her expression even more difficult. He suspected she had done that deliberately, on account of the many papers they'd written in the early days about facial cues for evaluating truth and credibility.

Either way, trying to form any kind of relationship with Molly from god knows how many light years away, *and* while in close proximity to his very long-ended ex, was not his idea of a smart move.

He got up, stretched his legs, and ambled back into the makeshift living area of the *Scamp Princess*.

Gaitune-67, Kitchen

"So where's Paige tonight?" Brock asked.

Pieter stuffed some fries into his mouth and then realized he couldn't answer. He chewed deliberately, bobbing his head and pointing at his mouth, then swallowed hard. "She's with Carl. Again."

Brock's face animated. "Wow, that girl must be getting some!" he sang in his lilty, playful way.

Maya placed her burger back in the open take-out box. "Hey, some decorum, Brock!" she chided.

Brock did his pretend serious face. "Ooops. Sorry," he said, a little sheepishly. "Looks like the sex police are out in force!" he added cheekily.

Maya rolled her eyes at him before adding more ketchup to her fries and continued eating.

Brock suddenly realized something. "Anyway, aren't you meant to be calling me Tallus now?"

Maya slapped her hand over her mouth. She said "shit" but it came out muffled between the mouthful of greasy fried potato and her hand smothering her face.

Sean had been chowing down quietly. He looked up, as if watching a soap opera. Shaking his head gently he uttered a single word.

"Amateurs."

Brock and Maya looked straight at him in annoyance and protest.

Pieter shoved another fry into his mouth. "He has a point. If you can't even remember for ten minutes when you're at home, how are you going to do it 24/7 when you're under pressure in a new environment?"

"Because," Maya explained, "we'll be *in* a new environment."

Pieter shook his head, looking to Sean for backup. "My money is on one of you two needing your asses rescued first," he said, waving his finger in Maya's and then Brock's direction. "Within the first week," he added, confidently.

Maya considered throwing a fry at him but then changed her

mind, choosing to instead play it cool. "Okay, betting boy. What you want to wager?"

Pieter suddenly looked caught off-guard. "Well, er... I..."

Maya waved her hand. "It's okay. Doesn't have to be money. We can just do something like... I dunno. Maybe you do my laundry for a month if you're wrong."

Pieter looked up at the ceiling, analyzing his options. "Okay. And if I win, you have to be my general house slave for a day."

Maya didn't hesitate. She stuck her hand across the table to Pieter to shake on the deal.

Brock interjected energetically. "Woah woah woah, girl. You don't wanna be doing that. You have no idea what nasty business he'll have you doing. Have you seen the state of his sleeping quarters?"

Maya chuckled. "It'll be fine, I'm sure. Geek-boy will probably just be having me organizing his hard drives or trying to get him free access to certain sites on Estaria."

Pieter looked shocked. And embarrassed. He said nothing, but shook her hand.

Brock tilted his head, his eyes giving her the don't-blame-me-when-this-ends-in-tears kind of look one's mother would traditionally give. "Well, Marissa d'Senigle, you're just going to have to not get captured on this mission," he told her decisively.

Just then, Jack walked in. "Ah great, grubs up!" she exclaimed, enthused.

Maya pushed her box of food across to her. "They didn't have onion rings so they gave you extra fries," she explained.

Jack's face lit up. "Nom," she commented, grabbing a fork from a drawer before sitting down. "Thanks, Marissa," she said as naturally as if it had been Maya's actual name.

"You're welcome, *Griselle*," Maya responded, a little less naturally.

Sean had been watching, and shook his head at Maya's

renewed attempt at adopting the new names. He took another bite of his monster burger and chewed quietly.

On board the *Flutningsaðili*, Uptarlung Space Port, Pike's office

Max Pike lounged in his console chair. His second-in-command, Pascal Randalf, ran through their list of operational items in preparation for the new crew showing up in a few days' time.

"Level four still off limits?" Randalf queried, a furrow playing across his forehead.

Pike nodded. "Yeah. Why?"

Randalf looked up from his holo. "Some of the new security detail were asking. Complaining they couldn't get through the doors to check the place."

Pike rocked idly in his chair. "Yeah, that's by design."

"So," Randalf tried guessing, "you just don't want anyone in there?"

"That's right," Max replied, looking off into the distance as if contemplating something entirely different.

"Why not?" Pascal pressed.

There was a pause in the conversation as Max came back to the room, and considered a response with mild annoyance.

"Because," he explained, "we are paid to keep secrets. And in that area there are secrets that I can't control if every Tom, Dick and Ralph have access to the area."

Randalf nodded, but kept his nerve. "Okay. I understand that, but …"

Max had stopped rocking and was now looking at the middle-aged Estarian administrator. "But?" he echoed.

Randalf's hand hovered over his holo as if waiting to check an item off. "Is there anything that I should be aware of in there? Like is it dangerous? Or something I need to tend to?"

Pike took a deep breath, contemplating.

"In case anything was to happen to you, I mean," Pascal added, his face even more contorted in concern now.

Max frowned, sitting up in his chair slightly. His eyes suddenly had a glint of suspicion in them. "Why are you asking all these questions all of a sudden?" he queried accusingly.

Pascal looked down and shuffled his feet a little. "Erm... I heard reports that you had, erm, brought a girl on board."

Max looked ready to explode. "Who told you that?"

Pascal put his hands out trying to calm his boss. "It's okay. I handled it. The person who mentioned it has been, er... called away. I assumed it was confidential." He paused for a moment. "I didn't think we were into that kind of thing, though." His eyes darted around a little, unsure of where to rest his gaze on this awkward subject.

Max stood up, a little calmer, and wandered over to the game ball on his shelf. He picked it up and toyed with it in his hands. "We're not," he reassured him firmly. "And it's not what you think. I'm doing someone a favor. The girl has value to them for what she knows. It's more a transfer of skills."

He twizzled the ball in his hands. "At least, that's as much as I've been told." He glanced back at his longtime friend and colleague. "You know how these people are," he explained, his tone softer. "So you just don't ask questions."

He headed over to his desk and sat down, hugging the ball to his body under his clasped hands, his elbows tucked in. "Besides, it's no different from the other two we're going to be transporting."

Pascal pinched his eyes with his fingers, his head down, no longer looking at the holo. "Yeah. And that's another thing we didn't get into this for."

Max shrugged. "Secrets are secrets, and precious cargo... sometimes has a pulse."

Pascal wiped his hands over his face, looking up and leaning forward in the low chair, his arms resting on his knees. "Well...

right," he sighed in resignation. "I guess this is what we're stuck with."

Max twizzled the ball in his hands. "You're not happy?"

Pascal stood up and glanced over at him. "You're damn right I'm not happy." He paused, controlling his tone. "But I'll get the job done," he added.

He closed his holo and then got up and stalked out of the office, leaving Max with his thoughts.

CHAPTER SIX

Uptarlung District, Estaria

Three pods hovered 800 feet in the air just on the outskirts of Uptarlung, before descending down to the surface near a tube station. The sky was grey and cold, and there was a dampness in the atmosphere that was uncharacteristic of the northern hemisphere of the planet.

Molly pressed her face against the side window of the pod she shared with Paige. "Looks like we're here," she remarked.

Paige didn't answer. She had a heaviness in the pit of her stomach. "What if they get caught?" she mumbled anxiously, as Molly reached for the button to release the front of the pod.

Molly stopped and sat back in her seat. "Then we'll swoop in and rescue their asses," she told her confidently. "Like we always do." Her voice softened. "They'll be fine," she added.

Paige smiled, unconvinced. But with nowhere else for the conversation to go, she allowed Molly to exit the pod.

Molly stepped out, greeted by the cold and damp. The area where they had landed seemed to have become surrounded in moisture.

I think this is what meteorologists call fog.

I believe so.

It's... ugh.

Molly shuddered and folded her arms against her, her atmo-suit already gathering water droplets.

I concur.

Molly watched as her team stepped out of the other pods, noting their reactions as they were each met with the foggy realism of their destination.

"What's with this weather?" Maya asked, hugging her arms around her and shifting the weight of her pack on her back.

Jack retrieved her luggage from the storage compartment of the pod and hauled it onto her back. "I know," she commiserated. "Last time it was like this I think I was probably still in school."

Sean plonked his pack in front of him, and rubbed his hands together briskly. He grinned. "Perfect weather to start an operation!" he declared with a strange glee.

Maya chuckled at his enthusiasm. She wondered how long it would last once he realized he was head auditor for the ship's cargo.

"Okay," Molly said, gathering them around. "This is it. You're each going to head into town from here, so there is no chance you are seen together. Take different trains and different carriages. Don't be too keen to introduce yourself to each other, or the others. Remember, you want to give the appearance of just wanting to keep to yourself and get the job done."

Maya and Brock nodded. Sean had his arms folded and was listening to their instructions carefully. Jack did the same.

Molly looked at each of them. "Stay in touch. Remember to do your quantum bead check-ins. Just a click is all we need to know that you're okay. Paige and Pieter are monitoring you 24/7, so if you need anything, let us know. Stay safe, and good hunting."

Each member of the team said their thanks and goodbyes before hugging both Paige and Molly, and then made their way over to the subway station. Each were careful to start behaving like individuals rather than a group.

Molly watched them leave. She realized that she was holding her breath. Taking a deep breath, she tried to release the tension she had been holding.

Paige's voice interrupted her thoughts. "Admit it," she pressed. "You're worried too." Paige watched her teammates disappear into the foggy version of suburban civilization.

Molly nodded. "I'm *always* worried about them. But they are the most capable and adaptable people I know, and I have faith in them."

Paige didn't respond. She just watched until they had all been swallowed by the fog, and then followed Molly back into their pod.

Brock had remained behind at the train station for another half an hour, so that they could stagger their arrivals. The mist was clinging to his skin, making him long for a nice hot shower, something that would soothe the travel tension he was already starting to feel.

Space travel and terrestrial travel are two very different things, he mused. *And honestly, when you take into account the standing about and the weather, space travel was the better option any day of the week.*

He paced up and down the platform trying to pass the time. If he kept moving, at least he was burning calories, so it wasn't a complete waste, he reasoned.

His mind flicked through to the last time he waited on a tube platform, on his way to and from school. It felt like a century ago. It was certainly another life ago. He sighed, remembering how his mother had come to meet him on his first few days of school. And then how as time went on she would barely remember she had a son. The alcohol tended to do that to a person.

He felt a heaviness in his heart. He had loved his mom. And yet, there was so much to still be angry about.

Good job I got out when I did, he consoled himself, rummaging in his pack for another layer to put on against the cold.

Maya sat on the tube, watching the insides of the tunnel, punctuated by total blackness, whiz past the tube window. For the first time in a long while she felt lonely. Sure, there were days in the safehouse when Paige had been at Carl's recently, and she had barely spoken to anyone the whole day. But this was different. This was a feeling of dread deep in the pit of her stomach.

Maybe Paige's instincts had been right, she thought. *Maybe this wasn't something she was prepared for. And what if this was the mission she didn't survive?*

There was a loud bang off at the end of the car. She snapped her attention round, ready to react.

It was another passenger struggling with his luggage that had fallen forward from the rack. She sat back around, and tried to calm herself.

No need to be so jumpy, she told herself. *Remember, you're meant to be a civilian. Start thinking and acting like one.*

She rested her head against the train wall, hoping to be able to relax. The vibration ran through her skull and as the carriage rocked the spot where she made contact kept moving. Uncomfortable and frustrated, she sat up again, resigning herself to the bolt upright position of the seats.

I wonder how the others are doing, she wondered idly.

Staðall University, Spire, Lecture Theater 21

Paige adjusted the holocamera settings and then realigned the floating autocue. "Okay, we're set. Wanna try again?"

Abigail Von took a deep breath and looked into the camera and smiled. "Have you ever wondered what the world would be like if we had leaders who were adept in negotiation and conflict resolution? Can you imagine a world where we are on the brink of eliminating war? What about a future where every person is fed, and cared for, and able to contribute in a meaningful way? Sounds like a fairy tale, doesn't it?"

Von started to move along the path Paige had chalked out across the front of the lecture theater floor.

Von continued to read off the script. "But what if it isn't? I can't tell you how many students who have attended my classes on interplanetary trade negotiations have asked me to teach them what would make the difference. Not just in trade. But in everything. And until now, it's always been a skill and subset of study that never quite made it into an official course."

Abigail had moved forward again as they had choreographed. The autocue continued to roll.

"My name is Abigail Von," she continued, "and I'm a professor of Interplanetary Relations, as well as the lecturer for Staðall University's new course on interplanetary negotiations."

The autocue ran out of words, and Abigail stopped talking, pausing so that they would have enough footage to clip the end of that segment.

"Cut," Paige called after a second. The camera automatically cut and then closed down ready for relocation.

Von's gaze shifted from the camera lens to Paige who was standing several feet behind it. "Are you getting what you need?" she asked anxiously.

Paige nodded. "Yes, you're doing extremely well!" she exclaimed brightly. "I'm ready to sign up for the course myself."

Molly had been sitting on the front bench behind the camera and out of Von's line of sight. Abigail looked over at her to get her reaction.

Molly nodded. "I think this is going to be really super." She looked over at Paige. "When I came to visit Abigail the first time, I was floored by how popular she is with her students. She can't kick them out of the lecture theater, even after her class is finished."

Paige grinned, taking in what Molly was telling her. "Wow. That's... incredible. I wish I'd had a teacher like you when I was at school."

Von laughed, a little embarrassed. "Well, I do think that the think tank technology has been an excellent addition to the teaching process," she explained modestly. "But, if you're actually interested in interplanetary relations you could always sign up for the course. I don't think it would be an issue with the university, since your boss is entirely responsible for the funding of it."

Paige glanced over at Molly, not wanting to put her on the spot. Then she looked back at Von. "If it doesn't look like it would interfere with my work, I may take you up on that generous offer." She flushed a little pink in the small of her neck. "I must admit, I wasn't the best student when I was at school, though."

Von winked at her. "I've always been told that there's no such thing as a bad student," she said.

Paige grinned, then turned to Molly. "And she blames the technology for the enthusiasm of her students." She rolled her eyes, teasingly.

Molly chuckled a little and shook her head. "I know, right?"

Von looked a little perplexed. And then embarrassed. Again. "So, we should shoot the next bit telling them how to register now?" she ventured, changing the subject to something a little more within her comfort zone.

Paige grabbed the camera and the autocue. "Yeah, I thought maybe we could do that out in the quad?"

Von frowned. "Even though it's dark?"

Paige nodded. "Yup. We have flood lights. And it will make it atmospheric. Besides... all your students have seen the prospectus videos with perfectly manicured lawns and bright daylight making the buildings look like something out of a utopia. I think it will be refreshing for them to see something different. After all, I'm sure there are many of them who are around campus after hours, and this is when they feel most like this is their university."

Von was taking it all in, impressed. She glanced over at Molly. "This one has a lot of insight into the psychology of relationships."

Molly slid off the bench, and started helping Paige pack up the other pieces of equipment. "She does. She has her own company she runs now and the media she runs through her sales and marketing departments is top notch. Outsells all her major competitors by at least 100%!"

Abigail looked even more taken aback. "Well in that case, I'd be honored if you were in my class. I have a feeling you have a natural ability for all things to do with communication and negotiations."

Northfield, Uptarlung Space Port

Jack arrived at the office, her pack weighing heavily now on her shoulder. It had been a long while since she had to travel like a cadet. Not that she was averse to hauling her own gear or putting in physical effort.

She found the registration office the Estarian at the station had sent her to. He'd said it was the fourth door on the right. As she approached the building she saw that the forth door was slightly ajar with a hand-written sign taped to it: REGISTRA-TION, BRAVO EQUIP.

That's the one, she told herself, bracing herself for talking to civilians. She slouched her shoulders a little, and pulled at her jacket so that she didn't look too orderly. Though she'd been in the military most of her life now, she hadn't lost sight of how military folks were perceived by civilians, and she wasn't about to give anything away here.

She stomped up the wooden steps to the slightly warped door and knocked before pushing it open. There was no one around, but a waft of the scent of sawdust and packing materials met her nostrils. She stepped up the final stair and shuffled in, slinging her pack down on the floor. She made a show of rolling her shoulder and loosening it from the load.

She heard movement off to her right, and a short Ogg appeared from the back room.

"Bravo?" he asked.

Jack wasn't sure she heard him right. "Pardon?" she asked. Then her ears caught up with her brain. "Yes, Bravo Equipment," she confirmed, mentally kicking herself for fluffing up straight out of the gate.

The Ogg didn't seem bothered. He simply opened his holo and started reading down. "Name?" he demanded.

She's been practicing this one. "Griselle Oriel," she announced, trying to sound natural, like she had introduced herself a million times.

He didn't look up, but poked into his holo and then closed it. "Sent you some registration documents. Medic is through there," he nodded to the door on the other side of the room. "He'll call for you when he's ready. You can wait over there."

He pointed at a bank of half a dozen hardback chairs. Jack glanced over at them, then back at the Ogg, and then down at her pack. Visibly unenthused by the whole situation, she bent over and lifted her luggage unceremoniously and hauled herself over to the chairs. She sat down, placing her pack on the floor in front of the seat next to her.

Crossing her legs, she opened her holo.

Here goes nothing, she told herself, as she eyeballed the bullshit paperwork she had gone to incredible extremes to avoid in her real life.

About twenty minutes had passed before a strange-looking

Estarian hobbled into the doorway of the other room the Ogg had indicated.

"Oriel," he called.

Jack sprung to her feet. "That's me!" she said, relieved to finally be getting on with something.

The Estarian nodded and ambled back into the other room. Jack assumed this meant she was to follow. She pulled her luggage into an upright position and half lifted, half dragged it across the bare floor boards of the temporary airport building.

Inside the room were two chairs, a desk, and an examination table. And not much else.

"Sit," the medic instructed.

Jack took the seat by the side of the desk, and the doctor pulled his chair out and sat himself down. "I have a series of questions to ask you, then I need a blood and urine sample for drug testing and then you'll be free to go. If there are any problems you will be notified by holo and your shift will be canceled. If everything is okay, you won't hear from us and you just report to duty tomorrow night. Do you understand?"

Jack nodded. "Yes. I understand."

"Good," he said flatly. "Onto the questions. Are you or have you ever been ..."

The next hour was filled with inane and ridiculous medical disclaimers that they wanted the workers' confirmation on. All of the rest of the information she gave was either something basic that would show up in the blood tests or in any of the DNA scans they would care to run.

After being poked and prodded, and having under gone an eye examination, and had her teeth counted, she signed a bunch of holo screens and was *finally* dismissed.

Picking up her pack, she didn't bother to tuck her shirt back in, because... well, not military now. She exited from the same door she had gone in, and noticed that in the time she had been in the exam room a number of other people had arrived. Her eyes fell immediately to the female Estarian sitting delicately between two Estarian males, who each took up a chair and a half by the time they had leaned and spread their legs comfortably.

Jack averted her eyes so as not to give anyone the feeling that Maya and she knew each other. Maya did the same, pretending to study the patterns in the dusty floorboards. Jack shuffled herself and her pack out of the make-shift office and traipsed down the steps. She dropped her pack that she'd been carrying like a brief-case, and checked her holo for the instructions that had come through in response to her registration paperwork.

She scanned the details and then swung her pack onto her back and headed off down the road to find the hostel they had been booked into for the night. She decided she would dump her gear, find out who else was around, make some acquaintances — or not — and then head out to find some food.

Her chest felt numb and heavy at the prospect. She'd done enough traveling with the military to know that space ports weren't the most inspired places for either accommodation or culinary requirements.

CHAPTER SEVEN

Tímabundið Hostel, Northfields, Uptarlung Space Port

Brock arrived at the Tímabundið Hostel and looked up at the old brown, ugly building. He assumed that the others had made it here before him since he hadn't seen any of them at the registration office. He hadn't dared ask anyone for fear of drawing suspicion.

He checked in and made his way up the staircase with the thinning carpet and entered the sparsely furnished shared room. The furniture consisted of a dresser, a chair and a bunk bed. There was gear on the bottom bunk, claiming it as taken.

Guess we don't get single accommodations on this gig, he mused, disheartened.

He pulled out the clothes he would need for the evening and his sweats for sleeping in, and then set about the task of finding the shower room.

He found the shower room down the hall, and after some faffing about gathering soaps and sponges and a change of clothes, he got himself showered and feeling almost human again.

Half dressed in his fresh clothes, his damp towel encapsulating all of his other things, he pushed his way back into his shared room.

There was a dark lump of a body on the bottom bunk. It moved, and he nearly jumped out of his skin. Still stunned, he quickly gathered himself so as not to appear scatty. Then he looked a little closer.

It was Sean.

His body flooded with relief, and he wanted to say 'Sean!' until he remembered: *Sean is called Rex.*

And Rex and Tallus don't know each other yet.

Sean casually rolled his head on the pillow to look at the person coming through the door. "Ah," he said. "Guess you're my roommate for the night."

Brock shuffled into the room and closed the door, smiling. "Yeah. I'm Tallus," he said, bowing in the Estarian way.

"Rex," Sean replied curtly. "Rex Baron."

Brock flushed a little, carrying the towel of shower things and dirty clothes. He glanced at the bundle and then shrugged awkwardly. "Nice to meet you, Rex Baron," he replied. "Good trip in?"

Without an obvious audience to their conversation Sean seemed to be going through the motions. "Tube ride in. It was dull."

He lay back again, his eyes falling to the bottom of the top bunk above him, and then closed his eyes.

Brock continued getting himself dressed and sorted his gear. "How did you get on with the medical? Tedious, eh?"

Sean grunted. "Yeah. But it's all for insurance purposes," he explained, almost as if he was embracing his role as the head administrator for the auditing company.

He seemed to think of something, and turned on his side, propping his head up in his hand. "So, what are you in for?" he asked with a slight smirk.

Brock spoke as he shuffled his things around, glancing up now and again. "You mean what is my job on the trip?" He slung his damp towel over a towel rail in the airing cupboard. "I'm a chef. So, food."

Sean lay back down again. "I see."

He paused. "Speaking of, we should probably go and find some food before we sleep. Maybe see who else in the crew has been put up here."

Brock's face brightened. "Good plan. Have you met anyone else yet?"

Sean had laid back down again, staring at the bottom of the bed above him. "I noticed a bunch of people who might be in the crew checking in earlier. Some Estarian chick said she was part of Bravo, doing computer maintenance."

Brock bobbed his head. "Hmm. Dirty work, that is."

Sean nodded. "Yeah," he chuffed, springing up off the bed. "Okay. Let's go do this then," he told Brock.

Brock, perplexed by the sudden decision for them to move out, grabbed his boots, his room key card, and checked his reflection before following Sean barefoot out of the room.

Gaitune-67, Base Ops Room

Molly sat in the dimly lit ops room. Paige sat by her side, clutching a mocha. Molly took the time to appreciate the sweet aroma wafting in her direction.

"Looks like it will probably be full by the end of the week," Von told them over the holo connection.

Molly's eyebrows raised up. "Seriously? All two hundred places?"

Von nodded. "Yep. I think we've hit on something that is very much wanted right now."

Paige was beaming. "That's excellent news. I think the video turned out to be very effective. I can't wait to tell Maya," she said to Molly, before turning back and explaining to Von who Maya was and that it was she who had written the script.

"It worked like a charm," the middle-aged professor agreed. "I don't think they're used to quite the same amount of thought going into a promotional video for a class. It certainly has stood out."

Paige was flicking through screens on her holo. "It looks like it has had five hundred times more views than the average video on the system. It's also been shared beyond just the students too."

Von frowned, suddenly looking a little uncertain. "You mean, beyond the university?" She noticed that Paige nodded. "How did you get hold of that data?" she asked.

Molly leaned closer to the holo. "We have access to a lot of resources through various channels. The thing is, most of the data is publicly available if you have the expertise and the willingness to pull it. I just don't think many people bother with it, because, well, they're not trying to blaze any trails."

Von's face relaxed again. "Ah. I see," she confirmed.

Paige was still flicking through screens on her device. "So, when did we say the course started?" she asked without looking up.

Von responded without thinking. "Two weeks from yesterday," she told her.

Paige bobbed her head. "Neat. This is going to be awesome!"

Molly smiled. "It is indeed." She turned to Von, her tone a little more businesslike now. "So, we should probably firm up the last few lecture topics you had on your last communication."

Von pulled up a screen in front of her camera, blurring her image a little. "Yes, shall we?"

Molly and Von discussed the ins and outs of where they wanted the material to end up, and what the final take-away they wanted the students to be left with. During the conversation, they had a few sidebar comments that made it clear they had much they could learn from each other in terms of both the concepts and the application. Paige looked on in rapt attention, her enthusiasm for the subject mounting.

Molly noticed and when the final lecture content was agreed on, she looked over at Paige. "I think you ought to take this course," she said, smiling. "If you think you can manage the workload, that is."

Paige's eyes lit up. "Yes, yes I can manage it. I'd love to, as long as you don't think it will be a distraction from the work we do here?"

Molly shook her head. "I think it's important that we support this material, and that we bring these understandings in house. Yes, you're here to do a job, but more than that, you're here to grow as a person, so you can do bigger jobs and take on bigger challenges for us in the future. It's my responsibility to give you the opportunity to grow into those future roles. Not just to get projects completed here and now."

Paige started tearing up. "That's... *amazing!*" Her voice was wavering, as the emotion welled up in her. "You're the best, Molly."

Paige lunged over the distance of the sofa between them and flung her arms around Molly. Molly stiffened at the sudden contact, but then after a moment relaxed a little and returned the hug.

Von watched over the camera, her face soft and head tilted to one side.

After a short moment Molly straightened up and Paige let her go, returning to her side of the couch. "Okay, so I think we're all set," she declared. "Paige will be there at your first lecture, and if you need anything between now and then, just reach out."

The ladies said their goodbyes and ended the call.

"I'm. So. Excited!" Paige squealed quietly, careful not to infringe on Molly's personal space again.

A moment later, Molly was watching her disappear out across the ops room, muttering something about needing to call her boyfriend.

Molly smiled, amused at Paige's capacity for happiness at the smallest of things. And her happiness at learning new skills. That was something she could get behind, one hundred percent.

Fjallabaki Bar, Uptarlung

Sean and Brock stepped into the bar.

Brock looked at Sean. "Sure this is it?"

Sean shrugged. "It's the only one on the right on this block," he said, recalling what the guy on reception had told them.

Brock took a deep breath. "Wow. Well, if this is where all the freight people come when they're in this hostel, then no doubt we'll find some of the people we'll be crewing with."

Sean ignored the commentary and strode deliberately up to the bar. "I'll have a pint of whatever moves the fastest." Brock joined him. Sean opened his hand to Brock. "What will you have?" he asked.

Brock considered for a moment, and then went with the safe option. "Whatever he's having," he said to the bartender, tipping his head in Sean's direction.

Brock turned around and surveyed the layout, looking for the others. He spotted Maya and Jack over in the far corner. He started to wave, and then remembered that without an excuse to talk to them there is no way that he should know who they are. He replaced his elbow on the bar, and continued looking around.

"Looks like some of our folks are over there," he said in a low voice to Sean.

Sean grunted something, and then when the man near them had moved away, he added quietly, "don't even look at them."

Brock turned back around, and pulled out a bar stool, sitting himself down. Sean did the same as they waited for their drinks.

They pretended to make awkward small talk, each mentally trying to figure out a way to make contact with the other two so they could start building a relationship.

Eventually their drinks arrived, and Sean used it as a way to hide his lips as he mumbled across to Brock. "Maybe it's better that we don't know each other that well until we've had a bit of time on the ship. It wouldn't be natural for a group of crew to meet just one night ahead of them shipping out."

Brock nodded. "Sure," he said, taking a sip of his beer, and then standing up. Sean looked at him a little alarmed.

Brock slapped his hand on the bar. "It's okay. I'm just hitting the head!" he chuckled, walking away.

Sean laughed quietly to himself as he took another swig of his beer, deliberately keeping his eyes in front of him and nowhere else.

Brock was back in no time, and was about to sit down, when an Estarian guy brushed past him. "Excuse me," Brock said spontaneously.

The guy turned around, and instead of nodding or muttering some similar polite apology he *glared* at Brock. He was holding a glass of beer, and it looked like he had slopped some. "Excuse you, indeed! You dreifbýlistútta (trans:= hillbilly) of a asswit!"

Sean tensed, but kept his eyes forward, not wanting to draw attention.

Brock however, had never been concerned about an audience. "Dreifbýlistútta, yourself!" he said in disbelief. "You bumped into *me*! I was just being polite." His colorful attitude, complete with hand-waving, snapped into action.

Sean shifted in his seat, trying to turn his face away so he wouldn't get pulled into whatever was starting to go down. This was the first rule of espionage. Become invisible. Unremarkable.

It was all he could do to keep from rolling his eyes.

The dispute escalated in volume, and the Estarian turned and put his beer down on the table, and started pushing the sleeves of his atmosjacket up his arm, more in a menacing gesture than it looked, like it was going to actually help his reach if he were to throw a punch.

Brock had his hands up. "Look, I didn't come here for trouble," he said.

"Yeah?" the Estarian said, stepping forward. "Well you found it anyway!" He lunged in Brock's direction, and Brock winced, closing his eyes and quickly pulling his arms around his head, and leg up to protect his body. He'd had enough ass-kickings in a bar to have developed a form of physical self-preservation.

Even if his mouth hadn't quite caught on.

Brock braced himself for pain. But the punches didn't come.

He opened one eye, and the guy was no longer in front of him. In fact, it looked like he had been pulled back away from him.

Cautiously, Brock lowered his leg and arms, and opened his other eye, to find Jack holding the Estarian by the scruff of his collar.

"I don't think so," she told the Estarian.

The guy scuffled a little and got free, turning to face her. "Oh yeah, and what's it to you?" he challenged.

Jack looked him square in the eye. "I don't like seeing other people fighting," she told him firmly. "Especially if I'm not a part of it," she added, a glimmer flicking across one eye.

Likely due to his state of inebriation, the guy was oblivious to Jack's confident movement and superior musculature. He hadn't bothered to notice the ease with which she had already whipped him around and used her weight to counter his lunge. Having not noticed her skill and cat-like balance, he could *almost* be forgiven for his next words.

Almost.

"Oh yeah. You want a piece of this?" he asked, dramatically raising his fist. "You and whose army?"

She smiled. "Oh, just me," she answered sweetly.

With that, the guy swung his fist at her as hard as he could. Jack adeptly and casually ducked, allowing his momentum to take him off balance. A second later he felt the wind being knocked out of him as he landed.

His head thunked dully on the floor.

Shocked, it took several moments before he could even feel the pain.

His body couldn't respond, but he was peripherally aware of Jack leaning over him. "The next time you want a fight, why don't you let me know, and I'll teach you the meaning of manners in civilized drinking establishments."

And then she had disappeared from view.

He lay there for several more minutes, aware of talking and activity around him, but still in too much pain and disorientation to do anything about it.

"Hi," Jack said brightly to Brock, extending her hand, human-style. "Griselle. Griselle Oriel."

Brock took her hand, not even bothering to pretend not to be impressed by her moves on the guy that was now sprawled out at their feet. "I'm Tallus. Copernican," he added.

"Nice to meet you, Tallus Copernican," she smiled, satisfied with herself. "Are you here on your own?"

Brock shook his head and turned looking for Sean. "No. I'm here with my new work colleague. This is…" Brock scrambled in his memory for Sean's new name. "Sorry, erm, I've forgotten your name," he said, tapping him with the back of his hand on his upper arm to get his attention.

Sean turned around in his chair to look at them. "The name's Rex," he said simply, nodding at Jack.

Jack waved back. "Ah great. So, you've just met?"

Brock nodded. "Yeah, we're here for Bravo Freight company. Shipping out tomorrow night."

Jack made an expression of mock surprise. "No way! Us too," she told him, indicating back over at where she had been sitting. "I've just met my colleague Marissa, over there. She's some kind of tech engineer or something."

Brock grinned. "Nice."

Jack looked awkward for a moment. "Do you... do you want to join us?"

Brock glanced back at Sean, who had gone back to ignoring them both. He turned back to Jack. "Sure!" he said.

Jack led the way back across the bar, and Brock slapped Sean on the arm. "Come on, man. Meet some of your new crew mates!"

Sean ignored him a moment more, taking another swig of his beer. And then he followed.

Just as the three of them were sitting down and making the introductions to Maya's alter ego, a female Estarian came hurrying up to their table.

"Greetings of the day. I'm... I'm sorry to intrude. But I just saw what you did to that guy over there. I'm so sorry for any trouble. He's not a bad guy, he's just been drinking all day. And..."

The woman's explanation came like a torrent.

Brock turned to face her better from behind Sean who was again, practically non-responsive to any kind of interaction. "You know that guy?" he asked.

She nodded. "Yeah. I've worked with him for years. He doesn't do well the night before we ship out. He hates the work and each time he swears he's not going on another run, but each time..." Her eyes hit the carpet, trying to avoid the feelings of shame she had over her friend's behavior.

Brock's eyes narrowed. "You're shipping out too?" he asked. "Who's your company?"

"Bravo," she told him.

"Oh, us too!" Maya exclaimed excitedly, pointing at each of the four of them. "I'm May... Marissa. This is Griselle, and this is Tallus, and, erm, sorry... I forgot your name already."

"Rex," Sean added, still less than enthusiastic about meeting another person, and not amused that it was becoming a thing for them to forget, or pretend to forget, his name.

Maya grinned at him briefly, waiting to see if he showed any signs of her little dig.

"I'm Jayne," the woman told them, waving and nodding at each of them.

Maya smiled at her. "You must join us," she said. "The more, the merrier."

Sean gruffed, "Unless you're talking about dickwad," tilting his head in the direction of the laid out Estarian on the floor in front of the bar.

Everyone politely ignored his comment, and rearranged themselves so that they could add another chair to the table for Jayne.

Jack picked up the conversation with Jayne. "So how long have you worked for Bravo," she asked.

Jayne's eyes rolled up to the ceiling. "Oooo, must be fifteen years now. The time just whizzes past. You say, I'll just do it for a few years, to get some experience, or money together, or whatever, and then it's just one more run, and before you know it, you're part of the furniture."

Jack bobbed her head. "Yeah, I know that feeling. I took this thinking it will be a change, though I know what it's like. It's all great while it's new and exciting, but then..."

Jayne rolled her lips inward, bobbing her head sympathetically. "So, what've you been recruited for?" she asked.

She and Jack continued their conversation, and the others chatted and pretended to get to know each other too. After another round, Brock and Sean returned from the bar with drinks and noted that the guy that Jack had laid out was no longer there.

Jayne looked immediately worried and excused herself for a few moments to go and look for him.

As soon as she was out of earshot, Sean shook his head. "Shoot me now," he said, his enthusiasm for this mission waning by the minute.

Maya grinned at him. "Come on, it will get better once we get into investigative mode. This is all just the preamble. It will be fun. Besides, it's kinda cool pretending to be someone else for a while."

Jack nodded. "Yeah. It's kinda liberating. Like stepping away from leadership for the first time."

Sean scoffed, raising his glass up to his mouth. "Like I get to know what that feels like."

Maya frowned at him. "Yeah, but you're never in charge. Molly is."

Sean shook his head. "Maybe. Of you lot. I still report to the General though, as well. It's like having two bosses—"

Maya shut him up with a warning glare that Jayne was returning.

Jayne arrived back at the table, this time with the drunk delinquent in tow. "Everybody, this is Auggie. Auggie, these are the nice people who will be your crew mates for the next several weeks. I suggest you use this opportunity to apologize."

Auggie took a deep breath and shifted his weight where he stood. His shoulders still slouching as if he were being dragged somewhere he didn't want to go, he turned to Brock. "I'm sorry I tried to pick a fight with you," he said. And then he turned to Jack. "And I'm very sorry for throwing a punch at you. I don't normally hit humans, given how delicate you are... so I'm glad you were able to stop me. I would have felt horrible if I'd actually hurt you."

Sean was rubbing his forehead, one arm folded across his

chest. He pointed at a chair at the next table. "Looks like you need a chair. Pull one over," he said, ending the social awkwardness.

Auggie was introduced to the rest of the party and given some water to drink, as well as being encouraged rather sternly by Jayne to sober up.

Gaitune-67, Molly's Conference Room

Pieter sat back in his seat with four telemetry feeds up on four different holoscreens. Each one looked normal. Or at least within normal parameters. They differed significantly from each other. Jack's heart rate was the most steady and stable.

Like her personality, he thought, wondering if its consistency had anything to do with that, or her regimented training routine.

Sean's heart rate was low. Supersoldier-athlete kinda slow.

If he weren't walking around breathing, I'd swear he were asleep, he thought, tapping on the desk at double the rhythm.

Maya's was a little all over the place. It sped up, then slowed, probably depending on what she was thinking or doing, or the emotional pressure of the situation.

Brock's seemed to have a musical rhythm to it. The display would shift and change, as if the guy were standing in front of him dancing.

Pieter smiled to himself, excited to be getting to know his team mates so intimately.

Just then there was a tap at the door, and Molly stepped in.

"Everything okay?" she asked, standing behind him, off to one side, looking at the array of screens.

"Uh huh," he confirmed, ruffling his hair and looking a little stressed. "They all checked in with their quantum beads about ten minutes ago. Maya was a few minutes late, and scared me a little, but I guess she's still getting used to the routine."

Molly pulled out a seat next to him. "Nothing unusual in the medical exams? Anything we should be aware of?"

Pieter shrugged. "I dunno. We opted not to activate the link until after they were clear, just in case the signals showed up. Only the quantum beads were live, coz well, they emit no signal."

Molly smiled, and Pieter glanced sideways at her noticing her expression. "But of course you knew that," he added blushing and sinking into his chair a little more.

Molly glanced back at him from the corner of her eye. "It's okay," she told him.

Pieter sat forward and poked at his holo, changing the displays one by one. "Hmm," he remarked, flicking through and zooming in on one of the graphs.

"What is it?" she asked.

Pieter frowned. "Looks like the conductivity of their blood has altered."

Molly leaned in, her eyes now scanning his screens for more intel. "They're all being poisoned?"

Pieter shook his head. "Nope. No. They're okay. They're out drinking and it's just kicking in." He sat back again, relaxing.

Molly turned in her chair to look at him directly. "And how do you know that?" she pressed, her eyes boring into the side of his head.

Pieter swiped at a screen, activating the audio feed on one of them. Sean's guffaw reverberated around the conference room, against a hubbub of background chatter.

Molly and Pieter chuckled.

"Okay," Molly conceded. "They're out drinking."

Pieter dropped the audio feed from the intercom.

Molly turned to get up. "Okay. So if all is well, I'll leave you to it. You and Paige have figured out a relief schedule, right?"

Pieter nodded. "Yeah, she'll be taking over for me in a few hours," he confirmed.

"Great," Molly concluded. "Keep me posted."

With that she got up and headed back out of the conference room.

Pieter swiped the audio channel back on, and listened to the chatter of his friends. The loneliness of the task, and their absence, somewhat abated by being able to hear them.

CHAPTER EIGHT

On board the *Flutningsaðili*, Uptarlung Space Port

"Looks like this is it, this time." Maya gazed numbly over at Jayne as they were told for the third time to strap into their crew seats.

Jayne cocked an ear listening to the sound of the engines for a moment. "Yep. I think so. They normally have a few tries at it before we actually get airborne. It's a dance they do with air traffic control here. I think the pilot has a rather fraught relationship with the staff over there."

Brock's ears pricked up. "Oh yeah?" he asked, injecting himself into the conversation in the hope of gleaning some insight into Crash's bizarre sparring with them.

"Yeah," Jayne continued switching into gossip-mode. "I think one of the pilots used to be married to the director or something. We never had a problem at any of the other ports," she confessed.

Brock bobbed his head. "Well, at least that's a logical explanation."

The three of them had chosen seats in close proximity to each other in the main personnel hold. There were about two dozen of them in total — that they could see. Plus, there would be pilots and engineers no doubt making the liftoff happen. Mind, it was a big ship. There could be other rooms where people were strapped in for takeoff.

"Is this your first time in space?" Jayne called over to Maya.

Maya nodded. "Yeah. I'm worried about space sickness."

Jayne made her professional "empathetic face." "Ah. It might be uncomfortable for a little while until we're out of the planet's gravitational field and until they turn the antigrav on, but after that it should subside."

Maya frowned. "Why do they have to wait to turn the antigrav on? I thought when ships went up they had it on the whole time?"

Jayne shook her head. "No, it messes with the escape too much. On the smaller ships it's not a problem, but if you consider the size of this thing, and the weight we're carrying…"

Maya nodded, her eyes quite grave. "I see," she said, now truly concerned about the space sickness.

The noise of the ship intensified, as did the vibrations. Moments later, Maya felt the ship lifting off. She gripped the hand rest on her chair.

Jayne glanced over at her. "It's okay. It will be over in about an hour."

Maya's eyes widened. "An *hour*?"

Sean noticed the look of horror in her eyes. He looked over at her, his look telling her that she had been spoiled with Federation travel all this time.

He, on the other hand, settled in for the duration, closing his eyes and pretending to go to sleep.

After the longest and most traumatic lift off Maya had ever lived through, the seat belt signs were finally switched off and they were given clearance to walk around the floor they were on.

They were still confined to just the upper floor until engineering confirmed that life support facilities were functional on all floors.

Jayne released her seat harness. "See," she said, "that wasn't too bad, was it?"

Maya looked at her in complete disbelief. "That was worse than I could have ever imagined," she exclaimed.

Jayne pursed her lips. "Do you still feel ill?"

Maya nodded, barely keeping it together.

"Tell you what," Jayne said, leaning in and lowering her voice, "once we get clearance to the fifth floor, I'll take you down to the med bay and give you a shot. Have you feeling right as rain in no time. Though you may need to sleep it off, too," she added.

Maya bobbed her head, still looking quite gray. "I'm okay with that."

Jayne checked her holo. "Okay. We should get a drink before the briefing. They tend to start promptly. Like to get their money's worth."

Jayne headed out of the back door, and Maya followed, curious to explore her new environment.

She noticed that Brock and Auggie had hit it off during takeoff and were now chatting away. Jack was mixing with other people who were also allocated to the cleaning and laundry functions of their artificially built community.

Maya slipped out down the corridor just ahead of a group of Estarians in overalls. They all seemed to know each other, and were talking in tones that seemed to suggest they were less than pleased about being on another run.

Jayne turned to see Maya following her. She smiled. "So, what were you doing before you applied to Bravo?" she asked.

Maya shrugged. "Bumming about, mostly." She paused, then qualified it. "Well according to my parents, who were sick of me ending up back home every time one of my contracts came to an end."

Jayne frowned. "I'm surprised you have problems with getting contracts in computing."

Maya sucked her lip to one side. "Oh, it's not so much about getting the contract. It's more like... *keeping* the contract."

Jayne glanced at her curiously as she led the way into one of the rooms off the corridor, which opened out into a small kitchen.

"Yeah," Maya continued. "Sleeping with the boss tends to end contracts fairly quickly."

Jayne burst out laughing, and then remembered to be sympathetic to the young woman who she seemed to have taken under her wing. "Oh, I'm sorry," she said, covering her mouth. "That must be... awful," she said, her eyes dancing with humor.

Maya grinned. "Oh yes. It's horrendous," she said, laughing at herself.

Jayne opened one of the refrigerator units, and pulled out a couple of shakes, handing one to Maya. "Nutri-shakes. The reason we don't land with malnutrition," she explained. "Can't just rely on the food they feed you in the mess hall."

Maya looked at the bottle, searching for an ingredients list.

"It's everything the body needs to survive, apparently," Jayne said. "Though I'd add in a few vitamin injections now and again, and of course water." She paused, breaking the seal on her own bottle. "And exercise." She added. "Though if your boss turns out to be tasty, I'm assuming you'll have that one covered!"

Maya's mouth dropped open and she quickly clamped her hand over it, amused and shocked at Jayne's playfulness. "Well," Maya said. "Nice to know who your friends are," she retorted, taking a sip of her nutri-drink.

The two women chuckled away, passing the time until they needed to reconvene in the briefing room they had just come from.

. . .

Gaitune-67, Molly's Conference Room

Joel scratched his head. "Okay, so if my calculations are correct, there are these forty-something companies that haven't been responding to our new measures."

"Yeah, looks like it," Pieter agreed glumly, taking a swig of an artificial power drink.

Paige glanced up from her array of screens. She was monitoring the undercover team, as it was her turn. But in the time when there was nothing to do they, had agreed it was plenty safe enough for her to be in front of the screens and working on other things — nail varnish related, or otherwise.

Joel swiped through a few of the screens he had selected. "It's a lot," he commented.

Pieter nodded. "Yeah. It's super sucky. I mean, this one. Zyto Corp. Didn't you pay them a visit early on when Molly first took it over?"

Joel closed his eyes repeating the company name in his head. "Yeah. I think so. Hang on, I'll have a note."

He pulled up another screen and ran a search.

"Yep, there it is," he said, his eyes scanning back and forth reading what he had written. "Yeah, and at the time it looked like they were going to play ball. Hang on," he said, flicking between two screens. "Looks like they've had a change of some of their key players."

He pushed the screen over to Pieter to see. Pieter read through while Joel studied another copy.

Both were silent for a few minutes.

Pieter ruffled his hair and leaned his arm on the desk, resting his chin in his fist. "You know," he said eventually, "I think I recognize some of these names."

He pulled up another screen and started tapping away cross referencing. "Ah ha!" he said after a few moments.

Joel looked up. "What is it?"

Pieter leaned forward reading off his screens. "There are

about five names which keep popping up, and they have an 80 percent occurrence in these forty-odd problem companies."

Joel stood up to wander round to the screens and see. "What do we know about them?" he asked.

Pieter pulled up the bios of the first three on the list. He read for a moment. "These guys all made a lot of money under the old system. Looks like they've been using their influence to get back into these companies and restart their old ways."

Joel rubbed at his stubble. "Yeah, looks like it. Okay, have Oz run the data. If we can verify this is what is happening then we have a starting point."

Pieter nodded, and continued working on the screens.

Joel went back to his work station to carry out his own analysis.

Sark System, Aboard the *Flutningsaðili*, Floor 14

"So, what did you make of the briefing?" Maya asked, idly wandering next to Jack as she made her initial checks around the fourteenth floor.

Jack shrugged. "The general briefing was interesting. But why it took them three hours to explain the cleaning crew duties I'll never know."

Maya fiddled with her holo, trying to get connected to the ship's Ethertrak. She frowned. "You were actually in there the whole three hours."

Jack touched her holo at the check point on the wall of the corridor, and turned to look at Maya, her eyes conveying the drama. "The. Whole. Three. Hours."

Maya had stopped walking. "To tell you to walk around your duty floors and check for things that need cleaning up?"

Jack bobbed her head. "Yeah, and to instruct us on general cleanups. The thing is, as soon as it's a chemical or bio issue, or anything more technical, we have to clear the area and leave it to the highly trained experts on board."

Maya grinned. "I see."

Jack sighed, and the two women kept walking.

"You know," Maya said getting her holo hooked up finally, "I think their security system wouldn't be too hard to get past, and then we can see what is behind some of these doors."

Jack looked around, making sure there was no one to over hear them. "You want to risk it? This soon?"

Maya shrugged. "We have to start poking about somewhere, right?"

Jack waved her hand, absolving herself of any responsibility. "You do your thing, honey," she told Maya.

Maya stopped walking again and studied her holo intensely. Then she looked up. "Okay. Pick a door."

Jack looked surprised at the immediacy of the request. "Seriously?"

Maya nodded.

Jack looked up and down the corridor, and then walked on a little further. "This one," she said, pointing the next door on their right. It looked more like a sealed container than the others. Though there weren't any warning signs telling them 'bio-hazard' or 'radioactive,' the key pad was heavy duty, and it was more like a portal into the next room, than it was just a swinging, or sliding door.

Maya looked at it, and then back down at her holo. She worked, poking at the screens, her tongue appearing out of the side of her mouth.

A moment later the door clicked open, much to Jack's surprise. "That looked easy," Jack remarked, looking back at Maya, and then back at the door again.

Maya shrugged one shoulder and hurried forward. "We should move. Dunno if these cameras are being monitored."

Jack looked horrified. "There are cameras?" she asked, as Maya bundled her into the room.

Maya nodded. "Yeah. But I've set them to wipe the recording as soon as it records. Doesn't get around that someone might happen to be viewing it real time though."

Jack shook her head at how cavalier Maya was about her protocols.

A few moments later the little tech wizard had found the light switch and then turned to survey the room they had just stepped into.

Granted, it was more a chamber than a room. Jack stood in awe as she peered into the darkness. "How far back do you think it all goes?" she asked.

Maya was only half aware of her question. She had been drawn magnetically to the first person-sized vat nearest them, and was inspecting it, daring herself to touch the steely exterior. "I don't know," she said, her voice breathless.

She rounded the vat and found the misty, see-through front panel her eyes vaguely aware of the security pad on the right-hand side of the door handle.

The vat was empty.

She moved to the next one.

Also empty.

Jack glanced back at the door, listening. "We should go," she said, but Maya had already scampered off out of sight investigating this strange wonderland they had just stepped into.

Jack tried again. "Maya!" she called in an urgent whisper.

Maya poked her head out from one of the vats two rows down from where Jack was standing. "It's Marissa!" she said, the half-light catching on her grin making her look a little maniacal.

Jack corrected herself. "*Marissa*, can we go please?" she said, a little more firmly, like a grown up playing the game of asking the child nicely before said child received a walloping.

"Just a second," Maya's voice called from between the rows of steel cylinders.

Jack looked up and down the width of the chamber, trying to guesstimate how many rows there were. The darkness swallowed them up pretty quickly, but from what she could see there were at least a dozen rows, and the one in front of her was at least five deep. Her curiosity begged her to venture forward, to head into the vats and see how many there really were.

Just then she felt movement off to her right and saw Maya reemerge from the sea of steel. "Okay," Maya declared, closing a holoscreen confidently. "Let's move."

Jack turned on her heels and in a heartbeat they were back out in the corridor, carefully allowing the door to close quietly behind them.

Jack started walking again in the same direction they had been heading before their rebellious little detour. "I think that's quite enough excitement for one day," she concluded. "Remind me never to let you do rounds with me again." She glanced sideways at her mischievous companion.

Maya had closed her holo down and clasped her hands behind her back, walking nonchalantly half a stride ahead of Jack.

"Sure," Maya agreed. "You'll just miss out on all the fun."

CHAPTER NINE

Aboard the *Flutningsaðili*, Mess hall, Level 2

Sean sat eating on his own, his supplements untouched in a dish to his left.

"You really should take those," a voice told him. Sean looked up to see Jayne looking down at him. She was still quite scatty in her appearance, her hair a little disheveled and tied in a short ponytail, just back off her neck. But the wisps framed her face gently, softening her look and almost countering her age.

Sean looked back at his food and took another forkful. After eating that, he answered her. "I don't like them. They spoil the food."

Jayne took it as permission to enter into a dialogue with him, and sat herself down at the table in front of him. "You've got months of this, though, and the food you're eating doesn't have..."

Sean raised his eyes to look at her. She stopped speaking.

He continued eating.

Jayne tried again. "You know... I get the feeling you don't like me very much."

Sean finished chewing a mouthful. He shuffled the gruel

around his compartmentalized tray and spoke without looking at her. "What gives you that idea?" he asked.

Jayne clasped her hands in front of her face, her elbows on the table. "Oh nothing. Just the way you are. Moody. Unengaging."

Sean looked up at her again. This time he allowed a smirk to appear on his face. "Unengaging?" he repeated. He held her gaze a moment.

Jayne looked awkward and then looked away.

Sean went back to his food. "I can see that," he conceded. "So how would you have me be instead? Life and soul of the party?"

Jayne shook her head. "No. Of course not. You can be however you want to be. It's just…"

Sean waited, deliberately not looking up. Deliberately not being too interested. He pierced a piece of synthesized protein and stuffed it into his mouth.

Jayne sighed. "I should leave you to it," she said, putting her hands on the table to get up.

Sean waved with his fork. "Nah. Get yourself some food and come sit. You can tell me all about how you came to be the ship's doctor on this floating hell. And I'll tell you how I got landed with heading up administration for the lamest auditing company in town."

Jayne flushed a little even under her blue skin. "Okay," she said smiling, and scrambling to her feet. She headed off across the mess hall to the food counter and picked up a tray. Sean watched her leave, knowing full well he'd make her into an ally by the end of the day.

"Yo, Rexy-baby!" Maya came striding over and plonked herself down at the table next to him. She looked at his food, and leaned over grabbing a piece of baked *'carboardhydrate,'* as she'd been known to call it back in the safehouse.

Sean looked a little taken aback, and his *carboardhydrate* was being munched before he had the chance to slap it out of her hand.

Jack arrived suddenly too, and sat in the seat opposite him, where Jayne was meant to be returning to. He looked bewildered. "Hey, someone's—"

Jack ignored him and reached for something off his plate. Once bitten, he reacted faster this time, slapping her hand before she could pinch anything. "Go get your own food. It's all there. Free of charge. Free for the taking." He waved over towards the food counters behind him.

Maya spun round on the seat and glanced over before turning back. "I will in a minute. In the meantime, guess what we found."

Sean sighed. "Surprise me."

Maya folded her arms on the table and leaned in. "You have to guess!"

Sean waved his fork "no." "You have less than a minute before Jayne gets back here."

Jack looked amused. And impressed. "Look at you, having dinner with Jayne already. You dark horse!" She winked.

Sean didn't react. "Fifty-six."

Maya frowned.

"Seconds," Sean clarified for her.

Maya nodded quickly and then got to the point, lowering her voice, and keeping her head low in confidence. "Fourteenth floor. We hacked our way into one of the rooms. Turns out it's a chamber full of cryostasis vats."

Sean shook his head. "Well, why wouldn't they have stasis vats on board?"

Maya raised her eye brows and turned her head a little. "There were *a lot* of them. All installed and functional. Empty. But usable."

Sean's brow creased up. "Yeah but this is a space-going ship, without any faster-than-light capabilities. They'll be needed to keep the crew from dying of old age before they get to where they need to be."

Maya shoulders slumped. "Fine. So it wasn't a discovery," she resigned, glumly.

Just then Jayne arrived and sat herself down next to Sean. "You're looking better," she said to Maya.

Maya nodded. "Yeah. I had a wander with Griselle and it seems to have walked off the most of it."

Jayne smiled, picking up her fork. "Well, if it comes back, or you have problems sleeping over the next few nights, come by and see me." She looked at the others. "Any of you. Really. I'd kill to have a patient on one of these trips!"

Maya was the first to get the joke, and then Jack. Sean either missed it or didn't want to waste energy laughing.

"So," he started, glancing in Jayne's direction, "Twenty-five floors. All of those are cargo stores?" he asked.

Jayne had started eating. She emptied her mouth before responding, shaking her head. "No. I don't think so. I think a bunch of them aren't used. But the facilities need to be maintained on them for regulations or something." She thought for a moment. "I think most of the warehousing happens on the lower floors, just because it makes unloading easier when we land."

Sean bobbed his head. "And do our guys get involved in the unloading?"

Jayne nodded. "Sometimes. Sometimes not. Depends on what is being shipped. Sometimes we have cargo that is sensitive, or technical and then the clients come and pick it up as soon as we land. We can sit about for days before we can get the rest shifted. Not that we all head out and start trucking stuff about," she added, chuckling a little.

Sean smiled. "Ah, the royal 'we' then ..."

Jayne nodded, a protein chunk on her fork. "Exactly." She continued eating, and Sean looked poignantly at Jack.

Jack ever so slightly nodded her understanding. She'd also clocked that there were shipments being taken off before the ship may have even officially docked.

Jack suddenly had a thought. "So, are there any areas that are off limits?" she asked. "The reason I ask is that little Marissa here seems to think that she can go poking around wherever she pleases. But surely that's not the case. Even if you have got skeleton key access?"

Maya shot Jack a look, which Jack promptly ignored.

Jayne shook her head. "Probably not. Though a cargo ship isn't the safest of places to just be wandering around. Especially not on your own, she said, looking at Maya now.

"The thing is," she continued, "when these ships get old, things tend to break. All it takes is for a burst exhaust pipe or a ruptured boiler, or, heck, even a box to fall on you and you're done. I'd stay in the main common areas unless you have to go crawling around fixing computers. And always take someone else with you if you have to go out away from the common areas."

Maya nodded obediently. "Okay. I will. Besides, this place is filthy. It's going to take a month to get clean once I get back to Estaria, if the grime under my fingernails is anything to go by."

Jayne sighed. "It's true. It's a problem," she said sympathetically to the young girl.

Gaitune-67, Safe house

Molly followed Joel out of the kitchen. "I'm just going to check in on Paige and Pieter. They should be doing a hand over about now."

Joel nodded. "Great. I'm heading that way too. And there was something I wanted to run by you about your Estarian portfolio."

Molly took a swig of her protein shake as they walked. "Okay, great."

They headed into the conference room together, causing Paige and Pieter to look up. Pieter grinned his haphazard kind of grin. "Looks like mom and dad have arrived at work!"

Paige giggled, as Joel made a playful swipe at Pieter's head.

Pieter ducked, nearly falling off his chair. "Missed!" he said victoriously as he tried to regain his balance.

Joel started to sit down, and a second later there was a thump as Pieter disappeared from view. He and Molly looked over to see Paige still snickering, and Pieter re-emerging from beneath the table.

"You okay, chap?" Joel asked, trying his best to keep a straight face, his bouncing chest giving away his laughter.

Pieter nodded, his face bright red as he hauled himself back up and sat properly on his seat again.

Paige's sniggering had escalated to where she was *killing* herself laughing.

Molly, oblivious to why everyone was laughing, glanced over with a look of confusion. Instead of asking for clarification, she reverted to the task in hand. "So how are things going with the crew?"

The mood sobered, but Pieter reported in brightly. "They're all okay. Everyone has been checking in on time. I've been monitoring some of the conversations here and there. So far, nothing untoward. Maya is doing some poking around, as you might expect."

Molly smiled. "Indeed," she agreed. "And everything working okay with the shifts and the hand-overs?" she asked.

Paige nodded. "Yep. No problems. Oz is also helping monitor things as well. If these guys so much as sneeze, we'll know about it."

Molly nodded her head once. "Good."

She turned her attention to Joel, who was smiling at Pieter, who was still looking somewhat embarrassed.

"So what is the deal with the companies?" she asked.

Joel's focus zoned in as he pulled up the screen he needed. "Pieter and Oz were doing some analysis of the companies that were under-performing, according to our remit."

Molly pulled her chair around to see his screen. "You mean things like profits and pay outs versus reinvestments?"

Joel nodded. "Yeah. It looks like some of the old guard have re-established themselves on the boards of a number of companies, and are drawing salaries and bonuses just as they were doing before."

Molly's face turned dark. "Well, this needs fixing."

Joel pulled his lips to one side, and nodded grimly.

Pieter chipped in, in a movie announcer voice. "I recommended termination, with extreme prejudice!" he interjected.

Molly raised her eyebrows. "I think that is probably the way to go."

Joel looked at her shocked. "You mean... kill them?"

Molly laughed. "No silly. Sack them. And then put a lock on them so they can't be rehired at any of our companies again."

"Ohhhh," Joel said, lifting his chin slightly as the understanding caught up to him.

Paige chuckled. "My, my, Joel. Someone is a little bloodthirsty these days. Maybe you should have headed out on the mission to get some ya-yas out?"

It was Joel's turn to blush. "I just... yeah," he buried his head in his hand for a moment.

Pieter patted him on the arm. "It's okay, mate. We all think stupid things now and again."

Joel looked at him sternly, and then at Pieter's hand on his arm. Pieter removed his hand. "Just sayin'," he added, defensively.

Molly had been reading down the list of names. "Yeah. I think I'll head on down there and sack them in person. It will send a clear message to everyone else in the companies too. We should also issue a statement citing our specific reasons why: failure to comply with company Ethics and Operating Agreement."

Joel made some notes as she talked. "Great, I'll start drawing something up and then Paige and I can firm it up before we send it out."

Paige looked up, nodded, and made a note herself.

"Great," Molly confirmed. "Okay. I'm off to get some training in. Then I have a meeting with Von."

Paige looked up in recognition. "Tell her I say 'Hi!'" she chirped.

Molly grinned. "Will do, teacher's pet!" she winked, disappearing out of the door.

Pieter glanced over at Paige. "Hahaa... teacher's pet!" he chuckled.

Paige harrumphed and turned her attention back to her work, and eventually Pieter did the same.

Aboard the *Flutningsaðili*, Pike's office

Max Pike sat in his console chair in his private office, just off from the ship's primary control room. He swiveled around, his feet on the desk, handling a game ball as he talked on the holo audio.

"What about our guests?" the client asked.

"They're safe," Pike confirmed. "None of the crew know about them. I'll be tending to them myself just to reduce the risk. But since they're sedated they won't be making too many demands."

The client was silent for a moment. "As long as their brain cells are functioning when they get here," he warned sternly. "Else there will be hell to pay. I don't suppose I need to remind you how much we have riding on this, do I?"

Max sat up, putting the ball on his desk carefully. "No sir, you don't. I understand exactly what is at stake, and will be doing everything to ensure this is successful. You have nothing to worry about from this end."

"See to it I don't," the voice warned. "Let me know when the shipment is due in port and I'll have my people come pick it up. I trust we have an adequate window?"

Max rested one hand absently on the ball, as if subconsciously making sure it wasn't going to roll off the desk. "Yes sir. At least twelve hours. Maybe longer. I'll know more when I get the updated flight plan."

"Very good," the client confirmed. "I'll wait to hear."

"Yes, sir. Of course, sir," Max replied.

And then the line went dead.

Max realized he'd been holding his breath, and slowly encouraged himself to exhale. He stood up, returned the ball to its little stand on a shelf, and then headed out into the control room, slowly regaining his nerve.

Staðall University, Von's Office

Are you sure this is right?

You know, for someone who is so damn smart you have a shitty sense of direction.

Well it's a good job I have a know-it-all AI in my head then, isn't it?

Yes, it is, rather. Turn left here.

Molly put on the brakes, jarring her ankle in her slightly heeled boots.

A bit of warning, Oz.

Okay, next turn is to the right, the next corridor you go down.

Okay. We got this.

...

...

...

Now where?

Seriously? You *still* don't recognize this?

Would I be asking you if I did?

Molly, it's the third door on the left.

Okay, well how was I supposed to know?

You *have* been here before.

Once. And I don't remember routes and places until I've done it at least five or six times.

Molly could feel her head vibrating with Oz's laughter. She grabbed the sides of her head to see if she could stop it, or at least stop her teeth from rattling. It made no difference. As she suspected.

She knocked on the door.

Pack it in Oz. Gotta talk with the Prof.

The vibration subsided.

"Come in," Von called from behind the door.

Molly opened the door and poked her in. "Greetings," she ventured.

Von ushered her in and offered her the seat in front of her desk. It was a small office. Just large enough for a desk and two chairs, and a storage server that probably housed her entire library and research. It was no longer prudent to rely solely on the ether-cloud, particularly since the collapse of '79.

"May I offer you some tea?" Von asked, gesturing towards the replicator.

Molly grinned. "Oh, yes. That would be great. Thank you."

Von selected the tea program and put a cup beneath it.

Molly watched the tea being dripped into the cup. "So, how's the course going?" she asked.

Von's expression was brimming with excitement. "It's going incredibly well," she started, chattering like an enthused child reporting on her day at school. "Obviously, we're only a week in at this point, but the students are responding fantastically. In fact, we have more students trying to subscribe all the time as word gets around about what we're doing."

Molly grinned enthusiastically. Von handed her the mug of hot tea, and placed another mug under the machine for herself.

She poked at the program she wanted and turned back to

Molly. "I'm thinking we're going to have to increase our capacity. Or at least run the course again."

Molly hugged her warm tea-mug. "That's wonderful. And yes, we must," she agreed. "I think we should probably start working on that now. Perhaps get the support of the Dean behind us and lock it into the academic schedule."

Von nodded excitedly. "Yes. I'm sure he'll agree to it. I mean, it's good for the university, and once the post-course evaluations are in they'd be mad not to."

Von took her freshly replicated tea and sat down at her desk.

Molly leaned forward, her mug balanced with one hand on her knee. "So, talk me through what needs to be done to make this happen."

Von flicked into business mode. "I think the first thing is to lock in a meeting with the Dean. Maybe even request an opportunity to address the board at their next meeting, which should be coming up fairly soon."

Molly made a note on her holo. "Okay. Great. I'll get in touch with him."

Von had an intensity behind her eyes. "Good. Then we need to put our case together," she added.

Molly made another note. "You know," she said after a moment, "it would be worth talking to each of the board members in turn. Separately. Before we get into the room. So that they understand what we're proposing and we have them on side individually."

Von clicked her fingers. "You're right!" she agreed quickly. She started making a note on her holo. "Let me take that one. I know most of them already, and some of us go way back."

Molly grinned. "Excellent. This is working out well."

The two continued plotting and planning for several hours, and by the time they were done they had what they thought was a solid action plan.

You know Oz, Molly said in her head as she navigated her way back through the corridors to rendezvous with her pod, *this may just work.*

You know Mollz, I think it might!

Molly stepped out into the Estarian evening. The Sark had gone down hours ago, leaving a coolness on the air. She took a deep cleansing breath, and looked out at the various old buildings of the university, feeling nostalgic for her misspent youth in academia.

Pod's here! Oz alerted her as it descended just off to her right. Molly sighed, and walked over to it, hopping in.

Staðall University, Radcliff's office

"Yes, send him in please, Amy."

The door to his office opened up and philanthropist Raj Ghettie stepped into the room. Amy hurried behind him and grabbed the door handle to close the door behind him again as he strode in to greet the aging Dean.

Radcliff stood up at his desk. "What a pleasant surprise!" he exclaimed, his artificial enthusiasm and charm oozing from his carefully maintained skin.

"Likewise," Ghettie responded, bowing slightly, before placing his hand on the chair that he had sat on before.

The Dean waved his hand, inviting the gentleman to sit, which he did.

"I'll get straight to the point," Ghettie began. "Our board of trustees have got wind of your new course. Something about interplanetary negotiations. Now, on the surface this sounds like a worthy course, but based on what we know of its content, and indeed the professor, it's something that we'd rather wasn't taught at an institution that we support."

Ghettie held Radcliff's gaze firmly.

There was a long silence as an addled Radcliff scrambled to figure out how to handle the request. He shuffled forward in his seat. "Erm... if I might ask," he began, "what is it that is disagreeable to your board?"

Ghettie drew in a deep breath and pushed himself back into the chair he occupied. "Well, to begin with, the professor in question has unusual methods of negotiation and manipulation. Plus, her politics aren't to our liking. She made some moves back when she was consulting that were not in the favor of the Ogg clans, and we would not like to see that kind of person poisoning the minds of the next generation. In fact, it's in direct violation of everything we agreed to when we started donating resources to this institution."

He paused, allowing the information to sink in for the Dean. Then, as if rehearsed, a superficial smile grew over his lips. He sat forward just enough to convey friendliness without sacrificing any power in the situation, and added, "I'm sure you understand our position."

The Dean shifted in his seat, feeling like cornered prey. "Yes. Yes. Of course," he replied amicably. "So, you'd like for me to put a stop to the new course continuing?" he clarified.

"We would," Ghettie confirmed, closing his eyes briefly as he spoke. "And of course, if this were to happen we'd have no problem to continue funding the institution."

Though still bewildered by the sudden demand, Radcliff now understood perfectly what he was being told. He made a decision on the spot. "Well of course," he said brightly, "I'd be pleased to look into this and make sure we keep our curriculum within acceptable bounds."

He stood, forcing Raj through social convention to get to his feet too.

"Very good," Ghettie agreed, a fraction taken aback by the sharp dismissal. "I'll report back to the group and we will continue 'business as usual,' as they say."

Radcliff bowed slightly as a farewell, and Ghettie returned the gesture and headed out.

The door closed behind him, and Dean Alfred Radcliff settled back into his chair. He pulled up the course enrollment and attendance statistics and sighed, weighing the implications of what he'd agreed to do.

Aboard the Flutningsaðili, Floor 2

Brock stepped out of the steaming kitchen, following Maya into the much quieter corridor. "So what do you think?" he asked, wiping his hands.

Maya crinkled her nose and tipped her head to one side. "I don't think she knows anything specific, but what she is aware of might help us piece something useful together," Maya confided, finishing up their conversation about Jayne.

Brock nodded, distracted, glancing up and down the corridor. "Good. Any idea where to start looking for our forced guests?"

Maya shook her head. "Not a clue. Jack and I found a chamber of stasis units, but there were hundreds. No way we could search all of those without getting caught."

Brock pursed his lips. "May have to. Seems like a logical place."

Maya sighed. "Yea. Would it surprise you that I've only just realized that?" She rolled her eyes at herself. "I was just suspicious about how many units there were, and what this ship had also been used for in the past."

Brock folded his arms, his chest bouncing up and down in quiet amusement.

"TALLUS!" A voice shouted from just inside the kitchen.

Brock stepped-back and glanced into the kitchen. "Yeah! Coming!" he called back in through the door before turning back to Maya. "I gotta go."

There was a clang and a thud. And then more kitchen noise.

Maya's face dropped. "Grr. I need your help though."

Brock looked amused. "Moi? But I'm just a lowly kitchen hand."

Maya slapped his arm. "I'm serious. I need a way to narrow the search. We need kidnapped victims and drilling equipment, remember?"

Brock glanced back at the door, taking a step towards it. Then he looked off into the distance, thinking. "Okay. So the hostages are going to be somewhere no one goes. Except, they'll need feeding. So someone has got to be visiting them. You're into the cameras already?"

Maya nodded.

"Okay," he said, thinking. A look of frustration passed across his face. "Oz could cross reference this so easily."

For a moment they both felt the absence of Molly and Oz.

Brock's brow creased up. "What about key card access? You could set up a search for where key cards are being accessed where no one else is."

Maya clicked her fingers. "Right. So I create a distribution of key card access and then look at the places that are only being accessed by, say, less than a handful of people."

The voice came from the kitchen again. "Tallus! You motherfucker. Get your ass in here."

Brock shook his head at the disembodied voice, and then waved a hand. He pushed his butt against the door and took one step into the kitchen. "Okay, sis. I got to go. Good luck!"

Maya waved as Brock disappeared back into the kitchen, yelling profanities back at whoever his work colleague was.

Dammit, she thought to herself.

This undercover thing wasn't turning out to be quite as fun as she thought it was going to be. She missed her friends.

Staðall University

Von glanced excitedly over at Molly as they made their way

across the quad. "I managed to have a conversation with about nine of the fourteen board members.

"That's great!" Molly exclaimed. "Were they all on board?"

"Mostly," Von confirmed. "I mean, some had their reservations about whether it fit with traditional academia and so on, but in principle they all liked what we were doing." She hesitated. "But then, some of them even admitted they were a little jealous of the buzz and the results we were getting with the students and course reviews."

Molly was partly taking it in. "Okay, sounds like a great start. Let's get in there and seal the deal," she added, smiling.

Von led the way into the building and down the corridor to where the meeting was being held. "Just in here," she said, opening a door, and stepping in as fifteen pairs of eyes turned to look at them.

"Ah, good. They're here!" exclaimed Dean Radcliff as the two women entered the room. "We're ready for your presentation if you're ready to get going straight away?"

Molly looked over at Von awkwardly, put on the spot. "Yes, of course," she said, caught a little off-guard.

Von nodded to her reassuringly, and showed her to a seat on the long side of the conference table nearest the door. Von herself then took the only other empty seat next to her. She made the necessary introductions and then handed it over to Molly.

Molly stood up and presented from the end of the room, using the holoscreens and charts and student clips that she and Von had spent hours assembling the night before.

She went slowly and carefully, laying out her idea and supporting evidence as carefully and methodically as any trial lawyer. She diligently maintained eye contact with each member of the group, ensuring that they were following and on board.

When she was done she stopped talking and surveyed the room. Her eyes were met with looks that were attentive, but blank. She tuned in trying to read the room emotionally.

There was something going on that she couldn't put her finger on.

It wasn't that there wasn't support for what she was proposing, but it was as if the support she should have was being stifled somehow. And yet, she couldn't tell how.

She raised her eyes to the end of the table where Radcliff was sitting back in his chair, his hands steepled in front of him. "Thank you, Ms. Bates," he said, unsteepling his hands and leaning forward.

"As is customary on all proposals brought before the board, we will now take a vote on how to proceed," he continued. "Those in favor of the proposal will raise their hands."

Two people at the table raised their hands.

Radcliff looked strangely satisfied. "Those against?"

Most of the rest of the hands went up.

Molly couldn't understand what had gone wrong. She scanned the faces of those present, some of whom had averted their gaze since raising their hand and declaring themselves to be against her. There was an awkward shuffling in the silence.

Then Radcliff spoke again. "The nays have it. Apologies, Ms. Bates. It seems that your proposal is just not what we're looking for here at Staðall University. I wish you luck with your future endeavors."

Von thanked the Dean, and the board members and stood up. She closed up her holo, encouraging Molly to do the same. As if in a dream, Molly did as she was expected, thanked the board for their time, and then allowed herself to be shepherded out of the room by Professor Von.

"What just happened?" she asked as they were half-way down the corridor and out of earshot.

Von's lips were tightened around her mouth. "I'm not sure. We should have carried that proposal, but... something else was going on. A number of those people I had talked to, even just last night, assured me they were on our side."

Molly shook her head in disbelief. "Something must have changed their minds. Or someone." She recalled the look on Radcliff's face. She stopped walking.

Von stopped and turned back to her. "What is it?" she asked.

Molly cocked her head. "How long before we went in were they convened?" she asked.

Von shrugged her shoulders, her face confused as to why the question. "No idea. Why?"

Molly started walking again slowly. "I think Radcliff didn't want the proposal to be accepted. I think he talked to them."

Von was confused. "But whatever for? Why would he not want us to go ahead and—"

"Ms. Bates, Professor Von..." A voice was calling from down the corridor. Molly and Von looked back to see one of the board members running down the corridor towards them.

Molly looked over at Von, puzzled.

Von's eyes widened briefly conveying that she had no idea either. She turned to the board member. "Mr. Atkins? Is everything alright?" she asked.

He was slightly out of breath when he came to a stop in front of them. "Yes, everything is quite alright. Apart from what just happened in there," he remarked, thumbing back towards the meeting room. "But I had a thought, and, well. Here isn't the place, but if you'd agree to meet me in a couple of hours, there is something I'd like to show you."

He looked from Estarian to human and then back to the Estarian professor.

Von nodded. "Yes, of course. She glanced at Molly to make sure she was in agreement. "We'd be glad to."

Mr. Atkins nodded his thanks and then turned to head back the way he had come.

Molly watched him leave. "So, what do we know about Mr. Atkins?" she asked.

Von shrugged again as they started walking. "Board member,

family man. Third generation alumni. Not really much to tell," she mused, racking her brain for some explanation or inkling of what to expect. "Let's go grab some lunch while we wait for him. He has my holo on the board contacts list. Besides, I'm in the mood for a milkshake after all that."

Molly grinned. "That sounds like a very good plan, Professor," she agreed.

The pair wandered off in the direction of the senior common room, churning in their brains to figure out what piece of the system they had so drastically misread.

CHAPTER ELEVEN

Aboard the *Flutningsaðili*, Jack and Maya's shared quarters
"*Two weeks* of traipsing around corridors," Jack complained, "and what have I got to show for it? Blisters!"

She collapsed on the lower bunk.

Maya sat cross-legged on the top bunk, working away on her holo. Her eyes never left her screen.

Then she looked up, realizing something.

"Hang on," she said. "You guys visit *every* floor?"

Jack had closed her eyes and was already almost dozing. "I don't think so. I'm allocated one through five, most of the time. I think there are three others of us. So, assuming they each do five, that leaves five unattended. Unless they're doing more."

Maya scratched her head, pulling her mouth to one side. "That's strange. And have you noticed anything odd on any of your floors?"

"Mess hall on two is a shit hole," Jack responded.

Maya grunted. "Yeah, I saw some interesting animalistic feeding at dinner the other night."

Jack muttered in her half-conscious stupor. "Yeah, I'd say it was because they were coming off nights, but I'm not sure those guys wouldn't be like that even if they were day workers."

Maya mumbled something, and then was quiet for several minutes.

"You know," Jack said slowly, "there is an area on four that I can't get through to. Terry finally explained to me today that I just don't have clearance after I bugged him enough to spit fire. Told me someone else is taking care of that sector."

Maya shifted on the bed above her, and a moment later Jack saw her scrambling down the ladder. "Show me," she instructed, opening a schematic on her holo.

Jack whimpered in exhausted protest and then hauled herself upright and sat on the edge of her bunk. She rubbed her eyes and Maya pointed out where the main elevator was.

"It's around this way somewhere I think," Jack said, still trying to stay awake. She paused. "Hang on. Something isn't right."

She turned the holoscreen around, and then back again. "Show me another floor?"

Maya pulled up another floor plan. "This is three."

Jack overlaid the two, showing that on four there was a whole segment missing, and that the ship didn't just end beyond the door she didn't have access to.

Just then, Maya's search completed and she pulled up the results, murmuring to herself.

"What is it? Jack asked.

Maya's forehead wrinkled. "According to my analysis of keycards, that door is never accessed. Which means either it isn't accessed—"

Jack finished her thought. "Or that your data doesn't include that access point."

Maya nodded. "And since I'm meant to have clearance for the whole ship, in case something goes down …"

Jack looked over at her, concern and excitement brewing in

her expression. "Then they've clearly only given you the official 'all-access pass' and not the real 'all-access pass.'"

Maya sat down next to Jack on her bunk. "Which is looking more and more like they have something to hide."

Jack fell back on the bed, putting her arm over her eyes. "Great. Lemme know when you've cracked it," she said.

Maya giggled and picked up a pillow and threw it on the exhausted Jack. "Fine. I'll see if Sean wants to come check it out with me."

Jack made a noise in acknowledgment. It was more of a mouthless sound, than a word. "Uhh."

Maya stored the map, closed her holo and then put some additional clothing and boots on for braving the world outside their shared sleeping quarters. It was nearly time for dinner and she needed to talk with Sean.

Staðall University, Senior Common Room

Molly and Von sat chatting and finishing their milkshakes as Gareth Atkins arrived, bustling in having come directly from the board meeting.

"Milkshakes here are to die for!" he remarked as a he approached their table. "Honestly, when I've been working late, I'll sometimes get them to add a shot of whiskey into the mix. Gives it a little something extra."

His eyes sparkled in a way that Molly didn't expect from someone who appeared quite straight-laced.

Molly grinned. "I think I'd like to try one of those some time," she confided conspiratorially.

Gareth smiled. "Well, maybe when we have something to celebrate we should all do that," he said quietly, glancing around to make sure that no one could hear that they were plotting something.

"I'm in," Von said brightly, her academic seriousness cast aside for a moment.

They chuckled.

"So, Mr. Atkins..." Molly started.

"Please, call me Gareth," he interjected.

"*Gareth*," she corrected herself congenially. "Tell me, what was so urgent for you to come running out of your board meeting for?"

"Well," he said, pulling out a seat at their table and sitting down. "Thankfully, the old codger called a recess after your segment, so I was able to hop out without raising suspicion, but I wanted to talk to you about a possibility that perhaps you haven't considered yet."

Molly, intrigued, nodded for him to go on.

"Well," he said again, including Von in the conversation by glancing at her now and again, "it seems that your course is getting so much traction, and the students are not just excelling, but finding a new way of interacting with the larger world... I, and a few others agree, that it would be a shame to have that ripped from them. I mean, if anything, this is something that we should be encouraging more of at a society-wide level."

Von's face lit up, eyebrow raised in a look of 'I told you so' directed at Molly.

Molly grinned. "It's funny you should mention that. This project began as a pilot. A proof of concept."

Gareth turned his ear closer towards her, genuinely fascinated. "A proof of concept for...?"

Molly glanced around to make sure they weren't going to be overheard by prying ears nearby. Satisfied, she continued. "A new type of university. One that could educate and inform not just the next generation, but the next generation of *leaders* in the system."

"Oh my!" Gareth exclaimed. "That sounds very much along the lines of what I was going to suggest!"

The excitement bubbled as the three talked, laying their cards on the table. After an hour or so of confabbing it became apparent that they all wanted the same thing.

"Okay, so how I thought I could help was with the buildings," he offered. "It will cost money, but we can figure that out. However, after today what is obvious is that your days here are severely numbered."

Molly nodded solemnly, hoping that Von wasn't going to be too disappointed by the realization.

Gareth continued. "I have contacts within my family. They control a trust which holds an old building within an estate. The trust's funds have been depleted by the building maintenance costs because ultimately, they have no tenants, but it used to be an old seminary back in the day. It would be perfect for a new university."

Molly's face lit up in sheer delight. "You're serious?"

Gareth nodded. "I am. I'd like you to see it." He looked to Von. "Both of you. Would you like to?"

Von clapped her hands together. "I would indeed!" she agreed enthusiastically.

Gareth grinned. "Well, no time like the present."

The three agreed and got up from their empty milkshake glasses and collected their belongings, and made arrangements to meet out front, on the road, so that Gareth could pick them up in his car.

As they walked back across the quad, Molly could barely contain her excitement. "If this works, this will be the beginning of something completely new. Something no one has ever done before!"

"It will, indeed," agreed Von.

It had been a short car ride to the buildings, and Gareth had made good time with his interesting driving skills. Heading through the main gates and up a long driveway, they pulled up in front of a main building. Though they had been warned it was deserted and in need of some upkeep it certainly looked majestic and more than functional.

"I love it already!" Molly exclaimed as they got out of the car and Gareth led them up the steps.

Once at the top he located a side door to the porch and used a keycard and key code to gain access. "Right this way, ladies," he gestured chivalrously towards the open door.

They stepped in, one after the other, via an old-style air lock.

Once inside, the porch opened out into a great hall. It was like stepping back in time. There were several floors bumping onto the central area like an atrium, which felt almost castle-like on account of all the stonework.

Molly looked around, awe-struck by the size and the grandeur. "It's incredible," she whispered, noticing there were old-style bookcases on the upper levels. By the looks of it, they were filled with actual paper-printed, books.

She blinked, then looked again, straining her eyes to see. She could barely believe it. No one used books anymore.

Gareth scuttled ahead of them like a kid showing his friends around his candy store. "Down here we have facilities like kitchens and common areas. Over this way there are a number of lecture theaters. And then," he waved his arms in the direction of the back, "over and around the outskirts of the gardens, behind the main building, there have been a number of buildings added over the years which have been used on and off as offices and labs."

Von put her hands to her face. "It's beautiful…" was all she could manage to vocalize.

They toured the site, allowing Gareth to point out the various features brainstorming what each area might be used for.

When they had been around the entire campus, Gareth walked them back to the front porch where they had started out.

"So, what do you think?" he asked.

Molly and Von looked at each other.

Molly grinned. "It's perfect," she said, beaming away. "I think our next move is simply to figure out how we can cash-flow it and what we need to do in terms of staffing and building up a faculty."

Von nodded. "No small feat," she agreed, her face bright, but clearly aware of the work ahead of them.

Gareth bobbed his head. "Of course, I'll work with you any way I can to make sure that the buildings are as affordable as possible. But as you already know, I want to see this project go ahead. This won't be a commercial venture for me, or the trust. It will be merely a way of making sure these magnificent buildings are put to good use."

The three chatted a little longer and then Gareth took them back to the university, where they promised to reconvene and do some more work on the project.

Molly mulled the possibilities in her mind as her pod whisked her back to Gaitune. She couldn't believe how wonderfully everything was coming together, and after the epic failure of her presentation to the board only hours before.

She smiled to herself. *Sometimes you just never know what you're being led to,* she mused.

Downtown Spire, Estaria

"Wow, that was... er, *interesting*," Pieter commented, stepping out of the airlock of the enormous office building.

Joel traipsed out behind him. "It was," he agreed grimly. "But you know, we expected some friction."

Pieter's eyebrows were high. He shook his head in dismay. "I know, but they treat it as if it's *their* company. Their industry. Their money!"

Joel nodded, starting off down the street to the alley. "I know. And this is one of the reasons they seem unable to grasp the new mandate."

The pair of them disappeared into the alley way, and their pod descended quickly. They headed over to it and hopped in.

Joel programed up the next destination. "I think they've just had it their way for too long. They've grown up thinking that fear and greed are just a fact of life, and this is all they know. Unfortunately, those on our hit list have shown us they're not willing to try anything differently, and we just have to respond to that."

Pieter nodded, looking down at his holo messages. "Paige has said that the statements are going out as we planned. One media release for each high-level sacking, and then a blanket cover announcing the enforcement of the operating agreements."

The pod lifted off in to the air. Joel watched out of the window as they ascended above the sky line. "It must be obvious by now that these companies are related. Has there been any commentary on that yet?"

Pieter ruffled his hair. "Lemme ask her."

He typed and waited, slouching back in his seat and only then remembering to put on his harness.

A moment later he got a response back. He shook his head. "No one seems to have put it together," he told Joel. "Paige suspects that it would be clear to anyone watching, but it's as if no one really cares. She also mentioned that Maya is on a ship in the middle of nowhere, so that takes our biggest journalistic concern out of the way."

Joel smiled. "That is true!" he agreed. "We're lucky to have her on our side, that's for sure."

He glanced down at his holo notes and the list of undesirables they were extracting from Molly's companies. "Okay, let's look at who we're sacking next," he muttered.

. . .

2nd floor, Rex Baron's office

Pascal Randalf poked his head round the door of Rex's office.

"Settling in okay?" he asked, grinning a wide grin, and showing his teeth, something almost unseen in Estarian facial expression.

Sean looked up, shocked to have someone engaging him in chitchat. When he was Sean Royale people knew not to do that. But as Rex Baron he hadn't allowed himself to lay out the ground rules or demonstrate that he was not a chatty kind of guy. "Yes. Thank you. Everything is tick-i-tee boo."

Shit. Maybe that was going too far? Damn, how do civilians talk these days? he wondered, watching Randalf's expressions for feedback.

"Good to hear," Randalf continued, completely unfazed by the tick-i-tee boo. "Any space sickness?"

Sean spontaneously started laughing, but then realized that this was a thing that people went through. He disguised his laugh as a cough. "Phahhahahaha! *Cough cough.* No. I've been fortunate."

Fuck. Not normal enough. The cyborg components correct for that shit.

He corrected his error. "I mean... er... I had a touch of it for the first day or so, but got my electrolytes up quickly and am feeling fine now." Sean watched again, holding his breath.

"Good, good," Randalf remarked.

Sean felt he needed to offer something back. "Do you still get space sick on these trips, sir?"

He couldn't believe he was calling someone who was not the General "*sir.*"

Randalf put one hand on his hip and leaned on the door frame as if he were the office Adonis. "Nah. Not anymore. But I've been doing this over a decade now. Don't worry, Sport. If you keep coming out with us, you'll hardly notice it after a few years."

Sean smiled, trying to contain his contempt for the sniffling man. "Right," he agreed.

Randalf turned to leave, and Sean suddenly thought of something.

"Ah, actually. Mister Randalf," he said, getting up from his desk and pulling up a couple of holos from his desk station, and dragging them across the room with him. "I think I've got something on the books that isn't quite matching up."

Randalf turned, frowning. "Ah, that's odd," he said. "Show me."

Sean showed him the screens. "You see, this shows us weighing in at 4:56 but the official paperwork has us at 4:30."

Randalf rubbed his chin. "That *is* odd," he agreed. He paused, thinking for a minute. Then, in his perfectly modulated supervisor's voice he spoke again. "Leave it with me. I'll see what's what."

Sean pretended to play the conscientious employee. "Would you like me to go through the inventory and see if I can find out what may not have been accounted for?"

"Oh goodness no, Rex," Randalf scoffed haughtily. "We have twenty-five floors on this vessel. That would take this trip plus the return journey, and of course we off-load when we get there. No. Leave it with me. Thank you for bringing this to my attention."

The matter was closed.

Sean bobbed his head, folding the holos away. "Yes sir. Of course. I still haven't got my head around quite how big this operation is."

He walked back to his desk. "It's one thing to look at numbers in a spreadsheet, or inventory on a search-able database back in the office ..."

Randalf nodded sympathetically. "Yes. It takes some getting used to," he said patronizingly. "You'll get there though."

He tapped the door frame and then wandered away down the

corridor that felt like it was made of cardboard overlaid on top of metal.

Sean sat back in his chair.

Gotcha! He thought to himself. *Now to prove it.*

Just then there was a rattling and jingling in the corridor, coupled with footsteps.

Maya, he predicted immediately, and just as he recognized the sound, Maya walked past, looking backwards as if she'd been checking all the offices she walked past, looking for him. Spotting him, she spun back around and strode straight into the room unceremoniously.

"Hey," she said, bringing the feeling of a whirlwind of activity with her.

"Hey," he replied, the stagnation of a day in the office in his voice.

Maya stopped suddenly, realizing the hell she had walked into. "You okay?" she asked, looking from side to side and coming to terms with his shoe box office.

He nodded. "What can I do for you, Marissa?" His natural impatient look had returned to his face now that he wasn't having to fool people he was Rex.

"I've found something," she disclosed quietly. "Well, I think I have. And I need your help. Brock, I mean Tallus, can't help coz he's on shift for the next three days. And Jack has just collapsed. I could go on my own—"

Sean shushed her. "No. I'll help. Just not right now." He discreetly touched his ear with a finger, and Maya nodded.

"I'll see you in the mess at feeding time," he told her, getting up and ushering her out of the office.

"Are you shooing me, Rex?" she asked, mock indignantly, as she was walked backwards out to the corridor.

Sean held her upper arm. "Yes, Marissa. I have work to do. See. You. *Later*," he said, gritting his teeth and glancing down the corridor to make sure no one had seen them together.

Maya rolled her eyes and straightened her atmosjacket. "Later, Rexy!" she called flippantly, twiddling her fingers in a wave and trotting away back down the corridor.

Sean took a deeeeeeep breath as he returned to his office, and then to his desk, to continue to poke around the files he could actually access.

Looks like she's having way more fun on this undercover lark than some of us, he thought, noticing how she was coming out of herself more on this ship than she had on Gaitune.

Maybe it's the act? Or maybe it's the liberation of not being herself.

Okay, Royale, back to work, he told himself, staring blankly at his holoscreen.

CHAPTER TWELVE

Staðall University, Lecture Theater 21

Von sat in the darkened lecture theater, the lights over the front bench giving an atmospheric hush that would normally enhance academic awe.

Molly strode in, dropping down the steps two at a time. "Paige says 'Hi,'" she said brightly as she arrived at the front where Von had been marking assignments on her holo.

The professor looked up. "Ah. Wonderful. She's an excellent student, you know. One of the best I've ever seen. And we get the cream here," she said with a glimmer of pride.

Molly smiled. "She'll be pleased to hear that," she responded, wondering how to convey the sentiment to Paige without sounding like she'd been to a parents evening. "So, you said you wanted to talk through some issues with the existing course? What's up?"

Von closed her holoscreens and looked up. "The course itself, and the students, are fine." She paused, correcting herself. "Actually, better than fine. They're excelling, and excited, and though we're several weeks in now, there are people still trying to sign up for it."

Molly grinned. "That's... awesome!"

Von matched her grin. "It is, isn't it."

Molly's smiled faded. "I sense a 'but'... "

Von's eye dimmed and she became more solemn. "Yes. There is a 'but,'" she sighed. "We're facing resistance within the department. Our head has suggested we cut it short, so still award the same number of credits but end it three weeks early. I think I've staved him off for the time being, but this may unravel quickly."

Molly's eyes widened. "Wow. They really don't want this material being taught!"

Von bobbed her head sadly. "It seems like." She stood up and started packing her things away. "I suspect they've gotten wind of what we're doing with moving to the new campus, and it's a little bit of sour grapes," she said slowly, as if contemplating the idea as she said it.

Molly sucked her lip into her mouth. "I guess it was inevitable they would find out," she said, contemplating how it might have become common knowledge.

"The other problem you're facing," Von explained gently, "is that these people walk around thinking they already know everything about everything. If you look at improving policies to help the masses, they call you a socialist. If you talk about not killing and not going to war for the sake of it, they say that you're unrealistic. They take no time to consider what you're actually talking about because they bring all their filters and pre-formed ideas to the table."

She shook her head, her eyes showing how hard this had been for all the years she'd been trying to make a difference with her work. "It just makes them unwilling — and in a lot of cases *unable* — to even hear what you're suggesting. They just filter it out and decide what you mean, based on their sound bites and prejudices."

Molly slumped down in a seat on the front row. "So what do we do?" she asked, frustration hanging in her tone.

Von tilted her head in a sort of surrender. "Deal with it, I guess. You're not going to change their minds by going head-to-head, or trying to have a rational discussion. I suppose the only thing you can do is keep doing your thing, and just engage with those who are truly willing to see a new alternative."

Molly smiled weakly. "So I guess that means the students then?"

Von nodded. "For the most part. I've had a few of the faculty be in touch privately to offer words of encouragement, except, for the most part, it comes with a warning: 'Don't be too XYZ, else they'll think you're this. Or don't push too hard with your ideas because they'll stop entertaining the idea of this course and shut it down…'"

Von sighed and perched on the front bench, as she often would when she was lecturing in this hall. "It's just the way it is with these things," she explained, shaking her head. "Anything that pushes peoples' buttons is going to be met with resistance."

Molly looked up, her face galvanized with a sheen of determination now. "I suppose that since we're going down this route, we just have to accept that some people aren't going to come with us."

Von nodded. "I think so." She got up and ambled over to take the seat next to Molly. "But you didn't start this whole thing just for entertainment. If you did, there were other courses you could support, courses that would have ruffled fewer feathers. You started this for a reason." She paused. "Because you had a bigger vision for what is possible."

Molly nodded, remembering. "Yep. I guess if the students want intellectual popcorn they'd be *taking* other courses too."

Von gazed at the floor for a moment. "So… we proceed?" she asked.

Molly nodded, without any new energy, as if it were just a continuation of her original concept. "We proceed," she confirmed.

. . .

Aboard the *Flutningsaðili*, Mess hall, Level 2

"Okay, let's go!" Maya said sharply from behind him.

Sean had been sitting down for about 84 seconds before Maya had searched him out, prodded him in the ribs, and then circled round the table to plonk herself down in front of him.

He looked down at his food. Assuming one could call it that. "I need to eat," he told her, his tone sounding more like a negotiation than a statement.

Maya pretended to be exasperated and huffed, putting her head down on her arm on the table. "Oh. My. Ancestors! You've got to work. You've got to eat. You know, you're taking this Mr. Rexy Boring thing waaaay too seriously."

Sean narrowed his eyes. "And you're taking this Marissa-floozy thing way too lightly," he said quietly, leaning over the table a little and lowering his voice.

She looked up, strands and clumps of her dark hair falling over her face in a haphazard way. She sighed. "Just coz I want to get on with this and get it solved."

"Patience you must learn, young one," he told her.

Maya sat up a little. "Okay. So, after you've eaten then?"

Sean nodded. "Sure. But where is it we're going?"

Maya looked over to check the queue at the food station. There were relatively few people. "Okay. Lemme grab some food and I'll fill you in," she promised.

She was up and making her way across the mess room in a shot. Minutes later she returned with a tray of food, plus her supplements.

"You actually eat those?" Sean asked her nodding at the colored pills in the little side tray.

"Yah-ha," she said, putting a couple in her mouth and slinging them back with a sip of water.

Sean shuddered.

"Why?" she asked.

He shook his head and continued eating. "Reminds me of my days on Teshov, when that was mostly all we had to keep us functional."

Maya's eyes widened in horror. "You're kidding? You mean no food? Like *real* food?"

Sean pulled his head to the side for a moment. "Nope. Anyway — what've you found?"

They sat eating, quietly catching up on Maya's activities over the last several hours. After they were done they cleared their trays away and left the mess hall, casually, so as not to draw any attention.

Once they were out in the corridor Maya spoke again. "You wanna go there now?" she confirmed.

Sean nodded, and Maya led the way.

Gaitune-67, Hangar Deck

Molly's mind was whirring following her emergency meeting with Von that evening. She was still distracted by it as she ambled absently back through the hangar deck after returning to Gaitune.

You know, the more I think about this, the more I think we just need to get on with it.

I thought that's what you were doing?

Yes, but I mean, put a stake in the ground.

Uhmmmm....?

Well, what if we were to start making offers to faculty members. Those that we want on board, regardless of whether they're at the university already or not.

That would certainly cause more of a rupture.

I think the rupture is already happening. But at least this might create some allies.

True. If they have the bottle to take the leap.

Molly contemplated it for a few moments, and walked straight past the steps back up to the safe house.

Where are we going?

Oh shit!

She stood trying to figure out what she was doing, and then spun around on the spot before she realized she had come too far. She backed up and found her way back up the stairs to the corridor and the demon door.

You know, thinking about it...

She stopped at the demon door and took a right into the ops room instead.

Oh, great. I know that feeling in your circuits.

Molly was in deep concentration mode. She headed straight for her usual console and connected a call with Von.

The holo flicked up, and Molly started talking before the image settled. "Professor Von, sorry, I know it's late ..."

A sleepy looking Abigail Von appeared on the holoscreen. "It's quite okay. Is everything alright?" she asked, concern wrinkling her slightly puffy eyes.

Molly didn't even bother to sit down. "Yes, yes fine. I've just been thinking on the way back home. I was wondering if you'd compile a list of people you'd like on the faculty. Say, your top twelve?"

Von answered slowly, her brain catching up with the processing. "Yes, I can do that." Her voice conveying her curiosity. "Are you thinking of approaching people soon?"

Molly leaned her hands on the console. "Yes, very soon. I'm thinking if we have a faculty and a full first semester of materials we could probably soft launch a program next cycle."

Von rubbed one eye, waking herself up some more. "You mean after this course has finished at Staðall, move the whole concept across to the new university?"

Molly shifted her weight onto one foot. "It would be out of

the way of the Dean and his cronies. We'd be free to teach what we wanted."

Von had leaned forward and rested her head in her hands. "But what about the students?" she questioned.

Molly shrugged. "Well, we've proven the concept. The rest will be down to marketing and smoothing the mechanism for anyone who wanted to transfer, but we could handle all that. Right now I just want to be in a position to approach those who we'd want on board and make them an offer. But *you're* the one who would know who we'd want in the mix." Molly leaned up and stood a little straighter.

Von nodded enthusiastically, dropping her arms to the table in front of her. "Yes. I would. In fact — oooo, this is going to be exciting!"

"Great," Molly said. "Well, I'll let you get some sleep, and look forward to your recommendations."

Abigail bobbed her head. "Very good," she agreed.

"Good night, Professor."

"Good night, Molly."

The call clicked off.

Molly stood in the darkened ops room, letting her brain catch up to where everything was moving.

I think this could work, Oz.

I have calculated a 92.9 % probability of success as defined by your previous comments of what success would look like.

That's good to know.

It is. And in the meantime, you are overdue for some rest too. You've been working hard on this, and I noticed you have clocked very little REM the last few nights... perhaps on account of the worry?

What worry?

Oh, I dunno. The pressure of suddenly starting a university. Having your team out in the middle of the system under-

cover. Not knowing what's happening with your realm jumping and the talisman thing.

Hmm.

I take that to mean you agree with my point?

I do.

Well good then. Time for bed, Mollster.

Molly ambled out of the ops room with less vigor than when she strode in.

You know it's true what they say: Tiredness hits you when you stop.

It appears so...

CHAPTER THIRTEEN

Aboard the *Flutningsaðili*, Level 4

Maya was midway through an information dump with Sean, once she was sure they weren't being recorded. "Okay, so the cameras are on the no-record loop. I've made it look like just a glitch in the system in case anyone notices. A few other cameras on other floors are also experiencing it."

Sean's eyes glinted with recognition at the technique she was using. "Ah, to avoid the no fingerprints syndrome."

Maya nodded. "I believe so, but that's a human history thing, right?"

Sean nodded. "I'm not sure. But it's been rehashed on Estarian crime dramas so I'm pretty certain."

Maya stepped out of the elevator onto the fourth floor. She started walking confidently, in case there was anyone around who might see them. Sean followed, suddenly having to widen his gate to keep up with her.

They made their way straight down the main corridor and then at the cross roads turned right and then left again and kept following it down.

At the end of the corridor she could see the double doors that led to nothing. "That's it," she muttered quietly to Sean.

He glanced around, trying to see if there was another way through. Then he looked up.

"You're kidding?" Maya gasped, looking up and seeing that he'd spotted a ventilation outlet.

"Do you want in, or not?" he asked, without even taking his eyes off it.

Maya looked around, realizing they had limited options. "I could hack the access. Given enough time," she attempted.

Sean looked down at her. "Okay. That's one option."

"Also," she added, "we don't know if there is breathable atmosphere on the other side."

Sean glanced down at her, putting his hands on his hips. "Except we do know someone is going in and out of there if there are living, breathing hostages."

Maya pursed her lips, thinking. "Unless the hostages are elsewhere. Like on ice?"

Sean bobbed his head. He was about to speak, but there was a faint bang off in the direction of the doors they had not yet approached.

Maya looked at him, the whites of her eyes showing. "Is someone coming?" she asked.

He moved, pulling her back in the other direction away from the doors. Looking back, he could see movement behind the glass.

"Shit," he mouthed to himself.

Maya, in a panic, had run ahead of him and whipped around the corner at the end of the corridor they had just come down. She turned left, away from the lift.

Shit, Maya, Sean cursed in his head, *wrong way.*

He rounded the same corner too and almost bumped into her as she'd pressed herself against the wall. He glared, at her, then stood on the other side of her.

Catching his wits, he checked down the corridor. There were doorways. With broken up shadows and recesses. He tugged at her arm, and pulled her along the corridor pointing at the doors. She understood and hid in one doorway. Sean took the next one down.

They waited.

Moments later they could hear the footsteps pounding up the corridor, almost amplified by the starkness of the passageway. They grew louder and louder. Maya felt her heart in her mouth pulsing with the anticipation of being caught.

The footsteps reverberated louder still as their owner rounded the corner.

They stopped.

Maya pressed herself against the door, trying to hide her head from view. A moment later they started again, and within a few paces Maya could tell they were going in the direction of the lift.

She cautiously tipped her head forward, stealing a glance at the suited, booted Estarian walking away from them. She waited, watching intently for his face as he rounded the corner. She caught a glimpse, and while she didn't know the person, she did recognize him from the initial briefing. He had been one of the key personnel on the dais at the front of the room, introduced to them as someone who was in charge.

She couldn't for the life of her remember his name.

She could sense Sean moving from his hiding spot and glanced over. He held one finger to his lips, and paused his own movement, listening. Maya held her breath, not daring to move.

After a few more seconds Sean started moving, relaxing a little. "Okay. He's gone," he said softly.

Maya pulled up her holo.

His eyes fixed on her holo. "What are you doing?" he asked.

Maya scrambled between screens. "If I can figure out who he is, I might be able to simulate his access codes and get us in the door."

Sean narrowed his eyes. "Did you get a look at him?"

She nodded. "Yeah. I just can't remember his name. He was on the platform for the briefing."

"Describe him," Sean told her.

Maya looked up into the top of her eye sockets. "Estarian. Male. Late forties. Large nose, but slightly drawn face."

"Max Pike," Sean said quickly.

Maya cocked her head.

Sean grinned. "I've gotten good at names and faces over the years. Plus, there is a training course the Federation has to help you," he said, looking at her as if she should have taken it already.

Maya smiled and returned to fiddling with her holo. "Ah yeah, that and the cyborg implants," she said teasingly.

Sean grinned. "Alright girlee," he said cajoling her, "you actually think you can get us in?"

She tipped her head from side to side. "Dunno yet. I can try. But it might trigger all kinds of alarms."

Sean sighed flatly. "Nothing is ever easy without an AI around."

She glanced up at him. "What about ADAM? Do you think he could help?"

Sean opened his holo. "Probably. Lemme see if he's available." He poked a message, and one was returned almost straight away.

"What do you need?" he asked Maya.

She grabbed at his wrist and started communicating with ADAM directly.

Sean looked around, straining to hear in case there was any activity around that they might need to react to. "Nearly there?" he pressed after a long minute, starting to feel like, under any other circumstances, he might not mind a female taking control of his holo that close and personal.

"Uh huh," she mumbled. "Let's go." She poked the screen again, and then closed it. "I need you nearby to pull the code over."

Sean followed her. "ADAM just wrote you a patch?" he queried, skeptically.

She grunted the affirmative and continued down the white corridor where their mysterious access point lay.

Sean shook his head. "Here goes nothing then," he said, taking one last glance around and following her.

Approaching the doors, Maya checked for cameras or sensors, hoping that something like that would light up on her schematics. She glanced down at her own holo and for the access she had. It all looked clean.

"Wrist!" She demanded, commandingly, holding her hand out for Sean to oblige.

Obediently, he complied and she pulled up the code she needed. Then, hurriedly, she poked around on the access panel, holding down key combos that she read off Sean's device, presumably also from ADAM.

"Uploading," she whispered.

There was a faint beep on the panel and she typed in 1234, and pressed enter. The door clicked open.

Without a hint of hesitation she pressed forward on it and headed through, Sean following quickly in her wake.

Once inside the darkness was illuminated in sequence, as lights came on down the length of the passage in front of them. "This is a lot of area to not have on the official schematics," she commented.

Sean whistled quietly between his teeth. "You're not wrong," he agreed.

The pair made their way down the corridor, moving as quickly as they could. There were doors on either side every now and again.

Maya's eyes softened in dismay. "We can't possibly search all of these," she said, a hint of defeat in her voice.

Sean slowed to a walk, and then stopped. "We may not have to," he said cryptically.

Maya turned and looked at him. "What do you mean?" she asked.

"Hang on," he said. "Calibrating."

Maya narrowed her eyes, trying to figure out what he was doing. She noticed he was looking at the wall and his eyes were moving slightly. "Hang on... you can see heat signatures? Like X-ray vision?" she pressed.

Sean smiled cockily. "One of the perks of being upgraded by the Federation," he told her.

A moment later, he pointed. "I've got three warm bodies, over that way," he indicated off in the direction of one of the rooms on the right.

Maya scanned the corridor. "But which door do we go through?"

Sean approached the one nearest him. "Try this one," he said, pointing at the panel.

Maya poked at the numbers.

1234 enter.

The door swooshed open, allowing them to pass through. There was a light on over in the far corner, behind what looked like a lab of hardware and equipment.

Maya jogged forward, towards the yellow light. "That must be them," she hissed quietly. Sean jogged after her.

They approached, finding a glass meeting room with three people locked inside. One of them came to the glass, recognizing that these people weren't their captors.

She was Estarian. And she looked exhausted and bedraggled. They all did. Maya straight away recognized the old guy from his profile picture. That was Dr. Brahms. And the girl at the window was Lana Rey.

She glanced at Sean who joined her at the glass. "Who's the other one?"

There was an Estarian girl, younger than Lana.

Sean shrugged.

Lana headed over to the door, pointing down at the access panel.

Maya punched in the code.

123-

Sean grabbed her hand. "Wait!" he told her.

She looked at him stunned.

Lana looked at him and then at Maya. She banged on the glass and then pointed at the door panel again.

Sean pulled Maya away. "We need to be smart about this," he told her. "We let them out, and then what? They just come up to the upper decks? And then we're no longer undercover, and they throw all five of us in there."

Maya turned back to the keypad, and tried to get her hand free. "Not if we integrate and give them a story to tell the rest of the crew. Whoever is doing this can't just disappear that many people," she responded defiantly.

Sean wouldn't release her hand. She looked at him, and then her hand, irritated.

Sean shook his head. "They can. And they will. And you're assuming the rest of the crew isn't in on this."

Maya hesitated. She dropped her tone. "Could we play dumb?"

Sean shook his head, letting her go finally. "Getting through all their levels of security? I don't think so."

Maya called through the doorway to Lana. "Hey can you hear me?"

Lana nodded.

Maya explained the situation. "We can't get you out. It's not safe. For any of us. Are you hurt? Are any of you hurt?"

Lana shook her head.

"Okay, we know you're here. We've been looking for you. Help is on the way. We know you're Lana and that is Ainstel. Who is the girl with you?"

Lana glanced over at the girl who was deliberately shying

away from the interaction, leaning on the wall, her back to the others.

"Her name is Anne," Lana said, trying to be heard through the glass. Maya could just make out her words.

"Anne," she repeated. "Who is she? Why is she with you?"

Lana shrugged. "She won't talk to us. She says she'll put us in more danger if she tells us."

Maya nodded. "We can't deal with this now," she muttered to Sean. "We need to get out of here and get Molly to extract us all."

Sean nodded.

Maya wanted to check one more thing. "Are they feeding you? Are you okay?"

Lana nodded.

"Okay," Maya called through, pressing her face near to the crack in the door, but still allowing Lana to lip read her through the glass too. "We're going to get help. Don't let on that we've been here. Everything is going to be okay, alright?"

Lana nodded. Brahms had headed over and put a hand on Lana's shoulder. He nodded his understanding too.

"Stay safe," Maya instructed. "We'll be back."

She tore herself away from the window and together she and Sean made their way out. As quickly as they could.

Without speaking they moved back down the corridor and out, heading all the way back to level 1 and the common areas for personnel where they were meant to be.

When they arrived, Maya sat down on a sofa and pretended to pick up a magazine. "What the fuck?" she exclaimed under her breath.

Sean sat near her, looking around, pretending to be people watching. "Yeah," Sean agreed. "Did you notice the equipment in that room, too?"

Maya continued to pretend to read, restricting her body language. "No," she responded.

Sean looked out across the common area. "Big machinery. Easily our drilling equipment."

"Uh huh," she acknowledged. "Wanna send a message to Pieter? I guess we have solved some of the puzzle."

"Yeah," Sean concurred. "I'll do that when I go to my bunk. The only other piece we need to sort out is who these guys are working for."

Maya frowned, and then pretended the frown was something in the magazine she was looking at. She pulled it closer and pretended to be reading the archaic printed material that some media companies started putting out during some renaissance of twenty years ago. "The only person who must know about that is the boss guy. What did you call him? Max?"

Sean wiped his face with one hand and slid the other arm off the back of the sofa. "Yeah. He's going to be harder to crack," he admitted. "Not like you can just start chatting with him over a beer and ask him if he's ever kidnapped anyone. And he's unlikely to offer it up."

Maya nodded discretely. "So what do we do?"

Sean glanced around the common area. "I dunno. Lemme think about it and I'll let you know."

He leaned forward, readying to get up. "I'll ping Pieter. But you need to go get some rest. I'll be in touch soon. Good job."

Maya turned the page on the printed material. "You too," she said quietly.

Sean got up and wandered out of the common area.

Aboard the *Flutningsaðili*, Level 2

Sean found his way back to his shared quarters. It had been weeks now and still the maze of identical corridors made it difficult for any normal person to navigate around.

Thankfully, he'd noticed various numbers placed on corridors or labeling facility points, like vents and electrical boxes, and used them to recognize whether or not he was in the right area.

He stepped into the shoebox of a room and paused while the dim lights came up and the door slid closed behind him. His roommate, Tallus, was elsewhere. Probably still working.

He glanced down at the smooth surface of the floor and then his boots, and sat down on the bottom bunk to take them off. Boots were essential around the ship. Apart from everything being hard exposed metal surfaces, most of the walkways and indeed unfurnished corridors were little more than grated grids of metal. Grids that should Paige show up with her high heel shoes on, she would rapidly find herself confined to briefing rooms for the entire trip.

He sighed, and started undoing the electromagnetic clasps, one by one. Then he hit his quantum bead with a double tap to hail Pieter. Or Paige. Or whomever was listening.

A moment later the audio connected in his implant.

"Greetings of the night upon you," came Pieter's overly exuberant voice.

Sean grunted. "Sounds like you're bored shitless, mate."

Pieter's voice came back through his ear. "How could you tell?"

Sean grinned to himself. "Practice," he told him. "So, I have news. We've located the two kidnapped victims, and found that in fact there are three of them. The two we know about, then a girl called Anne. Also Estarian."

Pieter sounded like he was scurrying and scuffling on the other end of the line.

Sean tilted his head, listening hard. "You okay, mate?"

"Yeah, I..." there was some more scuffling. "It's okay. I just slipped off my chair. All good now."

Sean chuckled quietly to himself, not wanting the overly-sensitive computer tech to think he was laughing *at* him. Or for anyone to overhear him have a conversation with himself.

He pressed on with the intel transfer. "I think we've also located the equipment too. In the same section of the ship. ADAM helped Maya get access so he'll be able to tell you the area."

Pieter was making active listening sounds and making a note.

"We need a plan," Sean told him. "We could take the hostages from their holding room, but then we'd have nowhere to go with them. We'd blow our cover and have no way off the ship."

Pieter frowned. "Okay. So you're ready for extraction then?"

Sean was quiet for a moment. "We haven't found out anything about who is in on this. Who is responsible. At either end of the chain."

Pieter scratched his head. "I think this conversation suddenly went way above my decision level," he decided. "Want me to talk to Molly and come back to you?"

Sean scratched at his day-old stubble. "Sure. Have a word and maybe ping me in a short while. I'm going to get some rack time and I can probably speak privately for the next few hours."

"Great," Pieter responded, his voice sounding relieved. "I'll give you a click in your implant when we're ready and you can hit your bead to confirm we can connect."

Sean stretched his arms out in front of him and leaned forward ready to make a move. "Okay. Sounds good. Talk soon."

The line went dead.

Sean hauled his cyborg ass to his feet and looked around for his shower gear. Locating it, he grabbed a towel, and slipped on his room shoes, which were just about protection enough from the hard-grated floor in the corridor, and wandered out in the direction of the shower facilities.

Staðall University, Senior Common Room

Molly, Gareth and Von sat around the outside table, their teas and mochas nearly done. The courtyard behind the Senior

Common Room was a little sark-trap, which got quite a bit of light at that time in the day. It was also a favorite spot for those who wanted to kick back and chill for a short while between the rigorous studying and marking of papers. Like a place of respite.

Right now it was deserted, apart from the three of them, allowing them to talk freely.

"I think we have a way forward," Molly said, looking up from the financial model they'd been working on.

Gareth nodded his agreement. "Yes. If I can get the trust to agree on this number here," he said pointing at the spreadsheet, "it all falls into place." He peered up at Molly. "Leave it with me," he said with a twinkle in his eye. "I'll get onto that this afternoon as soon as we're done here."

Von leaned on the table, smiling satisfied. "I think this is the easiest negotiation I've ever been involved in!" she remarked.

Molly grinned. "Kinda straightforward when we're all after a shared goal."

"Indeed," Von commented. "Although, I suspect we'll face continued resistance from the existing institutions. Unfortunately, they'll likely find this whole concept quite threatening."

Gareth's eye saddened a little as he nodded his agreement.

Just then Molly's holo started buzzing.

It's Pieter, Oz informed her. **It's important.**

"Excuse me, one moment," she said to her companions. She got up from the table and walked away a few paces amongst the empty tables in the little courtyard.

"Hello," she said, answering her holo.

It was Pieter's voice. He sounded anxious.

"Molly. It's Pieter. I've just had word from Sean. They've found the scientists. We could do with some direction on next steps. They're not in immediate danger but—"

Molly interrupted. "I understand. I'll be on my way right away. You can fill me in in the pod. Gimme a couple of minutes and I'll call you back."

Pieter's voice sounded a little less strained when he heard that. "Okay, great. I'll stand by."

Moments later, Molly had excused herself from her new friends and was striding out into the quad to rendezvous with her pod, which whipped down with speed. She hopped in, and then the pod disappeared up beyond the stratosphere.

CHAPTER FOURTEEN

<u>Gaitune-67, Hangar Deck</u>

Molly hopped out of her pod as soon as the door was open enough, and half walked, half ran across the hangar deck towards the upstairs conference room where Pieter was set up.

Is Joel on his way?

Already there.

And Paige?

On her way in.

Moments later, Molly burst into the room to find Joel and Pieter sitting in front of the telemetry screens.

"Everything okay?" she asked.

Joel nodded.

Pieter twisted round in his seat, his hair a little more unkempt than usual. "They're okay. Not in any danger. They've found the hostages and now we need to decide what to do next," he said recapping, the conversation they'd had in her pod ride back, making sure everyone was on the same page.

Paige appeared in the doorway and silently headed in and took a seat on the other side of the conference table.

"Okay," Molly said, composing herself. "Let's see if we can connect with Sean then."

Pieter sent a click, and received two clicks back. He connected the audio. "We're live with Sean's implant."

Molly had found a seat and sat down. "Sean?" she said.

Sean's half-asleep voice grated onto the call. "Yeah," he mustered.

Molly's manner was serious and businesslike. "I understand you have the hostages and the kit, but no intel on who is behind it?"

Sean's voice was a little muffled. "Yeah. We think the head guy on the ship is involved. Max Pike. Only coz we saw him visiting the hostages. But beyond that we've no idea."

Molly frowned. "What condition are the hostages in?" she asked.

Sean sighed a little. "They seem okay, considering. At least physically. Though I don't know how well they're being treated. They didn't look like they were being abused other than being locked up in a tiny room."

Molly bobbed her head. "Any leads that we can chase down that may help?"

Sean was quiet for a moment. "I suppose you could look into Pike. Max Pike. And any communications he's been having. He may have been in touch with either the client or someone involved even while we've been on board."

Molly nodded. "Sure. Anything else out of the ordinary?"

"Erm... only that Brock seems to be working harder than he ever has before."

Paige glanced up at them. "He's in the kitchens, isn't he?"

Sean must have heard her. "Yeah. I think he's pissed about all the long hours and manual work he's having to do."

Paige's eyes drooped in sympathy for him.

Molly tried to keep them on track. "So, are you ready for us to extract?"

"I'm not sure," Sean confessed. "I mean, we've only completed half of the mission. We've located the hostages, but we still need to find a way to get them out safely. Even if you extracted us, there will be resistance here. They have several armed security personnel. They could kill anyone — us, the hostages, anyone who boards."

Molly wiped her face with her hands. "Will more time help?"

Sean paused again. "I think probably yes. At the very least we can find a way to get us all to a safe place. And then even try and find out a bit more about who might be behind this.

Molly pursed her lips and nodded. "Okay. Well we'll do some digging into this Max fella and see if we can turn up anything from this end. Continue with the regular check-ins, and we'll reevaluate in a few days."

Sean's voice was still muffled. "Okay, sure," he said, half whispering. "It's a deal."

Molly had cocked her head. "Sean?" she asked. "Are you okay?"

Sean sounded puzzled. "Yeah. Why?"

"Your voice sounds different."

Sean paused for a second, and then there sounded like a ruffling on his end. "Oh. I'm doing a head stand while I'm talking to you."

Joel slapped his hand over his mouth.

Pieter closed his eyes, tightly, screwing up his face, laughing silently and trying to keep it together.

Molly remained expressionless. "Sean? Whatever for?"

His voice sounded like he was straining now. "It helps with the shitty antigrav on these things. Keeps the circulation in the brain working."

Molly frowned, evaluating the science behind his explanation. "Ah. Okay," she said simply. "We'll leave you to it then. Stay safe."

"Righty-ho," he responded. "Talk soon."

Molly made a slicing movement at her neck with her flattened fingers and Pieter killed the audio link.

Joel and Pieter continued to laugh, but more vocally now that the line was cut.

Paige joined in giggling. "I wondered why he sounded so odd." After a moment she cocked her head. "Do you think it's a cyborg thing? Or a real thing about antigrav?"

Pieter shook his head. "I've never heard of anything like that before. It might be something he's picked up in the Federation."

Molly tilted her head slightly. "Like a disease? Or a habit?" she asked, her face still deadpan.

Joel sniggered suddenly uncontrollably. "Remind me to ask him when he gets his ass back here!"

Aboard the *Flutningsaðili*, Level 5, Medical bay

"Okay, you're all set," Jayne said, putting the little bandage over where she had just given Max a jab.

Max put his finger over the bandage making sure it was secure. "Thank you, Dr. Jayne," he said, slipping off the examination couch.

Jayne busied herself with tidying away the needle and containers of nutrient injections. "Come see me in a week for the booster, and then you'll be good for another couple of weeks in artificial grav," she told him.

There was a long pause as Max rolled down his sleeve and perched against the couch. "How are our newbies settling in?" he inquired casually.

Jayne looked up briefly and then put her eyes back on her instruments. "Adapting. I think. I've not really spoken to the one in the kitchen since we came on board. But I see the two girls and the older guy now and again in the mess hall. They seem to be doing okay."

Max's tone dropped to being a little more serious. "Anything we should be aware of?"

Jayne hesitated. "I'm not sure," she answered slowly and quietly. "The girl. The young one. She was asking about who the client was the other day."

Max's gaze bore into her head from across the room. "And what did you tell her?"

Jayne shrugged. "Nothing. Just that we have lots of clients."

"Anything else?" he pushed.

Jayne thought quickly. "Well, I think I overheard her and the older guy in the mess hall mention something about drilling equipment."

Max stood upright. "That doesn't sound good."

Jayne bobbed her head. "No idea why they'd be talking about it, though."

Max folded his arms, and stroked his face with one hand. "Hmm. I heard he had found some kind of anomaly with the paperwork too. He was all for checking it out by going down there, until Mark put him off."

Jayne suddenly spun round. "Max. Why is it so important that no one knows what we're shipping? I don't understand what the big deal is."

Max glowered. "The big deal is that it's what our clients pay us for. Discretion. We don't know how this affects their business. Or the negotiations they might be involved in. We don't know what kind of impact this knowledge could have in the wrong hands."

Jayne had put one hand on her hip, and was now staring back at Max defensively. "So what, we just work hard to make sure *no one* finds out about it?"

"Yes. Yes, we do," he told her definitively. "That is why we are paid the big bucks, over any other freight service."

Jayne sighed, and turned back to what she had been doing.

"Okay, fine. But I just don't have any idea how they're finding this stuff out."

Max started walking across the treatment room to the door. "They must have come looking for it," he theorized. "I suspect, Dr. Jayne, we have some spies in our midst."

Jayne turned to follow his movement, the stress and concern showing around her eyes. "What do you want me to do?"

Max smiled. "Kill them."

Jayne looked horrified.

"Just kidding!" he said, laughing confidently.

Jayne started laughing too, relieved. Mostly.

"I'll do it," he added seriously.

Then he started laughing. "Kidding!"

Jayne pointed at him. "You got me!" she said waving a tongue depressor she had picked up off the side. Though she was laughing on the outside, something niggled at her amygdala. She didn't entirely feel safe around this man, and she didn't know why. Why did she feel like maybe he wasn't joking about killing these people?

Max continued laughing his fake laugh as he strode out of the med bay. The door swooshed closed behind him, and Jayne's laughing died immediately.

She sat down in a nearby swivel chair and rummaged in the drawer to her right. Finding what she needed, she pulled it out and unclipped the cap. She took the device up to her mouth and inhaled a drag of the substance, savoring it entering her lungs and her blood stream.

Max immediately pulled up a holo call as he strode down the corridor. "Yep. It's me. Yes, I think it's time to round them up. The younger one, Marissa, I think she told us her name was. And Rex, in accounting."

He listened to the person on the other end of the call as he walked. "Yes, I'll meet you down there. Do it quietly and discreetly. No need to alert the crew or any friends they have that we're onto them."

Max clicked off the comm and made his way up to the fourth floor. He approached the same stark white corridor as he'd walked many a time already over the last weeks. And, in fact, on many trips before this, for various reasons. He keyed in his ID code, and let the device scan his retina, and then passed through the heavy door into the previously secret and restricted area.

He strode through the darkened warehouse, the motion-activated lights coming on as he walked. "Looks like you'll be having some new company soon," he called out as he approached the glass-fronted meeting room where he had his hostages locked up.

The girl that was the most communicative came to the window. "You won't get away with this, you asshole! People will know we're missing. You'll be discovered. And I'll be there when they put you to death for kidnapping on Teshov."

Max looked down at his nails and leaned against a desk that had a few chairs piled upside down on it. "My, my, my… what little you know about Teshov. Death sentences are only handed out to the general populous to keep them under control and afraid."

He glanced casually up at her. "I wouldn't fall into that category. I'm far too valuable to the people who actually have the power out there. And on Estaria, for that matter."

The girl's eyes flared in furry. "You won't get away with this," she shouted, her voice straining painfully. The older man, Dr. Brahms came up behind her and placed a hand gently on her shoulder. She seemed to calm instantly, understanding that her position was futile. The older scientist led her back away from the window and sat her down at one of the desks with her back to their captor.

Just then lights started coming on again, guiding the path for the newcomers. There were scuffed, and uneven steps.

And boots.

Lots of boots.

A few moments later the party appeared from between the stacks of equipment and boxes, brandishing their weapons and their two prisoners in cuffs.

"Well, I suppose this is one way to meet the boss to vent your concerns," Max cooed as the two humans looked up at him.

They remained silent.

He continued. "I suppose you're going to deny any knowledge of what's going on here."

Sean called over to Maya. "Don't respond. To anything," he told her.

Maya nodded.

"Rex, is it?" Max asked, wandering over to him. "Fancy yourself as a hero, do you?"

Sean looked straight ahead.

Max's eyes narrowed as he looked Rex up and down. "Hmm. Do I detect military training in that disciplined defiance?"

Sean ignored him.

Max kept rambling, walking over to the glass window of the meeting room. "Well, you see the problem is, if I even suspect that you might know everything, then you're a liability. And must be treated as such. But if I knew that you knew nothing, then..."

Sean scoffed. "You say that after showing us that you're holding three hostages down here?"

"Ah, he does speak!" Pike turned back to him, looking the strongly built human up and down. "Tell me," he questioned after a moment, "you're not entirely human, are you?"

Sean didn't respond again.

"No matter," Max retorted, signaling to his guards. "You can rot in here until our scheduled garbage dump. And then you can have a trip out into the space. Get up close and personal with the vacuum."

Max paused, expecting one of them to crack and start blurting out what they knew.

Neither said anything.

Max waved for them to be put into the glass room and started to walk away. "Oh, and by the way, we'll be rounding up your friends on board and bringing them to join you too. Just in case you were worried you would miss them."

Sean stood glaring from the other side of the glass, and Maya walked into the room, putting her hands behind her head in frustration, pacing in a small area as the door was closed and locked behind them.

Max gestured for the security detail to clear the area, and then followed them out.

Gaitune-67, Carl Milberg's residence

"Yo yo! How you doing man?" Carl Milberg sat down as the call connected.

"Good, thanks," came the reply over Carl's audio implant.

Carl spun around on his anti-grav chair in his home office. "So, are we ready to reroute?" he asked as casually as if they were talking about sport, and not illegally rerouting a freight ship.

"We are," Pike replied on the other end of the line. "Go ahead."

Carl poked at his holo and then flicked over to another screen. "Okay, sending new coordinates and flight plan. As far as they know you're on the existing flight plan. This way though you'll arrive a day early, giving your client time to pick up their merchandise before any inspectors are expecting to see you."

Max made sure he'd received the new flight path data on his holo. "Great. Thanks Carl," he replied once he confirmed it was received.

Max hesitated for a moment. "One other thing," he started.

ELL LEIGH CLARKE & MICHAEL ANDERLE

"We've had to take two new personnel offline. Suspect they might be corporate spies."

Carl sighed. "Okay. We'll have to tighten up the vetting process. Maybe look at bringing it in-house if those folks over there can't get their shit together. That's the second lot in as many shipments."

Max's voice was serious. "Yeah. It's a concern. Especially with everything that is on the line."

Carl shifted his tone to match the seriousness of Max's. He continued to swivel idly in his chair though. "You don't need to tell me. I'll look into it. Want me to look into these guys while I'm at it?"

Max shook his head. "No. No need. They'll not be around much longer."

Carl chuckled in a single exhale of breath. "Lemme guess. You're taking out the trash?"

Max's voice lightened a little. "You know me so well, Carl Milberg..."

"I do," Carl answered. "I know where *all* the bodies are buried," he joked.

Max's voice had a slight edge to it. "As do I, Carl, my friend. As do I."

Carl felt awkward for a second. "So. Erm. Well, good luck with the trash disposal and... the unloading when you get there. Gimme a shout next time you're passing this way."

"Sure. Will do," Max replied, his professional-casual voice resuming. "We'll do a beer..."

"Plan!" Carl confirmed, thankful he didn't have to do these calls with video. It would be much harder to hide how he really felt about the guy. "Bye for now, then," he concluded.

The call ended, and Carl continued to swivel in his chair for another few seconds before closing his screens down and pulling up the next thing.

Just then then he heard the airlock activating and realized he only had a few minutes of productive work time left. He whizzed through his communications and responded to everything that needed attending to urgently. He closed down the screen just as he heard footsteps coming down the hallway to the office door.

"Hi honey," Paige called as she breezed on past en route to the kitchen. "You ready for a glass of something?"

Carl smiled and swiveled around, getting up from his chair and padding through to meet her. "Would love something. I think we've still got a bottle of red open from last night."

He heard the clattering of dishes and pans, and the fridge door opening. He stepped into the kitchen to see Paige already figuring out the most complex puzzle of the day: what to make for supper.

"So how was your day?" he asked, reaching over the central island to the bottle of red.

Paige sighed, straightening up and still looking at the contents of the fridge. "It was okay. Hard work. Lot's going on. Yours?"

Carl grabbed a couple of glasses from a shelf behind him and popped them on the side and started pouring the wine. "It was okay. Another shipment in progress, so just keeping an eye on things," he told her.

"How do you feel about mac and cheese, with broccoli on the side?" Paige asked, glancing over at him.

Carl wandered over with a glass of wine for her. "Sounds delightful," he said, passing her the glass and returning to the stool at the island and settling himself down.

Aboard the *Flutningsaðili*, Level 2, Mess Hall

Jack strode into the dining area glancing around. She spotted Brock sitting with Auggie at the end of a long table. His expression was one of a broken man.

She marched over. "Hey Tallus. Auggie," she said nodding at the second broken-looking soul. "You guys alright?"

Brock looked up. "Yeah. Just. I never thought that working in a kitchen could be so exhausting."

Jack nodded sympathetically, but continued to glance around the hall as they talked.

"What's up?" Brock asked, noticing her distraction.

Jack looked at the seat next to Auggie, and then stepped round to it. She sat down and leaned in, lowering her voice. "It's Marissa. And Rex," she said, glancing sideways at Auggie, trying to be discrete. "I've not seen either of them for a while. Have you?"

Brock shook his head. He had his arm on the table, his fork hanging over his food. He tipped his fork a little in Auggie's direction asking him the same question.

Auggie shook his head.

Jack's eyes carried an intensity and seriousness that Brock recognized as being unusual. "You want some help looking for them?"

Jack glanced at Auggie, and Brock immediately understood exactly what her reservation was. "No. No. I'm sure they're fine," she said, her tone becoming lighter and more casual. "I mean, where would they go on a ship in the middle of nowhere," she laughed.

Brock bobbed his head. "Yeah. Probably snuck off somewhere to chill out or something," he said.

"Yeah. I don't blame them," Jack agreed standing up. "I'll leave you to finish eating," she said.

Brock understood the words to mean *finish eating and make an exit that doesn't look suspicious.*

He nodded and she turned to leave. Just then Jayne appeared at the table with a tray of food. "Greetings, all," she said, looking at the boys and then at Jack. "You not eating?" she asked.

Jack shook her head. "Already ate. You haven't seen Marissa or Rex anywhere have you?" she asked.

Jayne hesitated for a moment. "No. No. I haven't. Why?"

Jack shrugged. "Just wanted to see if they were around to have a drink is all."

Jayne sat down next to Brock and settled in to eat. "Hmm. If I see them…"

"Great. Thanks!" Jack said as she waved, and then disappeared out of the hall.

Jayne watched her leave, a glint of suspicion in her eye as she picked up her fork to eat.

CHAPTER FIFTEEN

Flutningsaðili, **Floor 4, Restricted Access Area**

Maya sat down at the table with the other three hostages. Sean continued to pace.

"Why aren't they calling through?" she asked trying to keep the anxiety out of her voice more for the benefit of the others. Her eyes traced Sean's movements, watching him prowl like a trapped tiger.

"Probably a glitch in the tech," he responded. "No idea how this shit works ..."

Suddenly his facial expression changed. "They're connecting," he said, nodding at Maya.

Maya's face relaxed a little, and the three others looked from her to Sean and back to her again, hoping for an inkling of what was going on.

Sean put his hands on his hips and looked off across the room. "Hi, Pieter? Things have taken a turn over here," he started explaining. "Maya and I have been rumbled. They don't know how much we know, but they've put us in with the scientists, and they're going to eject us into space at their next scheduled trash dump."

"Shit," Pieter hissed under his breath.

Sean continued to look off across the tiny glass room. "Yeah, mate, I was hoping for something a little more useful than that."

"H-h-h-h-h-hang on. Let me call Molly," Pieter stammered. There was a shuffling on the other end of the line, and a moment later Pieter's voice returned. "She's on her way. Will be here in a moment. Are any of you injured?" Pieter asked.

"No," Sean's voice came back. "We're okay at the moment."

"Hang on, I hear Molly's footsteps. She's here," Pieter told him.

A moment later Sean could hear Molly's voice on the line. "Sean, what do you need?"

Sean glanced at Maya, who was starting to look scared. "We're ready for an extraction," he said calmly, trying to make it sound that they were in more control of the situation so that Maya and the others wouldn't be too nervous.

Maya could almost imagine he was calling for a car to pick them up from a shopping trip.

Molly was to the point. "Okay. We're coming for you. Do we have any idea how long you've got?"

Sean shook his head. "No idea. Could be minutes, could be hours or days."

Paige and Joel arrived at the conference room and stepped inside, quietly taking seats at the table so as not to interrupt.

Molly nodded. "Okay. Oz is looking into the garbage dumping on the ship. Since ADAM was already in the system with Maya's patch, he has some access, but it's going to take a little time to work it."

Sean exhaled. "Okay. Cool."

Molly, there's something that may be useful.

Oh?

Yeah it seems that there have been a few communications between the ship and Gaitune.

From here?

No. Not from us. Someone else on Gaitune. A couple of kilometers away.

Who?

Hang on.

Oz's voice paused, then the intercom sparked up again. "Carl Milberg's place."

Molly's eyes snapped on Paige.

Paige's mouth dropped. A stunned silence filled the room. After a moment Paige's voice found its way through her mouth. "Shipping," she said making the connection.

Molly nodded. "Oz, see what you can find out. Get Crash to start up the *Empress*. We'll be heading out shortly. Paige and I just need to pay Carl a visit. Sean," she said, lifting her voice a little so he would hear her clearly. "Hang in there. We're coming for you. Stay alive."

Sean nodded. "Will do, boss." He glanced over at Maya as he spoke. "See you shortly. Keep us posted about ETAs, eh?"

Molly was already half way through the door. "Sure thing. Oz and Pieter will keep in touch."

The line disconnected, leaving Sean staring now into space, feeling a little more nervous than he had been just seconds before when the connection was live.

He glanced over at Maya again. "They're on their way. But we need to figure out if there is a way out of here, just in case."

He wandered over to the table where the others were sitting quietly, bewildered by the unconventional rescue party. "How about you tell us everything you know so we can work on a plan to keep us all alive until our friends get here?" he suggested, looking into the fearful faces.

Aboard the *Flutningsaðili*, Level 2, Mess Hall

Brock left the mess hall, scuttling from one common area to another, looking for Jack.

He felt sure she wouldn't have gone far if they needed to powwow on this. He poked his head into the room that was used as a games room. It was noisy, with people playing computer games and simulations. She wasn't in there. He stepped out into the corridor again.

Just then, he heard a click in his implant.

Shit. Can't do this here, he thought to himself.

He marched down the corridor, looking for somewhere he might have some privacy to speak out loud. He found what he thought was a storage cupboard. He'd seen the cleaning crew use it before. He tried the key pad and it slid right open.

He slipped inside. A dim light came on, and the door closed behind him. The closet was about four feet by four feet, and fortunately there was no one else there.

He double clicked him quantum pearl and waited.

"Hey," he heard Pieter's voice.

"Hey yourself," Brock responded, a grin spreading across his face at the sound of a familiar voice. "What's happening? We can't find Sean and Maya, and I think I've lost Jack."

Just then the closet door opened. Brock's heart jumped into his mouth.

He scrambled to look at whatever was on the shelf so he could look like he was in here collecting supplies.

"Hey," whispered Jack, stepping inside and allowing the door to close behind him.

Brock breathed a sigh of relief. "It's okay. I've got Jack," he told Pieter.

Pieter's voice came through again. "Ah, well that's good news. Saves me trying to get you each separately. Lemme just loop her in, too. Okay, we're good. She should hear me too now."

Jack nodded. "I hear you, Pieter."

"Good," Pieter continued. "Okay, so it seems that Sean and Maya have been captured. They found the kidnap victims, three in total, and they're being held in the same place. We've been in

ELL LEIGH CLARKE & MICHAEL ANDERLE

touch with Sean, and we're on our way to extract you. Problem is, they could be ejected at any time. We just don't know. So we need you two to one, not get caught too. And two, see if there is anything you can do to get these guys free."

Brock's eyes widened. "No small order then," he remarked with a little irony in his voice.

Pieter's voice was sympathetic. "I know. I'm with you. It's intense. I'm sorry you're going through this."

Brock nodded. "It's okay. Any clue on how to do any of that?"

"Yeah," Pieter responded. "Turns out that before they got caught, Maya and Sean had ADAM create a patch for some off-limits area, to get them in. The code for bypassing the retinal scan and everything is 1234 Enter."

Brock nodded. "1234 Enter," he repeated, looking at Jack. Jack nodded, remembering the code too.

"Oz is working on figuring out their location on the ship. He'll have that to you soon. We're factoring in your relative positions based on your quantum beads. Should have an answer and a map soon."

Brock nodded. "But what about being seen accessing this secret area. This place has camera coverage everywhere."

Oz interjected. "Hi Jack. Brock. Oz here. It looks like Maya already implanted a patch to take the cameras from recording in places all randomly, but also where she wants to be. Pretty smart. It means that if they were to notice, they wouldn't just see it happening at the restricted access area. So we can use that patch to help you, once we've nailed your route."

Jack wiped a hand over her mouth, thinking. "We have another problem, Oz. Say we go ahead and get those guys out of wherever they are. Then what? We're on a ship with nowhere to go."

There was a silence on the line.

Brock leaned his head back against a shelf for a moment. "You know, we could see if there are any ships that we can use to get out of here."

Jack looked at him, her eyes gradually brightening. "Yes!" she agreed. "And a freighter has limited weapons. Mostly just for blasting rocks, and they have a restricted range to what, a few kilometers?" she guessed.

Brock nodded. "Yeah. About that. But all they're likely to have will be something for unloading cargo at best, and then trying to out run them in what is essentially a tractor."

Jack pulled her lips to one side. "Uh huh," she answered.

Brock bobbed his head. "Well, I guess that's it then. At least it will have more maneuverability than this beast, so we can head back in the direction of Estaria and wait for the *Empress* to scoop us up. It will take them hours to turn this thing around, so that's our best bet."

Jack nodded and shifted her weight, moving back towards the door. "Okay, it's a plan. Not an airtight plan by any stretch of the imagination. But better than sitting around waiting for them to execute Sean and Maya."

Pieter cut in. "In the meantime, Molly is on her way to you soon, and we'll be in touch with updates. Hang in there. We're coming for you. All of you. I'll let Sean and Maya know what's happening."

The line clicked off.

Brock and Jack stood in the half light of the closet. Brock suddenly got a twinkle in his eye. "You know, this is one of those times that someday in the future we're going to laugh about, and tell stories to rookies about tight spots that we got out of."

Jack smiled. "Yeah. I'm sure you're right. Okay. You wanna try stealing us some transport? And I'll find the restricted area and grab the others as soon as we get their location through?"

Brock nodded. "Sure thing. Stay in touch on holo message only. Better than getting overheard."

Jack turned to leave. "Defo," she agreed. "Count to ten before you follow me out," she said, and then she was gone.

Gaitune-67, Carl Milberg's residence

Molly rang the bell. Paige nudged her. "I have a key," she told her sheepishly.

Molly shook her head. "It's okay. This is an official visit. I want him to come and invite us in." She leaned on the bell again.

Nothing sounded on the outside, but since it lit up she assumed it was ringing inside.

Several moments later there was movement on the other side of the airlock. Once Carl recognized them through the two doors he waved at Paige, and beckoned them in, hitting the access switch on the other side.

The airlock door clicked and started to slide open in its circular swing. The two women stepped in, and it closed behind them, then normalized the pressure.

A moment later the other door swung open, allowing them through into the second semicircular chamber. Once they were clear, the door slid back, and the pressure normalized and the door into the house opened.

Carl had wandered away as they went through the airlock rigmarole. Molly looked left, then right.

"Through here," Carl called from the right. "Just putting the kettle on. You ready for a brew?" he asked.

Molly headed down the hallway following the sound of his voice. Paige followed, feeling more awkward about this than she would have guessed originally.

"We're not here for a social call, Mr. Milberg," Molly started as she stepped into the kitchen. "I'm afraid we've intercepted your communications with Max Pike, and we have reason to believe that you are involved in a criminal operation involving the kidnapping of a number of scientists as well as two of our crew members at this point."

Carl stopped what he was doing with the cups and turned around to face the two women. He'd heard a lot about Molly from Paige, but never had she described her as quite this formidable.

Mind, she perhaps didn't relay any tales where her boss was in a situation where her team had been captured and about to be killed.

Carl looked over at them with a shocked expression, a tea bag in his hand. "I'm afraid I have no idea what you're talking about," he told her.

"Cut the crap," Molly responded without missing a beat. "We've traced communications to here. You're in the shipping business, are you not?"

Milberg nodded once, and turned back around, placing the tea bag in a cup. He continued to make tea. "I am. Paige knows I am."

Paige took a step forward and placed her hands on the counter top island separating them. "I also know you have covert shipping operations. Just the kind of operations that would be facilitating things like illegal fracking of an inhabited planet."

Carl spun back around, his eyes defensive. "Hey, look. There are lots of people, lots of organizations that require covert shipping. Governments for one. If the Oggs are arming the Teshovians, or the Leath are doing deals with the Yollins under the radar, they pay for discretion. Heck, for all I know you people have used my services for bringing equipment onto this rock!"

He paused, then went back to the tea, muttering under his breath. "Not that I've ever been told anything about what you do for a living over there," he added poignantly.

Molly glanced at Paige, who was flushing a little on her chest. She sensed this was an issue in their relationship. "Sounds like you've both been keeping secrets," Molly commented. "The point is, we need to know everything you do about this ship in order to get our crew and the kidnapped scientists back safe and sound. You need to make this right. Transporting kidnapped victims... you'll be going away for a long time. You'll lose everything."

Carl had started pouring the tea.

Molly paused, and lowered her tone a little. "Can we count on your help?"

Carl paused pouring, thinking for a moment. Molly sensed his sudden anxiety, even though his back was turned.

Carl resumed pouring out the third cup. "Yes. Of course," he responded after a moment, keeping his tone even. "In fact, I think there is a way for everyone to get what they need out of this."

He carried the tea over to the island and handed them out, then returned for his own. He waved for them to sit down, and pulled out a stool for himself on the other side of the counter. "I'm assuming that by helping you I will absolve myself of any and all charges with you and whomever you bring into this?"

Molly took the tea, and toyed with it on the surface of the counter. "It really depends on how helpful you are. We want the safe return of our people and the victims. If we can achieve that, you won't be penalized."

Molly felt Paige relax a little, though she didn't turn to look.

Carl nodded. "Okay," he said, slurping his tea. He placed the mug down. "There are a few things you should know. Firstly, we've just altered the flight path. If you go after them now, they won't be where you think they will be."

Molly started to ask a question, and Carl waved his hand. "I'll get you the coordinates and the path details," he added dismissively. "The other thing is," Carl continued, "if you're in communication with your people who have been captured, you'll be aware that he has armed guards on the ship. Security."

Molly waited for a moment, studying his reactions. "What are you saying?" she asked.

Carl took another sip of tea. "I'm suggesting you need an

intermediary to negotiate a truce. If you show up there, guns blazing, people are going to die. They have weapons. And mercenaries on board. Lots of them. There is no way you will be able to get your people out of there alive without some kind of negotiation."

Molly turned her head slightly. "What do you suggest?" she asked.

Carl pushed his mug forward and wrapped both hands around it. "I'm going to propose he lets you take your people and leave him to continue with his shipment."

Molly didn't miss a beat. "My people, and the three hostages," she demanded.

Carl leaned back on the stool a little, his face looking drawn. "I dunno if I can swing that. Remember, he answers to some very powerful clients."

Molly held his gaze. "I'm taking the innocent people."

Carl chuckled a fake laugh. "Ha. They're not *so* innocent," he told her.

Molly frowned. "What does that mean?"

Carl shrugged one shoulder. "Well, they wouldn't be of interest to these people if they didn't have expertise in certain areas, like the illegal fracking of populated planets. For instance. Hypothetically speaking, if that is what they are doing."

Molly narrowed her eyes. "So you *do* know what they're doing," she remarked, reminding him that he had just incriminated himself. "I want the hostages, and my people. He can keep his equipment," she pressed.

The discussion continued back and forth for another few minutes, during which it became evident that they were unaware of Brock and Jack's involvement. He kept referring to her *two* people.

"Also, I have more than two people on that ship. And they're trained by the best. Federation military. Not just Estarian."

Carl swallowed nervously, and gathered his thoughts as his

eyes studied the cup of tea. He sighed. "Okay. Lemme see what I can do," he said getting up.

Molly watched him head out of the kitchen. "Where are you going?" she queried him.

He pointed out into the hall way. "Office. Need to make that call," he said. "Unless you want to waste some more time and let your friends be ejected out into space?"

Molly shook her head. "Okay. Go ahead. Leave the door open. We're listening," she said, getting up off the stool.

He headed out and got settled to make the call.

Paige had left her tea, untouched, on the counter. "You're not really going to let them keep that equipment that they're going to use to destroy the planet and those inhabitants, are you?"

Molly's face and tone were grave. "Right now," she said in a low voice, "the immediate problem is to get our people to safety."

Paige nodded solemnly, and followed Molly through to her boyfriend's home office.

Carl had already set up the call and was waiting for Max to respond.

"Max. Hi. Me again. Yeah. I know. Sorry to pull you off what you were doing, but we have a small problem we need to iron out."

Carl paused, listening to Max's response.

"Yeah, so it turns out that we've been compromised."

He paused.

"Let's not worry about that for now, but I'm sitting here having tea with a nice young lady who is responsible for those people you've got on board. Yes, the spies. Except it's not corporate espionage, I don't think. It's something much more serious that we don't want to get involved in."

He stopped again. Listening.

"Yes, yes, I understand that, but I think I've got a way for you to hold on to that and still make a delivery to the client."

Carl took a deep breath. "I think I can persuade her just to take her people. All of them. There are others we don't know about, and get them out of there... without getting any authorities involved."

"How many more?" He repeated the question he had just heard, looking over at Molly and Paige. Molly shook her head.

"I don't know," he answered. "But she'll take them all, and leave you be to deliver the shipment."

He muted himself out, tapping his ear. Shaking his head, he mouthed over to Molly who was now leaning on the door frame. "Not having it."

Molly stood upright again. "Okay. We'll just have to take it by force. Location?"

Carl held up one finger.

Then he started turning the finger over as if he's trying to hurry the guy speaking up.

He unmuted himself. "Max. You know me. You know I wouldn't be suggesting this if there was another way out. I think this is your best bet. No one gets hurt."

He paused again.

"Yeah. She has firearms. Lots of them. I don't know what kind of outfit this is, but if she shows up even your boys are in trouble."

"Okay. Okay. I'll give her your location. Be civil. Hand the folks over, and then let them leave. That's all you need to do."

He sighed. "Okay. Yes, I'm sorry too. We'll talk about that later on."

Carl clicked off the holo connection and rocked to upright in his chair. "Okay. You have your deal. Your people, the hostages, and you leave quietly. He delivers his payload and you two never cross paths again."

Molly nodded once. "Fine," she agreed. "Okay, so the location?"

Carl pulled up another screen on his holo and poked through a few pages. Then he offered his holowrist over to her. Molly opened a bump screen and stepped over to him. They bumped holos, transferring the data.

"Are we good?" he asked, looking at her, as if they'd just negotiated the sale of a desk holo, or a car.

Molly flicked through the new flight data and tilted her head. She paused for a moment, as if listening, and then nodded at him. "We're good," she confirmed, and headed out.

Carl's eyes fell to Paige, who was now leaning against the door frame. Molly walked past her and headed towards the airlock. Paige held his gaze for a moment, then followed after Molly.

Carl got up, following them through. "Paige ..." he called after her. "Can we talk?"

Paige turned to him quietly as the airlock slid open. "Not now. I have to go rescue my friends from being blown into space." Her eyes were dim, hiding the anger and disappointment.

She stepped into the airlock after Molly. Carl leaned his hand on the door, above head height, watching her turn from him as if he didn't exist anymore.

Seconds later they passed into the second chamber. And then when they were finally free, they headed out into the rocky terrain without looking back.

He watched them leave, running through in his head what he might have done differently.

CHAPTER SIXTEEN

Aboard the *Flutningsaðili*, Level 4, Restricted Access Area

"Are you sure that we're all going to fit through there?" Dr. Brahms looked up at the vent as Sean stood on the desk fiddling with the screws.

Sean glanced down at the rather bulky old man and then back up at the vent. "Should do," he gruffed. "Though, whether the vent will hold our weights is another matter."

He glanced over at Anne, Maya and Lana. "The girls will probably be okay. We should let them go first, just in case we break it, cutting them off."

He passed his key card to Anne. "Here, you take this. We'll send you through first. We've got a friend who is getting into the computer system on this ship as we speak. Once he has access he'll be able to let you through any door with that card. We've got another friend, Brock, who is going to get us a ship on level …?"

He looked out across the room, listening for Pieter on the quantum bead connection. "Pieter, what level was it again?"

Pieter's voice came over Sean's audio implant. "Level 1. Right at the top."

Sean looked back at Anne and Lana. "Level 1. Top of the ship.

You get to there, find him on the hangar deck, and he'll get you to safety. If we can follow, we will," he added glancing over at Dr. Brahms.

Anne took the card and closed her hand around it. She nodded without saying a word and then slipped it into her pants pocket.

Sean went back to the vent, and finished taking out the last screw. The vent cover hung down, leaving the open mouth.

Just then he heard footsteps. He jumped down off the table and moved it away from where it was obvious what he had been doing. The lights started coming on through the crowded warehousing area.

Sean looked over at Anne and Lana. "Okay, remember what we talked about. Girls, as soon as you get the chance, we're putting you in there. Maya," he said softy, "if you go with them, they'll have a better chance."

Maya nodded, then turned her attention to the oncoming footsteps.

There was only one set, though.

This could be interesting, she thought, *straining her eyes to see through the dimness who might be approaching.*

Aboard the *Empress*, approaching the *Flutningsaðili*

Pieter was the last one on board. He hurried in to the cabin of the *Empress*, his gear on his back and his atmosuit put on in a hurry.

Molly was standing in the cabin area running through logistics with Joel. "All okay?" she called over to Pieter.

He nodded, and stowed his gear away for takeoff.

She turned and headed through to the cockpit. "Okay," she told Crash, "we're good to go."

"Roger that," came his response. Crash had been quiet the whole time, working hard on various extraction scenarios. Molly knew through Oz that he was worried about Brock before they'd even left them on Estaria.

But Crash had his way of dealing with things.

Namely, not.

Within minutes the *Empress* was lifting off and leaving Gaitune. Molly strapped herself in next to Joel just as they reached the hangar doors. "I think this is probably the fastest turnaround we've done in this ship," she commented.

Joel had been looking straight ahead, lost in thought. He rolled his head to look at her, relaxing the rest of his body to the g-force. "No. It's not. There was the time when Sean took you to the *ArchAngel*," he reminded her.

Molly suddenly felt guilty for forgetting that. For what they went through. And for her part in it.

She swallowed.

Joel looked back at the wall in front of them. "It's okay," he reassured her, as if reading her thoughts.

In almost no time at all they were in space and Crash gated them through to a few hundred kilometers off from the location of the *Flutningsaðili*.

Crash's voice came over the audio. "Molly to cockpit please. Molly to cockpit."

Molly glanced at Joel and undid her restraints. "Duty calls," she said, eliciting a smile from him.

She arrived in the cockpit to see the ship up ahead of him.

Crash turned his head to her. "You want me to hail him? Have you got a code word or something?"

Molly shook her head, perching in the console chair next to him. "We haven't. But yes, let's hail him."

Crash opened a channel. "*Flutningsaðili*. This is the Empress. We have Molly Bates to speak with Max Pike."

He repeated the message a couple more times before getting a response.

"*Empress*, this is *Flutningsaðili*, we read you. Mr. Pike has granted permission for you to dock. Please proceed to dock 26 on the port side of the vessel, level 25."

The channel closed for a moment, and then reopened. "Level 25 is at the bottom of this ship, in case you're not familiar with cargo ships."

Crash rolled his eyes. "Like I'm an idiot," he muttered under his breathe. He reopened the channel. "Thank you *Flutningsaðili. Empress* out."

He steered the ship over and around. Molly watched on the screen as the enormous construct grew ahead of them, and then disappeared beneath them as they navigated over the top of it.

It took some time for them to find the correct loading bay. In the interim, as they drifted down one level after another, Joel joined them in the cockpit.

"So, is anyone else thinking 'Trap'?" he asked, waving his hands when he said the word trap.

Molly nodded. "Oh yes."

Crash responded. "Definitely."

Joel sat on the arm of another console chair, folding his arms. "Good to see we're all on the same page," he remarked.

Molly and Crash continued concentrating on finding the correct bay to dock in.

Joel stepped forward and leaned on the same console chair that Molly had a hand on. "So, do we have a plan?" he asked.

Molly cocked her head, then turned and looked at him. "Yes. I think we do."

Joel smiled. "You just made one up, didn't you?"

She smiled back. "How can you tell?"

Joel's smile broadened. "Coz I know you, Molly Bates."

Molly felt him connect with her. She felt a slight glow from him, despite the tenseness of the situation they were facing.

She turned to Crash. "Work with Emma and Oz, and find a bay that we can just dock in. Any bay that isn't number 26."

Crash nodded. "Aye, Captain," he acknowledged.

Joel looked at her quizzically. "So?"

"Weapons," Molly said simply. "We need to arm up. Let's go," she said, heading out of the cockpit and into the lounge.

Paige and Pieter were now sitting together, looking through the schematics that Oz had been able to pull together on the ship.

Pieter looked up. "We have locations mapped for everyone who has a quantum pearl. Jack is on the way to the others. Brock is on the way to their hangar deck to steal a ship."

Molly nodded, thinking. "Okay, here's what we're going to do."

Aboard the *Flutningsaðili*, Level 2 common area corridor

PIETER ARE YOU THERE? NEED HELP GETTING TO WHEREVER S&M ARE.

SEND.

Jack stood in the corridor typing out the message, wondering if she'd get shit from Pieter later for typing S&M in a message.

Pieter responded almost immediately in her ear. "Hey. Yeah. I've got you. Oz has just finished mapping the areas we're interested in. Can you get to the fourth floor?"

Jack didn't respond. Instead she turned and walked back down the way she had just come and headed for the main elevator.

Pieter understood that she was just responding to the instructions without speaking. "Got it," he said in her implant. "I'll just talk, and if you need to query me or respond, I'll look out for a holo message. Until you're able to talk."

Jack tapped another message as she walked.

CAMERAS?

Pieter paused, tapping away on some keys. "Yes. Yep we've got your back. Oz is plotting your route and will have you disappear from the elevator on a passing floor."

Jack suddenly felt so much safer. Like completely safe. It was suddenly as if this were just a training exercise. She took a deep breath, noticing what a difference it made to have her team in communication, backing her up.

So much easier! And to think I wanted to be a lone wolf once upon a time.

She wanted to kick herself for how she had been in the past, despite the intensity of the moment.

The elevator arrived and she stepped in, hitting the fourth-floor button.

Pieter was talking to her again. "Oz is going to have the elevator take you down to floor seventeen where there is a medium amount of activity, and then he'll do the thing on the cameras so it makes it look like you got off there."

There were a few other people in the elevator with her, and they got off at various floors before the machine swooped her down to seventeen. The doors opened into a dark corridor.

She didn't move.

After what seemed like an eternity they closed again and the elevator ran back up to four.

"Okay, you're up," Pieter told her. "You want to step out of here and then head straight down the corridor. Then take the second corridor on the right, and then first left."

Jack followed the instructions, now at a jog. "Can you hear me?" she checked, relieved that she could now speak.

"Loud and clear," Pieter confirmed. "Okay, you're approaching the restricted access area. You want to head to the panel and use the code to bypass…"

"Got it," Jack replied. She approached the keypad and tapped in *1234 ENTER*.

The door slid open, allowing her to step inside. The lights came up as she headed through. "Now where?" she said, seeing the dim outline of cargo boxes and strange heavy-duty machinery.

Pieter guided her through to the far side where the others were imprisoned in the meeting room.

Maya saw her approaching first, and came to the window. "Hi Griselle, what are you doing here?" she said with a smile, making light of the now redundant fake names.

Jack headed straight for the access panel to the room. "You know the code?" she asked, looking up through the glass at Maya and Sean.

"No, they don't," a bone chilling voice came from behind her. "But I do."

Jack spun around to see a figure emerging from the shadows. It was Max Pike.

"Time to let them go, Pike," Jack demanded with authority. "We have a truce. Our people are coming to get us."

Pike shook his head. "They may be on their way, and yes, we did agree on an unsatisfactory truce. And once they are here they too will become subject to our containment method." A smirk spread across his smarmy lips. Jack felt an urge welling in her. One which involved smacking him in the face right where his evil sneer was.

She took a step towards him.

A dozen of his security guards stepped out from the shadows of the heavy equipment in the room, and came forward, their weapons weighing heavy in the consciousness of the prisoners.

Jack frowned. "So you plan to kill us all?"

Max Pike smiled as he played with a key card in his hand. "*Kill* is such an archaic and brutal word, don't you think? I'm merely taking the necessary action to secure the interests of my client."

His holo beeped and he glanced down at the screen. "And there they are now. Right on schedule."

He looked back at Jack. "If you'll excuse me, I need to go and tend to something, but I'll be back shortly."

He waved at a couple of the guards to watch her, and then turned, taking a couple of his guards with him.

There was a sudden flurry of activity in the meeting room. Jack spun round, looking in, still unable to get through the door.

"Okay, now," Sean said quietly to Anne.

The security personnel came forward. "Stop. What are you doing?"

By the time Jack could see what was happening, she realized that Sean had managed to get the air vent in the room open, and Anne was being pushed up into it, her feet disappearing as she climbed in.

The guards were over at the door getting it open. Jack could see Sean whispering instructions to the girl and then closing up the vent after her.

The guards hesitated firing. They clearly had instructions to keep them alive for now. Jack used the moments of commotion to count up how many adversaries there were.

Six.

She stepped away from the glass as they came piling forward. They were all huddled in a smallish area now, and as long as there weren't any more in the shadows she knew what to do.

Coming up behind one she punched him in the neck, right where it would knock him out. He went down, and before he had hit the ground she had grabbed his weapon and turned it on their captors.

She checked for the switches, knocked off the safety and shot two of the security guards in the head.

Bam. Bam.

The others turned, completely oblivious to what had just happened. They saw Jack, just a young woman to them with one of their guns, and moved to open fire, except only the one in the doorway could get a clear shot. The others fired stupidly at the glass. The bulletproof glass.

Their shots smashed straight into the material and stopped there, breaking up the clear surface, and rendering them inert.

The one at the door received a shot through his throat. Blood exploded like a ketchup bottle, splattering over the body and around the doorway as it dropped.

Sean had already moved into action, taking one guard who had been busy firing rounds into the window, and breaking his neck before he even knew there was a threat behind him. Without hesitating he did the same to the one next to him.

That left one more in the room.

Jack started to move forward towards the door. Everything seemed to be happening in slow motion. The Estarian guard was aware that there was now a threat inside the cell and one approaching the door. Sean was closer. He started backing away. Just then, he felt his gun barrel being pushed up in the air. He turned and the last thing he saw was the other woman, Marissa, that had been one of the crew. She pulled her fist back and then everything went dark for him.

Sean stopped dead in his tracks, his grimace of combat turning to one of humor as he looked from the body on the floor and then to Maya.

Jack's run turned into a walk as she stepped over a couple of bodies to get a closer look.

The two scientists in the room looked aghast at what they'd just witnessed. Their eyes were wide, and mouths moved but made no sound.

Maya glanced down, regarding the heap of Estarian that she had just taken out with a single punch to the face. Her eyes lit up in excitement, and her jaw relaxed, turning her expression from one of determination into a celebratory smile.

"Well," Sean started, "looks like someone has been paying attention in their hand-to-hand combat lessons."

Maya grinned. "I can't believe it, I just saw the opening and did it. I never thought that I might be able to."

Jack took the last few paces over to the body. "You've knocked him out cold!" she announced proudly, prodding the body with her foot.

Maya did a little dance on the spot, and then her expression changed to one of pain. She lifted her hand. "Owwww," she said, looking at it. It was already starting to swell a little. "But it hurt like a motherfucker!" she said, clenching and unclenching it.

Sean reached over to inspect it for her. "Lemme see," he said flattening out her fingers, and feeling the knuckles and the bones on the back. "Hmm. Well, yeah. It's gonna swell. It's bruised. But the good news is you used the right part of your hand. Nothing broken. I'd class that as a win."

He patted her on the shoulder like she had suddenly become one of the boys.

Jack was already onto checking her ammo and returning the gun to its safety. She surveyed the scene. "See, if they'd been using stun bullets or trancs they'd all be alive now. Karma is a bitch," she added quietly.

Sean shrugged. "They didn't give us much choice." He looked out across the darkened space beyond the meeting room. "Okay. Time to move. We don't know if they have friends on the way."

Jack glanced over at him. "Pieter and Oz have had the cameras covered. As long as no one is monitoring real time we're okay, thanks to Maya's patch."

Maya looked up from her aching hand and smiled, her expression no longer as exuberant on account of the pain.

Sean nodded. "Okay. Let's move. Pieter?" he called.

"Here," Pieter responded in his ear.

Sean was already on the move as he issued instructions. "Let Brock know that he has one young girl, Anne, on her way to rendezvous with him. We're going to try for the *Empress* on 25."

Pieter started tapping away on his holo. "Okay. I'll let him know," he reported back.

Jack glanced back at Sean as they made their way through the rows of equipment. "Too late to call her back?" Jack asked.

Sean nodded. "We have no way of communicating with her now. But she seemed smart, and I gave her my access card, so Oz can track her as she uses it and grant her access. She knows someone is watching out for her in the computers, helping."

Maya was bringing up the rear, coaxing the bewildered scientists out with her. She sensed their hesitation at leaving.

She remembered the experiments with heffelumps tied up by a tiny rope they could pull through easily, but because they'd learned they were bound at a young age, they never attempted to leave. She felt they had a similar resistance to stepping through the door, even though they made it out, over the bodies strewn around.

Aboard the *Flutningsaðili*, Floor 25, Dock 26

Crash and Paige had been mulling the possibility of Paige staying with the ship, but after careful consideration it was decided it wasn't the best option.

Molly put her hand gently on Paige's shoulder. "Okay. Paige, you're with us. Crash, I need your expertise on the stick. You may need to undock or respond in some other way."

Paige's eyes looked terrified. She patted Crash on the arm. "It's okay. It's probably easier if I'm with them. I wouldn't know the first thing to do here, and if you're not here then no one gets out of here alive."

Crash nodded, and watched them leave.

Molly stepped out onto the hangar deck down the invisible staircase, her hands raised to show she wasn't holding a weapon. Paige followed her down carefully.

"Welcome aboard, Ms. Bates," Max called, his voice reverberating around the dock. "I trust you had a comfortable journey."

Molly scowled at him. "Let's dispense with the pleasantries," she suggested firmly. "You're holding my people captive. I'd like them back."

"Ah, yes," he said, pulling a gun from behind his back and

aiming it straight at Molly. "That's not going to happen. No one strongarms me."

Molly had reached the deck. There was nowhere to shield herself. "We had an agreement," she protested. "The hostages and my people off your ship, leaving you to continue your transaction with your client."

Max took a few paces forward, his tone becoming more and more patronizing. "Yes, well, you see, that's just not going to work for me. I give you the hostages, my client will not be happy."

Molly tried hard to keep the sarcasm out of her voice. "I'm sure someone with your abilities would be able to smooth that over."

"No, Ms. Bates," he argued, keeping his tone irritatingly even. "Alas, even I have my limits. My patience being one of them."

He raised his gun to her head. "Thank you for coming here and making the job of taking you out of the equation that much easier."

Paige stood glued to the spot, frozen in horror.

Molly felt a calmness wash over her. It was as if she slipped deeper into being in the body, and the present moment seemed to expand into eternity. Her muscles relaxed. Her whole being was relaxed.

She felt completely at ease, and dare she say it, even a sense of bliss.

Everything happened in slow motion.

She was aware of the changing expressions on Pike's face, contorted in meanness and anger. She could even see the hairs on his head move as he took the slight recoil of the pistol.

She saw the bullet leaving the barrel of the gun. She watched the bullet traveling through the air, and was fully aware of Paige's emotional reaction. She could feel her own horror on the surface of her being, but also felt her own sense of connectedness and complete peace with the moment.

CHAPTER SEVENTEEN

Aboard the *Flutningsaðili*, Floor 2

Brock slipped out of the closet where Jack had left him ten-Mississippis before.

He rolled his shoulders to relax himself and tried to look as natural as possible.

Reading off his holo he looked at the directions on the map that Oz and Pieter were feeding him.

He could hear Pieter talking through his audio implant. "You need to get to level 1," Pieter told him. "Oz is working on getting into the system to find you a ship that is functional and will hold personnel. Most of these are tractors, as you pointed out."

Brock didn't respond, but headed off in the direct of the other elevator set, in the opposite direction to the ones Jack had headed towards.

He passed a few people who he now knew by sight, nodding and waving casually as he hurried as fast as he dared.

"Yo, Tallus," a voice called from behind him. Brock turned around. "You up for that rematch, eh?"

It was Auggie.

Brock shook his head, scrambling for a legitimate excuse.

"Not right now, man. I've got to go lie down. My head hasn't been feeling right."

Auggie all of a sudden looked concerned. "You okay? What is it?"

Brock held his hand up to his head. "I think it's just overwork, and probably dehydration."

Auggie frowned. "Can I get you anything?"

Brock waved his hand and took a step away. "No. I'll be fine. But thanks," he smiled, giving his friend a thumbs up. "I'll catch up with you later," he added.

Auggie nodded, watching him scuttle away down the corridor, in the wrong direction for the sleeping quarters.

Brock's attention was back on Pieter's voice. "Turn right at the end of this corridor and then you just need to head up one level to their hangar deck," Pieter said in his ear.

Brock turned to the corner, glancing back, seeing Auggie still watching him.

"Shit," he muttered to himself.

Brock arrived at the smaller service elevator area, and hit the button. "I think Auggie is suspicious," he said quietly.

Oz's voice came over his implant. "You know why, right? You told him you were going to lie down and then continued in the wrong direction."

Brock slapped his palm on his head, and then remembered he was meant to be trying to look normal. He pulled his arms back down by his side, and rolled his shoulders again. "Dammit," he hissed under his breath.

Pieter chuckled lightly, despite the intense concentration. "It'll be okay. You'll be out of here super-soon. That kind of suspicion has a much longer lead time on it before it becomes an issue."

Brock shook his head, as if trying to shake the distracting thoughts from his focus. "Okay. Fine. You got me a ship yet?"

Oz came on the audio. "Yep. Sending you the details and access codes to your holo. It's situated on the far side of the deck though. I'd recommend staying on the peripheries and looking like an engineer if you can."

Brock stepped into the elevator as it arrived, scratching his head. "How the hell am I going to do that?" he asked, not truly expecting a response from Oz.

Pieter chipped in. "Improvise like your life depends on it. Because it does."

Brock exhaled a humorless chuckle. "On it," he said uncharacteristically dryly.

The elevator doors slid open onto another small elevator bay, and Brock stepped out turning towards what looked like a set of doors onto a hangar deck.

It was a strange feeling. Although the set up was different, the scene of fuel and oil and warp tech made him feel strangely at home.

He wandered through the doors and onto the yellow walkway. There wasn't a soul in sight. He followed the walkway, keeping his eyes peeled, and double-checking the make and model of the vessel he was looking for.

About 200 yards around he spotted a tool kit slung over the railings on the right. He walked passed, picking it up and slinging it over his shoulder as if he'd been the one to leave it there while he took a bathroom break.

He kept walking, his eyes flicking from one ship to another.

"You're nearby, just another 500 yards now," Oz told him.

Brock slowed his pace and started to wander off into the array of vessels, cargo movers, and antigrav forklifts.

He spotted the ship he was after, and checked the number on the side. "Bingo," he whispered, still keeping his awareness on high alert in case anyone else was about.

He marched over to it and activated the holo panel, punching in the access codes. The door opened on the tailgate only. He looked around and saw that was the only entrance on these models. He hurried around to the rear and stomped up the ramp.

Once on board he checked around, and then made for the cockpit. The inside of the ship was warm, as if it had been sitting here accumulating heat from the rest of the ship, and not radiating it out again. There was a smell of hot plastic and a scent of people, as if it hadn't long been used.

He sat down in the pilot's chair and started going through his best-guess checklist he could think of for this kind of machine.

"Oz. Anything I should be aware of on this model?" he asked quietly as he worked.

"Hang on," Oz said. "Okay, check your holo."

Brock glanced down at his holo to find the check lists for going into space on this ship. He opened the holo, pulling it out and laying the screen over his left leg as he ran down the list.

Within minutes he was ready.

"Okay Pieter, Oz. I'm flight ready. Where are the peeps. Wanna let Jack know?"

Pieter's voice responded. "Yeah. We've got a situation. Just hold on. We'll update you shortly."

The audio clicked off.

Brock sat in the cockpit and powered down the electrics so as not to draw attention. He sat there in the half-light with nothing to do but wait for further instruction.

Aboard the *Flutningsaðili*, Floor 22

Joel slipped through the dock door that Oz had just unlocked for him.

"Okay, now where?" he asked, looking up and down the corridor as a few dim lights came on.

Oz came over his audio implant. "It looks like this is all warehousing on this floor, with very few personnel. I suspect you could pretend that you belong here and if the folks aren't obviously carrying weapons, you'll probably be okay."

Joel straightened up and holstered his gun, looking up and down the corridor again.

"Go right," Oz instructed. "I'll get you down to Molly's floor so that when they dock you can come around the back of any resistance that seems to be accumulating."

"Sounds good to me," Joel responded, striding off down the first corridor, taking on the air of an employee of the freight company rather than a trained mission operative with a purpose.

"Also — for the record, it looks like Max Pike isn't planning to play ball," Oz informed him. "We've just had news from Jack that he's confessed as much, having caught her trying to free the others. She's there under armed guard, on the fourth floor, and he's making his way down to meet the *Empress* already."

"Okay, roger that. I'll cover Molly, then we'll head up to four to scoop up the others."

Aboard the *Flutningsaðili*, Floor 25, Dock 26

Molly felt the bullet approaching.

She could see it rippling through the air, and found herself fascinated by the pressure wave it seemed to make as it traveled on through the space between them.

She knew it was on a collision course for her chest. Just above her heart.

She knew she needed to move.

But somehow it just felt like there was no urgency. Her mind screamed at her, yet her body felt a complete peace.

And then something shifted.

Effortlessly she felt herself sidestepping out of the way. The instant she was clear, the speed of things returned to normal.

She turned and watched the bullet disappear into the force field of the *Empress* behind her.

The sense of peace remained though, clinging around her body like a swarm of magnetic butterflies, attracted to her skin.

Then she turned and looked at Pike. His face had turned from a look of aggression to one of shock as he himself hit the deck.

Molly tracked back in her mind what had just happened and she saw a shot hit him, from the direction of his left. She turned her head to see Crash coming out from behind the *Empress*.

"You okay?" he called over.

Molly nodded, suddenly aware of Paige screaming and crying. It sounded like her shriek kept catching in her voice, making it even more terrifying for her.

Molly ignored it for the moment, turning back to Crash. "Is he stunned? Or dead?" she asked quietly.

Crash looked down at the weapon in his hand to check the setting. "Stunned," he said, wandering over to where the ladies were still standing. "Settings were still on stun from the last mission," he shrugged.

Molly smiled.

Paige's tears had started to flow as her extreme terror had turned into relived sobs.

"Take her back onto the ship," Molly instructed quietly. "I'm going to find the others."

Crash put an arm around his tearful teammate and led her back the way he had come.

Oz, which way?

Straight out of here and turn right. Joel is two floors above you, heading for the elevator. Good job too, you have around half a dozen armed personnel coming from either direction.

What's the best way to deal?

Molly continued jogging down the corridor.

I'm opening a door. Slip in there. The ones from straight ahead are going to reach you first. Take those out. Then the ones from the other side. I'll bring Joel up behind you.

Okay.

That door. The one you just ran past.

Molly stopped and turned back, slipping into the door Oz had just unlocked for her.

Sure enough, not a few seconds later a parade of Estarian security personnel rounded the corner.

She began firing, just as if it were a training exercise. Again, amazed at how calm and collected she had become. And how easy it was to pick them off before they even fired a round. The feeling she used to have when her arms and legs would feel like lead when she was nervous pre-mission was a long distant memory.

Like a dream that was drifting away.

All that existed now was the confidence and presence that she felt, and the targets that gently appeared ready to be taken out.

She reloaded, concentrated on her breathing, and stayed in whatever zone she had slipped into since the bullet incident.

She turned, almost feeling the next wave of tangos coming around the next corner. They were further away. She tried to estimate the distance, but her brain couldn't kick in. She tried to remember the range on these Federation issue hand guns.

Again. Blank.

She took another breath and looked at her target, the oncoming security guards, with their rifles and black suits, ready for battle.

And then a sense in her body just told her that they were now in range. She raised her gun arm, keeping her body side on to minimize their target area of her, and fired.

The first round hit the first tango square between the eyes. Then the next. Then the next and the next, and the next. There was a pause as two more made their way over the bodies piling up, firing an array of shots in her direction, all of which felt like rain that would never hit her.

The remaining two came into range and she tapped the one behind, and then the one in front.

They both went down, almost as if they had just tripped.

She paused, sensing another body coming around the far corner. She raised her arm up to fire, but hesitated.

Something told her not to shoot.

A second later Joel rounded the corner. She dropped her arm and flicked on the safety.

Joel looked at the bodies in front of him, and stepped over them, making his way down the corridor, weapon in hand but aimed at the floor. "Guess you didn't need me after all," he said in a whisper. Then he looked on up the corridor and saw the other pile of bodies. He looked back at Molly. "You did all this?"

Molly nodded, half aware that she probably looked a little spacey.

Joel whistled through his teeth. "Remind me not to ever piss you off," he muttered.

Molly holstered her gun. "We need to get moving. Oz says the others are on the move. We need to find them before the other fuckwits get a bead on where they are."

Joel nodded, allowing Molly to lead the way.

Okay Oz, where now? Elevator?

Yes. Head for the fourth floor. They're just about to leave the restricted access area. Pieter is guiding them in. We'll stall them at the elevators so you can bring them down together.

Joel and Molly jogged the length of the final corridor to the elevator and waited for Oz to bring it down.

"You stay here and guard our exit," she told him. "No point in putting us all in the same spot."

Joel nodded, noticing her sudden increase in tactical awareness. "Good call. Be careful," he told her as she stepped through the opening doors.

"I will," she answered, still a little glazed in the eyes. Joel watched her as long as he could, the elevator doors closing and separating them once again.

. . .

Aboard the *Flutningsaðili*, Floor 4

The elevator doors opened on level four and Molly looked out into the stark white corridor. She could hear footsteps not far away.

They're coming down the next corridor. They'll be here any second.

Molly stepped out between the doors holding them open. A moment later the crowd of her people came around the corner. "This way," she told them urgently, beckoning with her hand for them to hurry.

Sean led the way. "Come on folks. Quickly," he commanded.

The group piled into the small metal box. Molly wondered for a moment if they had overloaded it, but after a second of anxiety the doors closed and they headed down.

"Good to see you," Molly smiled across at Maya and Sean. She glanced over at Jack. "Thanks for looking after them," she winked.

Jack smiled, and glanced sideways at Sean's reaction.

Brahms and Lana watched the interaction. "Who are you people?" Brahms asked in fascination and exasperation.

Molly grinned at him, and gave a little bow. "We're your friendly neighborhood rescuers. We'll explain more later. For now, let's get you out of here, eh?"

Lana nodded. "Thank you. That sounds... amazing!" Her face had relaxed, and though she was gray from the fatigue and conditions, she had already started to brighten with the hope of it all being nearly over.

Molly smiled at her, placing a hand gently on her shoulder. "We'll be out of here very soon," she promised.

The lift arrived at floor twenty-five and Molly pushed her way to the front ahead of the doors opening.

Aboard the *Flutningsaðili*, Floor 1

"Okay Brock. You're up," Pieter's voice came over his ear piece suddenly.

Brock suddenly sat up straighter in the little vessel he'd commandeered. "What's happening?"

Pieter was all business now, urgency in his tone. "You have one rescuee coming your way. A young girl. Her name is Anne. She was being held captive with the scientists. We don't know the full story yet but Sean was able to get her into the ventilation system and send her your way."

Brock hesitated. "What about the others?" he asked.

"Molly and Joel are going to get them. There was an intervention with some... errr... shooting," Pieter explained.

Brock was on his feet and moving. "Is everyone okay?" he asked quietly.

Pieter's voice relaxed a little. "Yeah. They're all fine. Just not out of the woods yet. I'd say hop out and see if you can meet Anne by the elevators. And then get her and you out of there pronto. Can you manage that?"

Brock checked outside of the vessel as he made his way down the ramp. "Yes. On it," he confirmed.

"Great," Pieter said. "Hail us when you're ready to leave and Oz will give you access."

"Okay, thanks," he said just as the line went dead.

Find Anne, he thought to himself, *and then get them both off this ship. I can do that.*

He felt perfectly confident, until he stepped out into the open of the hangar deck again.

He scurried out to the outer perimeter as quickly as he could without running. At least that was sheltered from view from the observation mezzanine he reasoned, as he broke into a jog.

He approached the double doors to the elevator area and then slowed to a walk again. He peered out of the door, hoping he wouldn't have to wait too long. Just then the doors started to open. He stayed behind the doors out of sight, just in case it wasn't Anne.

It was a good job he did. A second later two engineers stepped out of the elevator and headed his way.

SHIIIIIIIT!

He realized quickly he couldn't ask Oz for help, because they would hear him. He turned and headed back onto the hangar deck, looking around for somewhere to hide.

There were a couple of forklifts about twenty yards away. He hotfooted it over and hid behind them. Just as he disappeared the double doors opened and the two stepped in, talking.

"Yeah, but if they would just listen, I think we could turn up the efficiency," the first Estarian engineer prattled.

The second Estarian held up his hand. "Nah... seriously, you don't want to be doing that. Get too good at all this and half of us will be outta a job. You don't wanna go there."

There was a pause as they walked off in the direction of the ship Brock had hacked. "Yeah, suppose you're right," the first guy admitted. "But you know what would be neat ..."

The voices faded, and Brock peaked out from behind the fork lift. Satisfied that they were out of earshot, he crept back to the doors and then out in the elevator area.

Still no sign of any girl, he thought to himself.

He tapped into his holo.

ANY NEWS ON ANNE?

SEND.

The audio clicked in his ear. Pieter's voice came on. "Not yet. She hasn't used Sean's access card yet, so we have no idea where she is. Just hang in there. If we have to leave without her I'll give you a heads up and then you can make your way out. You have a few minutes. The others are just making their way down to the *Empress* on floor twenty-five."

"Okay," Brock muttered, wanting to pace, but knowing it would take him off guard if anyone were to appear. Heck, if someone were to come through those elevator doors he'd be done for.

He waited.

He listened as the elevators creaked and cranked, transporting people between other floors.

CHAPTER EIGHTEEN

Aboard the *Flutningsaðili*, Floor 25, Dock 26

"Oh my ancestors!" Jayne exclaimed, seeing Max strewn out on the deck. She ran forward to help him, oblivious to the ship docked in the bay.

"What happened?" she asked, wishing she had her scanner on her. She nearly always carried it, except she'd left it in the med bay earlier. She wanted to kick herself. *What kind of ship's doctor was she, anyway?* she chided herself.

Max tried to lift his head, but winced in pain. "Stun gun," he told her. "Those spies we had on board — they're making a run for it." His eyes fell on the ship. "Their friends have shown up too."

Jayne looked at the unfamiliar ship. "We need to get you out of here," she decided.

Max struggled, trying to get up, but did not have enough strength. "They need stopping," he insisted. "Get security down here!" he ordered.

She shook her head, her expression firm as she continued tending to him as if he were a child having a tantrum. "You've been lucky so far, but there's nothing to say they won't take you out once they have what they want. They'll be coming back through here any minute, I'll bet."

She glanced over towards the shadows and a storage area with some crates and debris that had been left strewn about. "Help me get you over there," she said signaling with her eyes.

She managed to slip her arms under his shoulders and chest and drag him into the shadows, out of harm's way.

Crash was on board the docked *Empress,* watching the screen.

Paige, still emotional, came into the cockpit to see what was happening. She viewed the screen over Crash's shoulder. "What's she doing?" she asked, her sobs subsiding.

Crash turned his head slightly to acknowledge her. "It's okay, she's unarmed. Just leave them be. Emma is keeping an eye on them."

He smiled, a rare expression on his face. "They so much as look in our direction wrong and she's got authorization to take them out."

Paige put her hand on his shoulder, tense now that there was another prospect of carnage, but distracted from how she had been feeling.

Aboard the *Flutningsaðili,* Floor 25

The elevator doors opened on the twenty-fifth floor to a corridor that was empty, apart from Joel.

Molly breathed a sigh of relief when she saw him.

"We're all clear," he informed her. "Crash says someone has shown up to help Pike, but Emma has a lock on them. If they move, she can blow them away. We're good to go."

Molly stepped out and instructed the group to move ahead.

Joel led them down the corridor — a chaotic mess of footsteps, some confident and urgent, some hesitant and bewildered.

Arriving at dock twenty-six, Joel went in ahead, gun sweeping the area in front of them checking for any risks. The others hung back, flanked by Maya and Sean, both of whom were still carrying the rifles they had taken from their captors.

"We're clear," Joel called back. Maya and Sean ushered their charges through and over to the open hanger door on the far side of the *Empress*.

Molly brought up the rear, spotting Max and Jayne watching them leave from several yards away.

Max called across from a sitting up position now. "Count yourselves lucky this time," he snarled. "Next time I see you, it will be your end. So," he said menacingly, "make sure we don't cross paths again."

Molly wandered over calmly. Serenely. She bent down and moved close to his face. Jayne had shuffled back in fear, leaving Max, half paralyzed to fend for himself against the approaching wrath.

"I think," Molly said quietly, "it should be *you* hoping we never cross paths again."

Pike froze in fear of her presence. Her tone carried no venom, and little emotion. It made her eerily dangerous.

Max shriveled from her, averting his eyes in surrender. Jayne, crouching a few feet back, watched the exchange, her face fixed in shock at what she was witnessing.

Molly quietly stood up, turned and walked away, her gun still holstered as if she felt no threat from him.

The ship powered up, and she disappeared into it before it gently undocked, reversed out, and then disappeared into the abyss of space beyond.

Aboard the *Flutningsaðili*, Hangar Deck, Level 1

Several more minutes had passed and there was finally a click in Brock's ear piece. "Okay man, you're going to have to get out of there," Pieter told him. "Leave the girl."

Brock hesitated. "Since when do we leave people behind?"

Pieter struggled to find his words. "We're going to have to. She could be anywhere. We still haven't got a trace on her. For all we know she isn't even on her way." His voice was full of remorse having to relay the order.

Brock racked his brains. "What if I were to just stay, and you guys go on ahead. I've got a vessel. I can catch up."

Oz clicked on this time. "Molly says she's not leaving you. So unless you want to put Molly in danger while she comes to — and I quote — *drag your ass back to the Empress*, I'd get going."

Brock huffed in frustration, his hands up on his face as he could no longer resist the urge to pace.

Just then there was a rattling, and a thumping from above. He looked up, and there was something moving behind the air vent. "Anne?" he called, in as loud a whisper as he dared.

"Yes?" came a girl's voice.

"Pieter, Oz. I've got her," he announced.

There was a sigh of relief on the line from Pieter. "Okay, great. Now get moving," he told him firmly.

Brock looked up, craning his neck, trying to see into the vent. "Can you get it open?" he asked quietly.

"I think so," Anne replied. "It hurts my fingers. I've had a few of these to do along the way, else I'd have been here sooner."

Brock stepped back, thinking. "It's okay. I'm right here. We've got a ship waiting. Just as soon as you get it open, you can drop down and I'll catch you."

Anne struggled some more with the grating and soon it dropped down, and two feet appeared. "Ready?" she asked.

Brock got underneath her. "Yeah, ready. Drop."

She wriggled forward and then dropped. Brock caught her, staggered back a few paces and then found his balance and put her down. "Wow, that went a lot better than I thought it would," he remarked.

Anne smiled. "Thank you," she said shyly.

"My pleasure," he responded. "I'm Brock, I'll be your escape buddy today." He held out his hand not to shake, but for her to take. She put her hand in his and allowed him to lead her off through the double doors to the hangar deck.

"Okay, now stay close," he told her quietly. "There are some engineer types around. We just need to act casual and if anyone asks, you're an intern, doing some work experience with me, right?"

Anne nodded, and continued to follow him back around the perimeter on the same route he'd originally taken.

They got nearly all the way round to where they needed to be, and Brock started leading her off the walkway and onto the deck.

"Hey. You there!" A voice called out across the deck.

Brock spun round to see one of the engineers. "Don't suppose you saw a tool kit on the railings out here, have you?"

Brock looked around where he was pointing. "Uh, no. Not just now, but there was one there earlier," he relayed.

The engineer nodded. "Yeah. Just left it there while I took a break and some bugger has nicked it."

Brock frowned. "Some people just need a good beating," he said, matching the guys tone of annoyance.

"Yeah," the engineer agreed. "You're telling me!" He scratched his head and continued looking around.

Brock pushed Anne on, and they hurried onto the ship. Brock went straight to the cockpit and started running the final checks. The tailgate closed and Anne came up to the cockpit to join him.

"Grab a seat," he told her. "And strap in, this may be a bit bumpy."

Anne did as she was told.

Brock hit the bead in his arm. "Okay Oz, an exit would be great right about now."

Oz's voice came through his implant again. "Okay, you're cleared for takeoff. Lift off when you're ready. I'm sending the shortest flight path out of here to your holo. You'll want to be going no faster than 20kph to clear their shield though. Any faster and it will think you're a rock or something and burn you up."

"Thanks for the tip," Brock responded humorously while focusing on the lift off.

Within moments they were up and out and then away through the opening hangar door.

Brock grinned to himself. "Okay Oz, we're clear," he announced, glancing down at Anne. "Heading in the direction back towards Estaria to rendezvous with the *Empress*."

"Great stuff," Oz acknowledged. "We'll be picking you up any minute."

Flutningsaðili, Floor 25, Dock 26

From the shadows Max and Jayne watched the *Empress* pull away.

Max was still unable to move and had been propped up against a wall by Jayne for comfort. She had called for help but it was going to take several minutes for someone useful to arrive. Plus, it was a matter that they wanted hushed up, so Max had insisted on everything going through Pascal to coordinate.

They sat waiting in the shadows of the now-empty dock. Jayne looked out absently. "I knew there was something off about that Marissa girl," she mused, thinking back to all the conversations they had had and kicking herself that she hadn't known.

She glanced down at Max. "So, what exactly are we transporting that is causing all this fuss? And who were those other people? I didn't see them at takeoff."

Max grunted, and then winced in pain, trying to shift his position slightly. "It doesn't matter anymore. We're fucked. When we show up without the personnel, the client is going to well and truly fuck us over."

Jayne looked at him. "You mean, we're transporting people? Not just equipment?"

Max avoided her eyes. "The less you know ..."

Aboard the *Empress*, heading back to Gaitune

Molly watched the screen as the little vessel Brock had escaped in gently touched down inside the *Empress* cargo bay.

"Okay, she's in," Crash announced. "Doors closing."

Molly got up and headed out into the lounge area. "Sean, Joel," she called. The two looked up at her awaiting their instructions. "Brock has just docked with us. He has the girl with him. She'll be in need of treatment. Could you go help him get her down to the med bay?"

They nodded and headed off to the back of the ship. Jack had already taken the two scientists down to get them checked out and treated.

She turned her attention to Paige and Pieter. "You two okay?" she checked. They both nodded.

She looked over at Maya, who was settling in to relax with her eyes closed. "Maya," she called. "Get ye down to the med bay and let Emma take a look at that hand," she instructed. "Paige, you can help her. And hop in a med dock for a diagnosis yourself while you're there."

Paige nodded and silently got up and led Maya down the aisle back towards the corridor between the cockpit and the lounge.

Oz, can you get Emma to look Paige over? She might need some down time in a med dock. I think that was quite a shock for her back there.

Sure.

...

...

And for the record, it was quite a shock for all of us. Myself included.

Why?

Because you dodged a bullet. Somehow. Emma and I calculated the trajectory and you were in the path of that bullet. And then you weren't.

Uh huh. And your point?

My point is, that was not normal.

Good job for us, eh?

I'll say. But—

Yeah, we should talk about it. But later, okay?

Okay.

Sean carried Anne into the med bay, where Emma already had both Paige and Maya in the med docks. "Well Emma, this is looking like old times," he remarked as he stepped inside and opened the nearest dock for Anne.

He placed her gently inside. "It's all okay. We're just going to let Emma take a look at you. Make sure you're okay."

He smiled at her reassuringly. She stared back at him, her eyes wide but expressionless, as if half out of it and half fearful. She nodded, and weakly tried to return his smile.

"Good girl," he told her, as Emma started the scan.

A pink gas started to fill the chamber, and a force field came over the open top to keep it in. Emma spoke to the girl softly through the audio in the dock. "I'm just going to give you a mild sedative to relax you a little. Breathe deeply. It's good for you."

The girl glanced at Sean. He nodded. "Go ahead. It's all okay. Emma is going to take good care of you."

Within minutes the girl was asleep.

Emma's voice came over Sean's implant for privacy. "She's okay for the most part. She has a mild head injury, which I've started treating. Severe dehydration and moderate malnutrition. Also suffering the effects of bad artificial gravity. My guess is she had been on that ship long before it picked up the other two scientists. I'll have Oz cross-reference its passage prior to our team boarding. Might give you something useful to work with."

Sean's shoulder noticeably relaxed and dropped a little. "Great, thanks Emma."

"Sure thing," the ship's EI responded.

He folded his arms, hugging himself. "How are the others?" he asked, glancing over at Maya and Paige.

Emma pulled up some charts on a nearby holo for him to look at. "Maya's hand is a little bruised, but healing nicely," she told him. "She'll be fine in half an hour. Paige is in shock. I'll need to treat her for a few hours. You can leave her on board when we land at Gaitune and Oz will give you a nudge when she's awake again. Might be good for her to have a friendly organic around when she comes around."

Sean smiled, making a mental note to be around. "Okay. Sure thing. Thanks Emma. What happened to traumatize her though?"

Emma responded matter-of-factly. "Oh, well... from what we can gather she saw Molly get shot, and dodged the bullet."

Sean's mouth dropped open. "Shit. You're kidding?"

"I'm not."

Sean frowned as he wandered along the row of med docks, checking on the girls. "Is this part of the realm jumping super powers?"

"I think it might be," Emma responded, still in his implant.

Back upstairs, Molly headed to the cockpit again.

"Okay Crash, let's get these scientists home," she said brightly. "If you might avoid gating for the moment, I'd like to see if we can figure out who Anne is and what her story is before we turn her over to the authorities. I'm assuming she was also taken against her will, but she hasn't said much to anyone so we're just guessing."

Crash rolled his head to look at her while he was steering the ship around some space debris. "Sure thing. I'll let you know when we're twenty minutes out so you can decide what to do. We've got a couple of pods on board for dropping people to the surface."

Molly patted his shoulder. "Thanks, Crash. And also," she turned back to him. "Thanks for having my back earlier. I appreciate it. A lot."

Crash looked up at her. "You're welcome," he told her. Their eyes locked in an understanding only comrades in arms have, and then he turned his eyes back to the flying, as if the moment had never happened.

Molly patted him once more before removing her hand from his shoulder and heading out into the lounge.

CHAPTER NINETEEN

Aboard the *Empress*, Lounge

Molly sat back in her seat, trying to rest her body while they figured things out. "Is she awake?" she asked.

Sean shook his head. "Not at the moment. Emma needs another half hour with her."

Molly rested her head back, closing her eyes. "Did she say anything to you while you were in holding?"

"Not much," Sean confessed. "Only that she had been kidnapped from her room in Estaria. Some kind of religious boarding school."

Molly shook her head gently from its tilted back position. "But what would Pike want with her?" she mused.

Sean shook his head.

She lifted her head and looked at Sean. "Do you think *she* knows?" she asked.

Sean raised his eyebrows and then sat back himself. "I think she knows more than she's saying, but I think she's having problems trusting anyone." He crossed one ankle over his other knee.

Molly sighed. "What's the best call? I mean, is she a minor? I didn't get a good look at her."

Sean frowned. "No, she's technically an adult. I think she's just a little... strange. She *told* me she was nineteen."

Molly frowned. "She looks much younger. Maybe she's just small. Let's see if Oz and Emma can get an ID on her and any background."

Emma is grabbing her prints and DNA right now.

Great. Thanks Oz. Let me know when you find anything.

An hour later, Anne was brought up to the lounge to sit with Molly and Sean and come clean about what she knew.

She looked down at the mocha Molly had made for her. "It all started when my abilities started accelerating beyond the norm. And beyond what they could reasonably expect us to achieve," she explained. Sean was mesmerized that the mostly mute girl he'd known up until this point was suddenly so coherent and eloquent.

He made a mental note to find out what Emma had done to her to make her suddenly so... chatty.

Anne continued her story. "The teachers at the academy notified the elders, and they suddenly decided that I was a danger. But they said I was *in* danger, and should be locked away for my own protection. They're very powerful. I always thought that they wanted us all to learn to ascend, but now that I suddenly might be able to I don't think that is the case. I'm scared. And I don't want to go back."

Molly had been listening with rapt attention. "Is there anything else you can tell us? Anything that might help us find out who might be after you?"

She shook her head.

Molly sighed. "But you think it is someone other than the elders?"

Anne nodded. She had wrapped her hands around her mocha, and now she had stopped speaking she took a slurp, carefully so as not to burn her lips.

Molly stood up. "Okay, give us a minute," she said to Anne. "I'll be back shortly."

She tilted her head for Sean and Joel to follow her out to the cargo area, leaving Anne sitting in the lounge.

The two guys stood around her, waiting for her decision. Molly shook her head, taking a deep breath. "I think there is something she's holding back," she shared.

Joel nodded his head. "I agree. But we can't blame her. I think she needs time."

Molly shrugged, pulling her shoulders almost to her ears before relaxing them. "So what do we do?" she pressed.

Sean folded his arms. "Anything from Oz."

Molly shook her head. "Only the usual stuff, and confirming what she told us about being enrolled in the academy."

Sean frowned, shifting his weight as the three huddled conspiratorially. "We should probably let her come with us. It's what she was asking earlier."

Molly bobbed her head. "We'd have to clear it with the General."

Joel cocked his head a little and turned to watch the girl through the door again. "There's something about her that I can't put my finger on," he confessed. He glanced at Molly. "Don't you get a sense of that, too."

She nodded. "I do. But I can't put it into words. And right now, my brain is foggy from everything that is happening."

She folded her arms and looked down at the insulated floor. "If we can get the okay, I think we bring her back to base, and that will at least give us time to figure something out."

Sean nodded. "I concur. There is nothing to suggest she's a threat to us."

Joel nodded. "Great. Well, keep me posted, in case I have to add one more into my training exercises." He winked at Molly as he headed back into the lounge.

They all chuckled, and Molly and Sean headed back in.

Oz, can you get agreement from the General via ADAM for us?

Sure thing. Gimme a few. He's been a bit slow responding the last few times I've tried him.

Molly chuckled to herself. *Maybe he's just behind on his holos,* she thought, remembering what it was like back in the day of being a part of an institution with demands that weren't mission urgent.

Oh, you might also want to give them the 'Go' on the Teshov mission.

Will do.

Estaria, Spire

The group clustered around between the pods they had used to get down to the surface.

"We really can't thank you enough," Dr. Brahms said, shaking Molly's hand, and arm, as he gazed in amazement at the pod he'd just got out of.

Lana descended from the second pod, helped by Joel. "Yes, thank you so much. To both of you. Or rather... all of you," she said pointing up at the sky. She laughed nervously. "I really thought I was going to die on that ship at one point."

Molly smiled. "I don't think that was ever their intention," she told the very relieved Lana. "Okay," she said, turning to them both, "remember what we said about your rescue. You can't describe us. You don't know who we are. We just helped you get off the freighter and brought you back here, and that was it. Agreed?"

The two nodded. "Yes, of course," Dr. Brahms said.

Molly continued debriefing them. "Okay, now you're going to walk around that corner and up the steps into the precinct and you're going to ask for ...?"

"Detective Chaakwa Indius," the two scientists said in unison.

"That's right," Molly beamed. "Okay, so off you go. Have an amazing life!"

She waved at them as they walked off, looking back and

waving uncertainly. Millions of questions played across their eyes, and yet the relief in their faces was palpable.

Joel looked down at her. "Good job, Ms. Bates," he told her. "Anything else need doing while we're down here?"

Molly thought for a moment before answering. "No, but did I tell you I called my parents like you suggested?"

"No, you didn't." Joel looked at her in astonishment, his tone positively impressed. "What happened? How did they take it?"

Molly smiled coyly. "Oh, turns out they already guessed I was still alive. Dunno how. And yeah. It was fine."

"And?" he pressed.

She shrugged. "And nothing."

Joel tilted his head towards her. "So no plans to meet up?"

Molly shook her head. "Not really. I mean, I'm not totally against it, now. But you know, one step at a time. The point is, I took your advice." She patted him gently on his chest.

Joel grinned and draped an arm over her shoulders as they ambled back to the pods. "I'm glad you did."

The pair hopped back into their respective pods, and buckled up.

As the pods lifted back up to the *Empress*, Oz came on over the audio. "Looks like we've got the all clear for Anne to stay with us for the time being while we figure this out."

"Excellent," Molly replied. "Have Sean let her know." Molly caught Joel's eye through the window in his pod. She smiled at him and Joel smiled back, putting his hand gently on his window.

Molly returned the gesture, and a moment later Oz had whipped them back up out of the atmosphere and into space.

CHAPTER TWENTY

Gaitune-67 Safe House

It had been several days since the team and Anne had arrived back on Gaitune. Things were slowly returning to normal, and Anne, though she had secrets, had been working on sharing in dribs and drabs and generally she was integrating with the others well.

Paige, on the other hand, took a few days after her time in the med dock on the *Empress*, and had barely stepped foot out of her room.

"You think she's okay?" Brock asked, his concern showing in his eyes.

Pieter shrugged. "I dunno. From what I hear she's been stressed trying to run the nail varnish business, her normal job, and then this course. And then whatever happened with Carl, and that incident during the rescue. It's a lot."

Maya waved her hand at him to get him to lower his voice. "She's only down there," she said pointing at the corridor to the sleeping quarters. "You don't want her to hear us talking about her."

Pieter nodded. "Sorry."

Maya pursed her lips. "But you're right. She's been through a lot. And goodness knows what's going through her mind about Carl."

Brock leaned closer into the huddle of close friends sitting in the common area. "D'you think someone should go and talk to her?"

Maya glanced over at the corridor and then back. "Maybe?"

Just then the odd sound of outdoor boots clunked through the corridor and into the foyer. It was Paige. She was dressed in full atmosuit and carrying an empty bag.

Maya sprang to her feet. "Hey sweetie. How you doing?"

Paige smiled weakly. "I'm okay. Just off to Carl's."

Maya cocked her head. "Everything okay?" she asked, unable to keep the concerned tone out of her voice.

Paige nodded, her eyes filling with tears. "Fine. I just need to pick up my things."

Maya could hear the gasps and murmurs of the other two behind her. She stepped forward towards Paige. "You okay?" she said gently.

Paige didn't fold. "I'll be fine. Thanks. I'll see you later."

And with that she had headed out of the airlock and disappeared across the rock.

Maya turned to the others, now sitting in stunned silence.

Gaitune-67, Carl Milberg's residence

Paige came through the airlock, her heart in her mouth, wondering how easy or difficult this was going to be.

"Greetings!" she called, without any humor or lightness in her voice.

She heard movement. And then footsteps coming through from the other room. Then Carl appeared. His face was ashen, and his skin generally was dull. He looked like he hadn't been sleeping. "Greetings," he said flatly, his eyes fixed on her.

"I've come to collect my things," she explained, holding up the bag.

He nodded. "Of course." He paused, uncertain of himself. "I... erm... I thought we might talk, when you're ready."

Paige shrugged. "We can talk," she said quietly.

He ushered her through to the kitchen where he set about making tea as a distraction. Paige noticed some things she'd left lying around. Jewelry and nail varnish samples. She gathered them up into a pile on the side, ready to put into the bag.

Carl had his back to her at the kettle as he spoke. "I'm really sorry about what your friends went through. I'm sure it's obvious that I had no intention of anyone getting hurt in all of this."

Paige sat down hesitantly on a stool. "Yeah, I'm sure," she agreed.

He turned to face her as if surrendering. "I'm sorry. I feel awful. And I miss you. I don't want you to take your things and leave."

Paige felt the sadness rise in her heart. She didn't want that either. "The problem is," she explained slowly and quietly, "you do this for a living. You have secrets and you look the other way. You don't operate on a code of right or wrong. Your business operates no matter who gets hurt or what evil you might be helping." She paused, glancing down at her fingers, her words weighing heavy in the air.

A tear escaped one eye, and she swiped it away. "I can't be a part of that. I can't be with someone who operates in this gray area."

Carl had left the tea and was at her side. "But I don't know what else to do. I don't know how to put this right. Tell me, and I'll fix it."

Paige shook her head, her mind all jumbled and her heart consumed with a stabbing pain. "I, I don't know how to fix it. I thought I'd just come for my things and see what happened over the next few weeks. I... don't have any answers."

She turned and picked up the things she had gathered, and popped them in the bag. "Maybe you could gather anything else into a box and I'll pick it up in a few days?" she said, closing the bag up and getting ready to leave.

Carl nodded, his face expressionless. "Sure," he said, a little more coldly now.

Paige shook her head, chastising herself for coming here so soon. She made a beeline for the front door and was away into the airlock before Carl could think of the next thing to say.

The kettle finished boiling, pulling his attention, but he didn't move. He just stood, motionless, in the empty kitchen.

Gaitune-67, Safe house, common area

"What *is* that noise?" Sean asked, wincing.

Joel paused the video game they were playing. "Ohhh, that," he chuffed. "It's the front door bell. I think Molly or Oz set it to be the sound of that spaceship on that show she loves... Doctor something or other."

Sean frowned. "Sounds like a robot dying. And who would be ringing it. We don't have friends who just pop round."

Joel shrugged as Sean got up, moving carefully so as not to knock over any beer bottles. He shuffled over to the door in his house socks and saw Carl on the other side of the airlock. Surprised, he hit the button to allow him in.

"I'll just get Paige," he said, mouthing through the airlock door to him.

Carl shook his head, looking agitated. He tried to mouth something else.

"Molly?" Sean asked, trying to make sense of what he was asking.

The second chamber equalized and Carl stepped through. "Molly," he repeated. "I'd like to speak with Molly, if I may?"

Sean looked confused for a moment, a series of scenarios flashing through his head. Paige and Carl. Molly and Carl. Paige and Molly and Carl. His processing slowed. Paige *and* Molly. He quickly shook his head, dispersing the distracting thoughts.

"Just a second. I'll try and find her," he said, leaving Carl to step through the second part of the airlock into the foyer.

Sean connected his holo with Molly's. She answered straight away, and he explained that Carl was here to see her.

"She'll be right through," he said. "Would you like to wait in here?" he suggested, indicating through to the double doors, then leading the way.

Carl followed, and Sean deposited him in Molly's conference room before padding back over to his video game with Joel.

He crashed back down on the sofa and picked up his holo-controls.

Joel looked at him quizzically. "Was that Carl?"

Sean nodded. "Yeah. Wants to talk to Molly." He paused, contemplating again. "That's odd, right?"

Joel took a swig of beer, watching Molly appear from the basement. She turned left into the corridor where her conference room was. "Yeah. Very," he agreed.

Molly's conference room

Molly stepped into the room to find Carl turning around to greet her.

"Carl," she exclaimed, unable to keep the surprise from her voice. "I... wasn't expecting to have a visit from you."

Carl nodded gravely. "Yes, I'm sorry for the intrusion. I was hoping we could have a chat."

Molly waved at a seat and he sat down. She then settled in a chair a few seats down the table from him.

Carl took a breath and fiddled with his fingers. "You must think I'm an awful person," he started. He looked back up at her from his hands. "And I really want to apologize for my part in everything you and your people went through."

Molly bobbed her head, not entirely sympathetically, but patiently hearing him out. "That's not why you're here though?" she pressed, trying to get to the real issue.

"Er... no," he said, hesitating. "I'm here because I need your advice."

Molly frowned, confounded.

"About Paige," he added.

Molly couldn't quite understand what he was asking, but she sensed a sadness deep within him. In fact, tapping into his feelings, she found it difficult to hold a grudge against him. "What about Paige?" she asked.

"I know I've failed her. And she came by to pick up her things earlier. But ..." His voice kept catching in his throat as he battled against the feelings in his chest.

He took a breath and composed himself a little. "She's disappointed in me. But I don't know how to fix it. I understand why she doesn't want to be with me. I get it. But I don't know what to do about it."

Molly felt a little overwhelmed. Not just by the sensations of feeling his emotions that were running through her circuits right now, but by the enormity of the task he was putting to her. How should she know how to fix this shit? This was precisely the kind of thing she'd ask Joel about.

Joel, she thought. *Maybe I should get him in here?*

She breathed. *But he isn't asking Joel. He's asking me. Paige's friend.* She looked down at the desk, thinking.

Eventually she spoke, choosing her words as carefully as she could. "I don't know the solution to your problem. This kind of thing isn't my forte. And I don't really know you at all. But what I do know is Paige. And she is an amazing person. She's kind, and forgiving, and she sees the good in everyone. So here's what I think you should know."

Molly's certainty and conviction in her words seemed to grow as she spoke. "Number one: she *is* worth fighting for. Period."

She counted her points off on her fingers. "Number two: you have to just try. And keep trying. Show her you can make better choices. Get her to help you, and include her in whatever changes you want to make."

Molly's tone was confident now. "If you two are going to make it as a couple, you need to be talking through these things, and figuring them out together. Even if you're both hurt, or mad. Even if you've fucked up."

She could see Carl's demeanor shifting in front of her, from one of despair, to a man with hope. "Don't run from the pain," she told him. "And even if she rejects you at first, I refer you back to my first point: she's one hell of a woman, and worth every effort you exert fighting for her."

The room was silent as Carl sat awestruck, looking at Molly and churning her words in his mind. After a few moments it was like he suddenly remembered to breathe. He took a breath, and the spell he had been under seemed to lift a little. A couple of tears trickled down his blue skin and he wiped them with the back of his hand.

Slowly he started bobbing his head, as if rehearsing it and integrating it into his psyche. "Yes. Yes. You're right. She is sooo worth fighting for. And she is so kind and sweet. If anyone is going to help me work through this, it's her."

He put a hand to his chest and deliberately forced himself to breathe again. "Thank you," he said, looking deep into Molly's eyes. "I came here lost. And you've shown me the right track. I know what I need to do."

He went to stand up and Molly got to her feet too. They bowed slightly, and Molly accompanied him out into the corridor and then to the airlock.

"Thank you again, Ms. Bates. This has really meant a lot to me. And I hope to be seeing you again soon. Under better circumstances than when we first met," he added, his embarrassment showing.

Molly smiled. "I'll look forward to that," she said, hitting the airlock button and watching him pass through and out.

She could hear Sean and Joel duking it out across the common area. She glanced back at the Estarian making his way across the rock to his truck.

Can't believe someone thought I could help with something like that.

It appears much is changing, Molly Bates. You're not going to be able to keep pretending you don't know the answers for much longer.

Molly chuckled to herself. *Perhaps...*

She headed over to the common room where the boys were messing around in full competition mode. She spotted the beers on the table. "Can you spare one of those for the boss?" she asked, pointing at the beers.

Joel paused the game, much to Sean's frustration. He leaned over the table, picked one up, popped the lid off it, and handed it to her. Then he picked up his own and cheered her.

She slumped down in the adjacent sofa and watched as Sean and Joel continued their duel.

Aboard the *Flutningsaðili*

Max Pike watched from the control room as the pilots took the freighter down into Teshov space.

"The client should be here within the hour," Pascal Randalf reported from the console chair next to him.

"Good," Max responded. "Have alpha crew around and ready to start unloading level four. We need to have this done before the authorities arrive for inspection. This escapade has already delayed us several hours."

Randalf nodded, and turned to open up a channel from his console to get the ball rolling on the orders.

"Sir?" the pilot reported back through the channel on Max's console.

Max hit the speak button. "What is it?" he asked irritably.

The pilot spoke his message as efficiently as possible. "Sir. We've got the go ahead to land, but we're being told that we'll be subject to an inspection right away."

Max sat up. "On who's orders?"

"General Reynolds of the Federation," the pilot answered.

Max's face paled under his blue skin. "The Federation? What are they doing in this system? Let alone this shit little planet?"

The pilot assumed it wasn't a rhetorical question. "I have no idea, sir," he responded politely.

"Pull up," Max instructed.

"Sir?"

"Pull up. Don't land."

"But sir ..."

"I don't care, just pull up," Max insisted.

The pilot's voice wavered in fear. "We haven't the fuel, and if we don't comply we'll be in breach of a direct order. They will be within interplanetary law to fire."

Max racked his brains, clawing at his head trying to think of a solution.

The disembodied voice pressed. "Sir? Your orders?"

"Land. Land. Land the damn thing," Pike responded, angry like a rat backed into a corner.

Randalf had heard some of what was going on. He watched nervously as he ended the connection with the team leader in charge of alpha crew. "What is it?" he asked.

Max shook his head, dropping his face into his hands. "We're fucked. That's what," he declared getting up out of his seat.

"Where are you going?" Randalf called after him.

Max barely heard as he wandered out of the control room. It

CLOAKED

would be a matter of hours before their secret was discovered and he was taken into custody.

And around the same time his client would find out, and be forced to take ultimate action to protect themselves.

He had known the risks when he signed up for this. He thought he'd accept the consequences. And yet, now it was unraveling his mind churned trying to find a way out. A way to go back.

He opened his holo and tapped a message to Carl.

FEDERATION AT TESHOV. WE'RE DONE. GOOD LUCK!

SEND.

At least that would give him a head start. After all, it would only be a matter of time before the Federation traced the flight plans back to Carl and his company.

Maybe Carl would get a few more weeks with a heads up.

He wandered down the corridors back towards his quarters. The crew bustled around him just like any other trip. Working hard, busting their asses for their next paycheck. Their next promotion.

The reality of it dawned on him as he walked, as he realized how pointless it all was.

Gaitune-67, Safe house

Carl hopped up into his truck, feeling emotionally spent, but with a new optimism growing inside of him.

He'd fucked up. That was true. But Molly was right. This was Paige they were talking about. He couldn't just let her walk out of his life.

He was going to fight for her.

No matter what.

He started the engine, and then realized a holo communication had come through. He paused, and swiped to open it up.

He read the message. It was from Max Pike.

FEDERATION AT TESHOV. WE'RE DONE. GOOD LUCK!

He read the message several times, each time the implications became more and more real. The sensation of hope that he felt just moments before had been obliterated. Gone. A distant memory.

He had no choice.

He had to run.

If the Federation were involved it was only a matter of time before they traced calls and connections back to the person who had been organizing the whole thing.

Him.

But it wasn't the Federation he was worried about. It was the people he had been shipping for. The clients. Governments. Dark ops. Criminals. Terrorists. He didn't ask questions, but they knew who he was despite his low profile. They could find out where he was.

And if they even suspected the Federation was onto him, they would make it their business to find out where he was, so they could 'manage the risk'.

Which meant a bullet in his head.

He looked at the message again.

They probably already knew. The second that ship was boarded, they knew.

There was probably someone on their way here now.

He turned off the engine and rested his head against the headrest, his mind scrambling for something - *anything* - that would make this go away.

Anything that would mean that he didn't have to run and leave Paige behind.

Anything that would mean he could escape that bullet to his head within the next twenty-four hours.

"Fuck," he whispered under his breath.

The frustration and trauma escalated. He slammed his hand against the steering wheel.

"FUCK!" he screamed, feeling like his heart was being torn out.

He banged on the steering wheel again and again, the blood rushing to his head, making him blind with rage and panic.

"FUCK FUCK FUCK FUCK FUUUUUUUUUCCCCK!"

CHAPTER TWENTY-ONE

Staðall University, seminar room

"Good evening, Doctor Jones. Glad to see you with us." Paige handed Dr. Jones his name badge and showed him into the medium sized meeting room.

She had set up chairs enough for those expected and a few more. There was a podium at the front of the room and two aisles down between the chairs for easy access to the rows. Several of the invited had already arrived.

Paige turned back to the table with the name badges laid out, her thoughts drifting back to Carl and what she might say to him next time they talk. Her heart weighed heavy, and her brain was thick with uncertainty.

"How you holding up?" a familiar voice asked her, pulling her back to reality.

Paige peeled her eyes off the thick navy carpet and saw Abigail Von looking at her kindly. "I'm okay," she lied. Changing the subject, she turned to people already arrived. "Looks like almost everyone we approached is going to be here."

Von smiled and joined Paige looking out at the rows of seats.

"You did a fantastic job at vetting them and extending the invitations. It's made this process so much quicker."

Paige smiled a little. "Thanks. It was good to have something to throw myself into."

One of the new faculty members who was sitting in the audience turned around, recognizing Paige and waved. Paige waved back. "Plus," she added, "it gave me a chance to meet a ton of really interesting people. At this rate, I think I'll be signing up to all the classes this university is going to run!"

Von chuckled. "Well, that would be more than a full-time job in itself!" Her chuckle subsided. "But then, in all seriousness, it would be good for someone in your position to be fully trained in everything we're going to teach, not that I fully understand the reach of your role. Just what I could gather from snippets Molly has shared."

Paige nodded. It was neither the time nor the place to get into that, and she had no idea what Von was cleared for. Though if last week's homework had been anything to go by, she had no doubt that Von would make a great strategist to have on their team.

A tall, burly Estarian wandered into the room. "I'm Dr. Augustine," he told Paige, eyeing the name badges. "Lot more people here than I thought there would be," he commented as Paige found his badge and handed it over.

Paige exchanged some pleasantries with him and then showed him into the room. Von noticed the quiet sadness behind her eyes as she worked.

Soon all the name badges were distributed and the room was buzzing. Paige went to the front of the room and introduced Molly, who introduced Von, and proceedings went from there.

Molly looked out at the twenty or so individuals in front of her. "Some of you will be joining us right away, and a number after this academic year has completed. For now, I'll just introduce those who are starting immediately, so you can locate them if you need to, and everyone else will be named in a confidential register you will have access to since you've signed the agreement to keep this information to yourselves."

Molly glanced around to make sure there were no objections and that everyone was on the same page. She continued. "Dr. Augustine is joining us this coming semester to teach Sarkian Social History. He'll be joined by Professor Duffledorf, who is instructing our students on non-combative military strategy. Professor Lakin," Molly nodded in the direction of a rather studious-looking middle aged Estarian, "will be teaching the Installation of Effective Governance, having had extensive first-hand experience in the field. Dr. Jones joins us to head up Environmental Sustainability in Urban and Colonized Settlements."

She went on down the list, introducing a number of others, each one of whom stood and acknowledged their peers, to approving mummers and welcomes.

"You all have incredible resumes," Molly declared, "as well as practical experience that will serve our students well as they look to take what they learn out into the real world."

She made eye contact with as many of her new faculty as she possibly could, while reading off her scrolling holo screen. Her manner was collected, and verging on regal. Paige had never seen her quiet so... together, before.

"As you know, our goal is to shift this world to make sure that those without a voice currently are looked after by those in leadership roles now and in the future. This is what we stand for. This is why we have formed this institution. And though we will face opposition from those who have a vested interest in the old way of doing things, and indeed those who just like their education, and system the way it always has been, in the end the lives we save and the better life we can give the individuals in this system, will be worth it."

The emotion welled in Molly as she spoke, and some part of her could sense that as she shared her vision for this new institution, those in the audience were ready to go with her. To face the odds, and succeed. She could feel their passion stirred by the chance to finally be able to make a difference.

"Never lose sight of what we are working for," she declared emphatically. "Education, equality, and life. These will be our basic tenants."

She held them in rapt attention. "If you're sitting in this room it's because we have felt that you can contribute to this shared goal. We believe that you have not just the expertise, but the personal passion to help students learn these ideas and take them out into the world.

"And I'm grateful to every single one of you who has decided to take the leap and become a part of this institution. Not all who were invited were courageous enough to see the possibilities. And that was okay."

Molly stopped, her eye catching a familiar face at the back of the room.

And then another.

The two figures hovered in the door way, watching the proceedings and scanning the backs of the heads of the people assembled.

She stopped her speech, and fixed her eyes on the two intruders at the back of the room. "And now I see that not all of you here were invited."

The entire room of new faculty members turned to look where Molly's gaze had landed.

The two figures stepped out of the shadows of the doorway and into the light of the room.

Molly's face broke into a smile so wide she could eat a banana sideways.

She left the lectern she had been speaking from and made her way across the floor to greet them. She flung her arms around the Estarian woman, hugging her tightly, tearing up. Then she turned to the middle-aged looking human in a tweed jacket. He wrapped his arms around her, and didn't let her go for several moments. In the meantime, Paige had emerged from her seat on the front row and greeted the woman.

The room erupted in ahhs, and then applause, still oblivious to who the newcomers were.

When they had made their hellos, she turned to introduce them to the new faculty.

"My apologies," she explained, obviously pleased to see the strangers. "May I present to you Professor Giles Kurns and Arlene Bailey. Giles is probably the most experienced and learned space anthropologist you will ever have the pleasure of meeting, and Arlene is likely the most advanced tech person on the planet right now, who is also versed in interplanetary sociology, and Estarian spirituality."

The two received an applause which they acknowledged as gracefully as if they'd been in the spotlight their whole lives.

Most advanced tech person, eh?

Yes Oz.

Except me, you mean?

Yes, except you, Oz.

So maybe you should say the most advanced *organic* tech person.

Molly turned to the audience. "Oz, my on-board AI with whom many of you have communicated with already, would like me to clarify that she is the most advanced *organic* tech person. Oz is claiming the top spot."

"I think that's fair," Arlene said loudly to the audience. Then she whispered to Molly. "I'm so glad to see you. We'll talk later, but your name has become something of an enchantment for Mr. Giles," she winked.

Molly froze and pretended not to hear Arlene's last comment.

Molly showed the newcomers to some empty seats on the front row and Paige sat with them while Molly returned to the front of the room.

Molly took a moment to compose herself and then turned back to the now-hushed assembled academics. "And honestly, not to put them on the spot," she grinned mischievously. "But one has to get a pitch in when one can."

There were chuckles from the audience.

She turned to where Arlene and Giles were sitting to address them indirectly. "If they are planning to stay for any length of time, I would be honored if they would consider joining this esteemed faculty."

There were 'hear, hears' and 'ayes' from the audience who, unlike any other academic community Molly had experienced, were become quite engaged and enthused by what was unfolding before them.

Giles and Arlene exchanges a few words between themselves and then Giles stood up and cleared his throat. There was a tittering around the room as the other academics were taken aback by the sheer amount of excitement. "If I may respond to that, my dear Molly."

Molly waved her hand, palm open, inviting him to speak.

Giles looked around the room. "Arlene and I have returned from some pretty intense adventures, the subject of which we can get into another time. But our investigations have come to a brick wall. An impasse. And with nothing else planned for the foreseeable future, our happening on your gathering was no coincidence."

It was you, Oz, wasn't it. You knew they were going to be here.

I did.

And a heads up wouldn't have killed you.

No, but it would have spoiled the surprise. Giles made me promise.

Hmm. You and I will talk later!

I'm sure we will.

Giles continued. "If there is space for us to contribute to the cause and the molding of young minds, we would very much love to take up teaching posts here."

The room erupted with applause and Molly clamped her hands to her mouth in surprise and delight. She couldn't believe all the information that was coming to her. For some reason, she felt thrilled that Giles was back, and wanted to be a part of what she was building.

Her chest welled with emotion, and her eyes teared up again. She was still smiling as a lone tear trickled down her face.

Since she couldn't talk anyway she stepped into the small audience to hug Arlene and Giles again.

"I'm so glad you're staying," she said to Giles, without really realizing what it was she was feeling.

"Me too, Molly. It's going to be good to spend some time in this neck of the woods," he agreed.

Gaitune-67, Safe house, Paige's Quarters

Carl glanced around the array of nail varnish samples and trinkets on the shelf in Paige's quarters. "I've never been in your room here on base," he commented.

Paige sat down on the small sofa on the other side of the room, exhausted from the evening's event down at the University. "That's because there are people around and, well, you know."

He nodded. "I know," he said quietly turning to her. "You work here."

He seemed to suddenly remember why he was here. "So I was hoping we could talk." He looked even more beaten down than when Paige last saw him the previous afternoon.

She didn't move. "Sure," she said.

He looked down at the floor, and then back up at her with resolve in his tone. "Something's come up," he said, as if confessing. "And it's not good."

Paige's face creased up in concern. "How do you mean? What's happened?" she asked, spontaneously getting to her feet.

His face looked pained. "I have to go away," he told her. "This thing with Pike. The Federation got involved to stop the fracking on the planet that his client was involved with. It's just a matter of time before they call on me."

Paige shook her head, frowning, trying to comprehend what was happening.

"And there have been other things, too," he added. "Where I've turned a blind eye, but I've suspected other things were going on. And if the Federation come after me, all of that information is a risk to someone. To a number of someones who were paying me to... you know ..."

He went quiet.

Paige took a moment to process what he was telling her. "Maybe we can help?" she suggested, her voice weak and quiet.

He shook his head, his eyes looking at the ground again to avoid her eyes. "It's the Federation," he insisted. "You *work* for the Federation. There is no way to make this right. I've been involved in so many of these things. If I stay, the Federation will come for me. And if anyone knows the Federation is onto me, they will take it upon themselves to take me out."

He sighed, his face almost wincing, as if just breathing were painful.

"Either way, I'm dead," he told her. "If I run, I get a few weeks. I've got a small chance that I might even get away clean and maybe I get to just survive. Somewhere."

Paige was in tears now. "Please," she begged him. "Just talk to Molly. I know she —"

Carl shook his head. "It's no good. There's nothing she can do. At this point, even if the Federation don't bring me in I'm exposed as a risk. Just being associated with Pike and his getting caught is enough."

He glanced back towards the door. "I have to go."

Paige took another step towards him. "I know we've had our problems, Carl. And maybe I should have been …" she shook her head, trying not to lose her thread. "But you can't just run."

Paige felt like her chest was going to implode. Carl stepped towards her and held her by her arms. "Believe me Paige. If I had *any* choice I wouldn't be running." He looked deep into her eyes, tears now welling up in his. His voice started to waver. "I'd be staying put and winning you back. I'd be changing and making better choices. But my choices have already caught up to me. It's too late."

He pulled her to him and hugged her as tightly as he dared for fear of his conviction breaking her.

She sobbed. "When will I see you again?" she asked, peeling her face from being buried in his chest.

Carl shook his head. "That's just it," he said, leaving the rest of the sentence for her to fill in in her mind.

He kissed her forehead and turned towards the door. Opening it, he looked back one last time, and for a moment Paige thought he might be changing his mind. And then he was gone.

The door slid shut.

She stood there staring at it. Numb. Unbelieving. Waiting for him to reappear and tell her it was all a mistake.

But he didn't.

The door stayed closed.

Paige's knees buckled beneath her as she fell to the floor, sobbing. In pain.

EPILOGUE

Gaitune-67, Paige's quarters

"He lied, and he was a bad person. And I just couldn't tell," Paige sobbed. "What is wrong with me?"

"Nothing," Molly confirmed decisively. "He wanted to be a better person, for *you*. You made him a better man. In just the short time he was with you, you gave him a reason to question it all."

Paige lay on her bed, barely able to move.

Molly sat in the chair normally reserved for discarded clothes that weren't ready for the laundry basket. "He came to see me, you know?"

Paige lifted her eyes in Molly's direction, unable to spare the effort to turn her head to actually look at her. "No. When?"

"Yesterday," Molly told her. "He wanted to know how to fix things with you."

Paige dropped her eyes again and relaxed back into her semi-catatonic state. "What did you tell him?" she asked, her voice monotone.

Molly crossed one leg over the other and shuffled down in the seat some more. "To talk to you," she paused, and shrugged. "And to get his shit together. No gray area, yadda yadda. But one thing was clear to me as we were talking... he was doing it all for you. He was prepared to change everything just to be with you. Just on the hope that you might give him one more chance."

Molly paused again, wondering if any of it was getting through to her. Her eyes defocused as she remembered the conversation for a moment and then sighed.

"That's the kind of guy you let stick around." She looked down at Paige. She still hadn't moved. "I know it would be easier to hate him for what he did. And then for leaving. But that wouldn't be fair to either of you. Or to what you had."

Molly moved over and sat on the bed next to the heap that was Paige. "It *will* hurt," she told her. "Maybe for a long time. But don't let it become poison."

Paige smiled a little, tears streaming from her eyes and soaking the bed linen. "You suck," she said finally. "Can't you just tell me he was a jerk, and the next one won't be."

Molly stroked her hair. "He's a jerk, and he doesn't deserve you."

Paige chuckled and sobbed at the same time. "Thanks," she said, humorously.

They stayed like that for several minutes.

Eventually, Molly rubbed her shoulder and moved to stand up. "Ice cream?" she offered.

Paige nodded. "Ice cream and then beer," she added. "Lots of beer."

Molly grinned. "We can do that. Come on then," she said, encouraging the broken-hearted girl to haul herself off the bed and to her feet.

Paige grabbed a wad of tissues and dried her face, then disappeared into the bathroom to pull herself together. She reemerged, her face damp from washing it, and then throwing a wrap around her, the two girls headed out of the room to raid the fridge and freezer in the kitchen.

FINIS

AUTHOR NOTES - ELL LEIGH CLARKE
SEPTEMBER 17, 2017

Thank yous!

As always massive thanks must go to Yoda/ MA for his constant support. A lot goes into producing and publishing these books and he deals with all of it – some of which can be emotionally draining and stressful. I'd like to acknowledge him for his endless patience and persistence even while he's flying around the country fielding all manner of responsibilities. Thank you Yoda.

Uber thanks must also go to our awesome JIT team and Zen-Steve. Because of tight time-scales and conflicting schedules, they received this manuscript (version 1) unedited. I'm immensely grateful to them all for their hard work in turning this around and making it happen in time for our deadline.

I was also mega impressed by Steve Campbell's optimization of the process. I managed to restrain myself from putting in the slack channel that his new tweak to the process was sexy.

Oops. So I guess I wrote it here instead.

Oh well. ;)

[EDIT Michael: Hahahahahaha! I wonder if Steve will read this?

THEN I wonder, if you read this Steve, will you add your OWN comment to this?]

[EDIT Steve: Oh crap - How did I get roped into this??? I'm calling this 'sexy' new optimization tweak the George Clooney process. Big thanks to Kelly O'Donnell and John Findlay for playing the role of George Clooney for this one.]

And as always, I owe a debt of gratitude to you the reader, who reads the stories (sometimes more than once!), writes the five-star reviews, and provides an endless source of encouragement over on the Facebook page. I cannot explain to you what a boost it is to hit the Facebook page in the morning or during writing breaks and see your comments, your jokes, and your interaction with the random stuff I post.

You keep me writing.

Without you, these stories would not be told.

Thank you.

Additionally, I'd like to thank everyone who voted for us for the SXSW panel. We haven't heard anything back yet, but looking at the number of likes, comments and shares, we certainly out-did the competition on that front. And it was thanks to you! Whether we get selected or not, I know that we (which includes you) did everything possible to stack the odds in our favor. The rest it up to the judges now. I'll keep you posted.

Thank you for supporting us in all the ways you do!

Dr. Mojito continued...

So, there I am, midway through another root canal.

(You may ask why so much dental work. Nope – it's not because I eat sugar or sugary drinks. Turns out these root canals and fillings were done so badly in the UK that lots of work is required to get me back to normal. Sucks for me.)

Dr. Mojito: do you know what this is, dear?

Ellie: (mouth open, full of instruments, sees him holding a threatening look syringe) 'o. 'hat?

Dr. Mojito: chloroform.

Ellie: (gasps.)

Dr. Mojito: It's okay. I'm just using it to break down some of the filling.

Ellie: 'o, it's coz you 'ant 'o 'op me giggling...

Dr. Mojito: Hahahahhaa. Yes. This is true. Here, let me give you another injection.

Ellie: (tries to smack him but misses).

Later, to MA...

Ellie: You know Dr. Mojito gave me chloroform today!

MA: Sounds like he's trying to find a way to sedate you that actually might work.

Ellie: Hey! I wouldn't be laughing if no one else was messing about.

Healed

The last couple of root canals it seemed like the Author may need to take an antibiotic, something she tries to avoid if at all possible. But each time she walked in the week following the risky work, and Mojito asked about infection and antibiotic, here's how the conversations went:

First time...

Mojito: Any swelling?

Ellie: A little, for a couple of days.

Mojito: Did you take the antibiotic?

Ellie: (shakes head) I didn't need it.

Mojito: How come?

Ellie: I healed it.

Mojito: (frowning) How?

Ellie: I stopped eating sugar and sent it nice thoughts.

Mojito: (frowning even more). Seriously?

Ellie nods.

Mojito: (grunts and grumbles) Well, okay. Let's have a look.

Second time...

Mojito: Any swelling?

Ellie: A little, for a couple of days.

Mojito: Did you take the antibiotic?

Ellie: (shakes head) I didn't need it.

Mojito: Why not?

Ellie: I stopped eating sugar and sent it nice thoughts.

Mojito: **Can you *please* stop healing it?** I want to get a read on how good my work is!

Ellie: (collapses into a giggling fit which spread to whole staff).

Plus, for some reason, his brother (another dentist) came in to say "Hi" while I had my mouth full of metal instruments. The author was perplexed, but was later informed it had something to do with her laugh.

(Update: Ellie is still puzzled, but this week Mojito asked her if she wanted his brother to finish the last tooth).

Dental Porn 2.0

So, there we are sitting looking at x-rays and Mojito is admiring his work.

As he does.

Ellie: You know, I told my friends about the dental porn.

Mojito: (laughing) Really? You told them about the curves and dental porn?

Random consultant shows up at the door to speak to Mojito, mouth open, eavesdropping, and laughing — probably wondering what he's walked in on.

Keto Dramas

I'm sure you'll be hearing more about this over the next few podcasts we record (and when MA actually gets started with it) but here's what's happened so far.

Last time MA and I were actually in the same room was a while ago at a writing conference. He and another author were talking about wanting to get into a certain type of good-looking jeans and made a pact to work on it: i.e., lose weight so that next conference they could be looking 'all that and a bag of chips.'

This Author was invited into the pact, but from some of the hell they were talking about in reference to the keto diet, it sounded like a form of self-flagellation that wouldn't end well.

She opted out.

"I'll cheer you on from the sidelines," she agreed.

Fast forward several months to a few weeks ago and MA brings this up again. Wanting to lose weight. By this time, this Author has been through hell and back already and no longer eats grain anymore. Thinking "Well, I'm half way there already, and having recalled that Dr. Awesome had mentioned it as a next step," she listened carefully as MA talked about his hopes and dreams with keto.

For the uninitiated, Keto is short for the Ketogenic diet.

Basically, it's a super effective method to trap the body into burning fats rather than subsisting off carbs for fuel. (From the research the Author has done recently, done right, this is actually a more efficient way of fueling the body – and more importantly for a writer, the BRAIN!).

So when MA mentioned it again, the Author said: "Okay. I'm in. But lemme figure out how to hack the transition because I want to minimize the hell."

MA agreed.

About a week later, the Author had ordered up a shit-ton of materials to help the transition, including a super-informative scientific summary of everything relevant to 'going keto.'

The arrangement we had was that the Author was going to try

the various hacks, and if they worked, would pass them on to MA, who would then also implement. (This also limited the amount of science he had to hold in his brain to implement each thing.)

[Edit - Michael: For the record, I was so damned excited that Ellie was going to sciency the shit out of this, I damn near wet myself.]

The official reason is because he was travelling and didn't know where to have the stuff shipped to.

Anyway, Ellie transitioned in about a week, and only lost about 3 days of effective writing time.

MA is still eating pizza and tacos.

[Edit Michael: For the record, I was good for 5 days. I've now sucked for 3 out of 5. I'll get back on it!]

There are lots of ins and outs to this process, which we will update you on very soon on the podcast (www.lawnfaries.com), but the Author is noticing a massive increase in energy available for gaming and productivity. She is also able to focus longer and better. (The adaptogens and mushroom coffee are also proving indispensable in this too.) She is consuming waaaaay fewer calories and not feeling like she wants to chew her own arm off.

And she's more emotionally stable.

Mostly.

Disclaimer: A ketogenic diet probably isn't for everyone.

MA suggests that he'll be doing it and then cycling back out of it when he's into those Levi-whatsit jeans. But Ellie thinks that maybe this is a new way of being in the world.

Time will tell.

Sword vs Light saber

MA: I can't believe you sent me a sword!

Ellie: It's not a sword. (in her head, she added the word *dumbass* and *heathen*). It's a light saber (patiently).

(I mean, who the fuck doesn't know what a light saber is? And why wouldn't you be excited about it? Oh, right... not everyone has the same level of geek. Sigh.)

MA: It's a big red dildo.

Ellie: Well, good luck with *that*. I think at 5 feet and however many inches girth that's one hell of a dildo.

[Aside: Ellie, puzzled, wonders: Is this what they mean when they talk about women not being able to park because guys tell them that six inches is yay small? :-0]

[EDIT Michael: I think I said 'glowing' not 'big'... But I may have. This fucker is got to be 8" in circumference or something. It looks a lot smaller in pictures than when you have to put it together.]

Author Shenanigans Podcast

As you may have seen if you've been on the Facebook pages MA and I have started trialing a podcast.

The true origins of this project are still disputed (MA is adamant that I twisted his arm, though I distinctly recall being laid out on the floor, unable to move, not knowing if I was even going to be able to continue writing let alone doing anything else, and saying that we'd have to revisit it when I was feeling better).

Anyway, it's happening. As long as you keep listening/ watching, we'll keep producing them.

So what is this podcast all about?

Mostly the shenanigans and stuff that happens behind the scenes when we're talking business and/or story.

What you see is not far off our normal average conversations
...

We've had a few episodes we've recorded about the differences between English and American (bastardized) English.

MA has also explained some southern expressions which have confuddled me beyond belief. (Honestly how ANYONE can use the expression "ridden hard and put away wet" and not go bright red from embarrassment is beyond me. I'm blushing just typing it!)

[EDIT Michael: OMFG! She is SO bright red on the video... You have to go just to see that part. I think I warned her, too.]

I saw today MA slip some other phrases into our special slack channel for squirrels and shenanigans. He followed them with instructions: DO NOT READ.

So I can't tell you what other topics he's planning.

But if he gets his arse in gear about the keto stuff I'm sure we'll have more drama to report on that front.

What is already becoming clear, as a number of people have pointed out – if this is indeed representative of how most of our conversations go, the fact that we get any work done at all is... well... astounding.

And yet somehow stories get published.

In our defense, as I recall telling MA waaay back when he first brought me on board and taught me to write, what's the point in doing anything if it's not fun?

And work isn't work if you love what you're doing. It's just play.

So this is how we roll.

And long may it continue.

You can join in the fun here: www.lawnfairies.com

And at some point soon I'll get an opt-in up so you can put in your email address and hear about new episodes as soon as they go live.

General Fuckery

You may have seen this on MA's website, but he thought it might be fun to add in here. When I first joined the KU I was asked to fill in some questions asked by the Actors Studio.

Here are my responses...

What is your favorite word? FUCK. Especially when uttered by a very smart guy. [3 #fuckingmagic

What is your least favorite word? See you next Tuesday... (can't even type it!)

[EDIT Michael: Holy crap, I had to phonetically say that, then the "See" screwed me up a few moments... "S? What S?... OH! "C" "U" NEXT TUESDAY... Wait a tic.]

What turns you on creatively, spiritually or emotionally? Smart guys/ Time Lords.

What turns you off? Judgmental people.

What is your favorite curse word? Fuckery, or fuckwit. Fuckwit on Wednesdays.

What sound or noise do you love? The sound of a cello in an empty hall.

What sound or noise do you hate? Starbucks blenders

What profession other than your own would you like to attempt? Time Lord's companion

What profession would you not like to do? Anything that requires a 9-to-5

If Heaven exists, what would you like to hear God say when you arrive at the Pearly Gates? Come, let me show you the control room for this place.

[EDIT Michael: Oh, that's a GOOD one!]

AUTHOR NOTES - MICHAEL ANDERLE
SEPTEMBER 17, 2017

First, let me THANK YOU for not only finishing this book, but making it past Ell Leigh Clarke's author notes and reading mine now, as well!

Unfortunately, we have spent all of our wonderful 'snippy comments' on our videos (which you should totally watch, because they are fucking hilarious!) So, I'm going back through some of our normal notes since the last time we spoke, and catching you up in what I am calling...

"The life and times of an Indie Author..."

No, that sounds pretentious...

How about "The World According to Mike."

Wow, talk about a snoozer just waiting to happen. Here we go.

"Notes from reality, two authors work to go on Keto, talk back and forth and frankly have fun while writing stories."

Or not.

35 Evil Minion Memes
https://www.pinterest.com/pin/437764026262451406/

So, Ellie is harassing me about the minion that she has. Remember, that gift bit me in the ass. Either way, I go off and find this wonderful website that has funny as hell Minion memes including ones such as (they have pictures of Minions, but I figure I can't place them here for legal reasons) :

Of course women don't work as hard as men... They get it right the first time! (Selected by Ellie – big surprise!)

She follows this up with:

How to stop time: Kiss

How to travel in time: Read

How to escape time: Music

How to feel time: Write

How to waste time: Social Media (then she adds 'squirrels' to the end of it.)

I'm thinking *YOU SENT ME THE SQUIRREL!*

Ellie is complaining (errr, I mean commenting) about coffee and other stuff and says "i wish i could hurry up and get enlightened so i don't have to bother with all this shit!" which I found rather funny (reminds me of "God give me patience...and I want it NOW!")

I went and found the Minion meme:

You laugh, I Laugh!

You cry, I cry

You take my COFFEE? May God have mercy on your soul!

The next day, she sends me a picture of her two pillows...

Now I tell her she has a very strange sense of humor and she just needs to come out of the closet. This is the very picture I talk about in one of our video author notes.

Her sense of humor drives our fans to share their own humor with us. Especially in the reviews...

Random Ellie Comment: Reading some reviews.... one reader said: . I also look forward to your collaboration on the Michael series, and the future of Molly. Don't stay up too late looking at root canal porn. ;-)

Not so Random Ellie Comment (related to post showing the minion I sent):

FB comment on minion post - "MA just replaced himself..."
bwhahahahahahahhahhahaha

i think it's the best performing post so far

See? This is the type of verbal stuff I get behind the scenes. I know all of you are besotted by her English accent (so is half the world, it's scientific) but you have to know, she can be downright competitive.

ELLIE LIES THROUGH HER TEETH

So, another day, another message comes my way from Ellie.

Ellie: omg - ive found the best yoda mug for you. What's your postal address?

Mike: When are you thinking it will arrive?

Ellie: next few weeks...

Mike: Because I'm in and out between here and Texas .... uh....

Ellie: You'll still be vegas?

You want it for your Vegas office really... ;-)

<EDIT: I should have paid attention to the wink..>

So, she is worried the gift won't arrive until I've left for Texas and we figure out it should hit before I go from Las Vegas to Texas.

No big deal.

The day comes when I get notified that I receive a package that is being held downstairs in the mail center for our condo building.

Seems legit. I didn't expect a mug to be in a box small enough for the regular postal content anyway.

Hours later, I go downstairs to get my Yoda mug. I'm kinda excited. I go to the security station and ask for the mail and I'm told I have two boxes. No biggie, I ordered something from Amazon.

The rather petit security guard walks into the postal room and I follow. Then, she unlocks the door to the postal storage and I wait. There is some box movement and then the door opens, and she sticks a foot to stop the door from closing on her and wrestles with a box.

Now, I'm starting to clue in. I'm *thinking "This lady shouldn't be wrestling with any boxes that are coming to me. What the hell is up?"*

So, then I see it, and my mouth drops open. She is wrestling with a box THAT IS FOUR FEET TALL.

<< *Ellie Edit: it was bigger than four feet. Keep reading, then do the maths...>>>*

Ell Leigh Clarke did NOT send me a Yoda mug...Oh no.

No, no, no, no, no, no!

Ok, I don't have a big office in my condo. I have a SMALL office in my condo and now, I have a HUGE red light-saber light thing and I am in shock. Why, you ask?

I'll tell you.

Cause I *believed* her. I actually believed that I was getting a nice little Yoda mug that might sit on my desk and instead, I have a five-foot-tall-evil-red-lamp-sword.

It takes me a little while to get through the shock. But then, I'm starting to warm up to the idea of a big lightsaber lamp. I'm starting to think... "Shit, I'm going to decorate this room and this lamp is going to be one of my main pieces!"

And THAT is how I came to own a massive red lightsaber lamp and I am (now) happy to say I have a pivotal piece to help me decorate my office in Las Vegas.

<Note: When I tell her the story of my shock, she laughs hysterically.>

<< *Ellie Edit: mwhahahahahahaha... Hang on. Why wouldn't anyone be THRILLED to be sent a fucking awesome light saber?? >>>*

LOW-CARB / KETO DIET

I'm probably going to save more of these for the next book. But I have to share this one.

<< *Ellie Edit: ... the reason he has to save it because he hasn't really started the keto bit yet! >>*

If you have ever gone on a low-carb diet, there is a SHIT time when your body is pulling off of carbs, and you feel like crap. Ellie was researching the hell out of stuff to help get through this, and I'm behind her (and even more now) with getting my shit done.

So, I've done the diet twice now, and I know what to expect (which is why I'm trying like crazy to hack a way to not feel like shit.)

It's Ellie's first time.

<<RANDOM AUTHOR COMMENT>

Ellie: hey - i have some things i need to clarify for Michael. (vampire Michael, not you.) Lmk when you might be able to run through a scene with me to just make sure i've got this squared away?

<<//RANDOM AUTHOR COMMENT>

So, she is starting her Keto stuff and like 8 hours later I get this:

Ellie: Re keto... death is always an option, right?

18 hours later:

Ellie: Hello. Life is worth living again. Keto salts finally showed up. YAY! Oh and they work. At least they have been for the last ten minutes.

Couple days later:

Ellie: i'll have to get my shit together and get some writing done!

[11:29]

plugs brain in... and watches it misfire a few times

Oh Shit!

It's my birthday coming up, and I get this message...

Ellie: morning! (by the time you see this). I need two pieces of info from you. 1. where will you be on your bday. and 2. if it's

AUTHOR NOTES - MICHAEL ANDERLE

texas, I need your mailing address, si vous plait. I promise i'm not sending a light saber, so you can relax. It's all chill.

Needless to say, I wasn't convinced.

During this time, Hurricane Irma hits Florida which is where Stephen Campbell and Julie live. They have to evacuate after a little while to a friend's house north because they have no power.

I get a package from the mail. It isn't four feet tall, so she wasn't lying about the no lightsaber... No, this time is is a gorgeous hardback book "The Personal Story of my Life." With my name printed on the front in gold lettering.

I open it up and it has a TON of questions about my life ... that aren't filled in. I quickly realize she sent me *HOMEWORK* for my fiftieth birthday!

I'm lazy, I don't want to think this hard. But, it's such a beautiful book I'm damned tempted to start filling it in.

...but it is *homework!*

I can't believe she did this to me.

<< *Ellie Edit: cracks whip... come on geek-boy. I wanna read these entries about your pivotal life-moments...How about you have it filled out by your 51st? And then you can do another one when you hit 100. (tee hee)* >>>

I just went and looked at the book again a few minutes ago (it's on my office desk.) I just know I'm going to get hand-cramps writing in it. My hands don't know how to write more than "thank you" and my signature anymore as I either type or dictate everything.

I'm so screwed.

I regale you, the fans with these stories but know that I appreciate Ellie for my gifts, and I really am going to make the lightsaber something that is going to help influence the decoration of my office!

Author Shenanigans...Cause I had three (3) that we forgot about.

Most of our hilariousness was put into our Author Shenanigans (I just love that word) podcast. However, three of them were saved for YOUR enjoyment.

We hope you like them!

Ellie and I are discussing the author blurb for book 06 Retribution.

Michael: Ok, I'm not wanting to make this blub sound too *"KILL, KILL, KILL!"*

Ellie: good....

Michael: Pause (not receiving any instructions to create a killing blurb, not create a killing blurb...)

I guess that's another author note. (trust me, this was funny as hell when it happened.)

So, we were talking about Oz and Molly having a few more scientific discussions in the story when out of the blue Ellie spouts this off...

Ellie: I got to get my "ya ya's" out about using worm holes to travel on the Michael (MD) Cooper's podcast... So, I don't have as much frustration about that.

I *HAVE* to ask more questions about worm holes and my poor little Indie Author head *explodes.*

YOU HAVE TO READ THIS IN AN ENGLISH ACCENT FOR ELLIE... It is SO much funnier that way!

Ellie: I have changed my phone to the correct English swearwords...

Michael: That is such a Molly thing to do.

Ellie: Like "ass" changes to "arse"

Pause... (she notices me not paying attention.)

Ellie: You are writing this down, aren't you?

Michael: Yes, this is too good to pass up.

I sent Ellie a Minion due to her need to effectuate efficiency by providing tasks. To others, namely *me*. (Ok, probably not me much, but I'm hypersensitive to being given tasks.) She now named this Minion "Mikey" and I realize the practical joke bit me on the ass.

Ellie is playing w/ "Mikey" and waving at the video.
Michael: Don't make me regret sending him to you.
Ellie: I thought you already did?
Michael: …. *More.*
If you have not looked at our Author Note videos, check them out here: http://lawnfairies.com/

BOOKS BY ELL LEIGH CLARKE

The Ascension Myth
* With Michael Anderle *

Awakened (01)
Activated (02)
Called (03)
Sanctioned (04)
Rebirth (05)
Retribution (06)
Cloaked (07)
Bourne (08)
Committed (09)
Subversion (10)
Invasion (11)
Ascension (12)

Confessions of a Space Anthropologist
* With Michael Anderle *

Giles Kurns: Rogue Operator (1)

Giles Kurns: Rogue Instigator (2)

The Second Dark Ages
with Michael Anderle
Darkest Before The Dawn (3)
Dawn Arrives (4)
Deuces Wild
with Michael Anderle
Beyond The Frontiers (1)
Rampage (2)
Labyrinth (3)
Birthright (4)

CONNECT WITH THE AUTHORS

Receive updates from Oz by registering your holo/ email
address here:
ellleighclarke.com

Facebook:
http://www.facebook.com/ellleighclarke/

Michael Anderle Social

Website:
http://kurtherianbooks.com/

Email List:
http://kurtherianbooks.com/email-list/

Facebook Here:
https://www.facebook.com/TheKurtherianGambitBooks/